# BREAKING THROUGH THE SHADOWS

Romola Farr

Cover illustration by Lucy Perfect
lucyperfect.com
instagram.com/lucyperfect

*I'll never forget the moment I met you.*
*I didn't know how fortunate I was going to be.*

*Thank you, B*

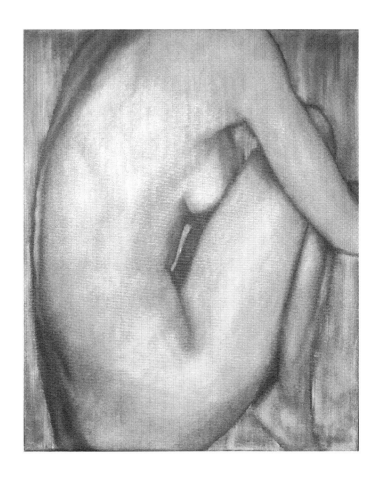

Breaking through the shadows takes more than raw courage...

# 1

It was her birthday. 29th September, 2019. Libra. When she was a child she celebrated it with pretty dresses, pretty friends, pretty cakes. Aged fifteen, she giggled through her first kiss. Aged twenty-five, she woke up alone as she had done for nearly two years.

Waiting.

Waiting.

Waiting.

Her mother had persuaded her to return to the family home in Hawksmead. She had new friends in London. She had a good job. But there was a gap, a chasm, that no amount of birthday cards and presents could ever bridge.

*Tina laughed as she flicked her blonde hair and ran beautifully manicured fingers down her long, slim calf. It was her twenty-third birthday and she was ready for her present.*

*The door to the rented flat banged shut and her whole body stiffened. She listened. There was movement in the hallway.*

*'Police. Anyone home? Come out, come out, wherever you are.' It was a young man's voice.*

*She waited, not moving. The handle to the bedroom*

door squeaked and it swung open. Almost filling the frame stood a police officer. He wore a white shirt, black tie, stab vest with pouches, radio, camera, and a utility belt with handcuffs, extendable baton, CS spray, medical kit, and torch.

'Good evening, officer. How may I be of service?'

'Is dinner in the oven?'

'No.'

'Is beer in the fridge?'

'All gone.'

'Do you have anything to confess?'

'Oh yes.'

He smiled and removed his heavy vest, dropping it on the carpet. He unclipped his belt and it fell around his feet.

'Boots,' she said.

'If you insist, madam.' He bent down and swiftly loosened both laces and pulled off his heavy footwear.

'Now go and wash your hands.'

He laughed. 'It was all going so well.' He left the bedroom and returned in no more than a minute drying his hands on a small towel and stripped down to a T-shirt and boxer shorts. 'You look beautiful, sweetheart.'

'You look pretty buff yourself, Detective Sergeant Burton.' She loved her police officer; he was tall, toned, determined to achieve more than the target, to go the extra mile, and some. Of course, she had gone more than the extra mile for him by leaving her great job, her childhood friends, and her parents, to travel hundreds of miles to London.

'It's the Met. The big one. The dream.'

'The next station stop is Hawksmead,' announced a man's voice through the carriage speakers.

She hadn't checked her Facebook page or Instagram.

She couldn't focus on her novel. Her eyes stared out of the carriage window but she had been oblivious to London's ugly suburbs giving way to England's green and golden, late-summer hues. Her mind was far away on the District Line as the tube came into Southfields station, decked out with flowers and tennis paraphernalia to celebrate Wimbledon fortnight. She'd got off early from work to give her time to prepare dinner for her handsome husband. She had suggested inviting the couple who lived in the flat below to make it more of a party, but Gary was suspicious of them.

'The problem is, I cannot get any info on the guy.'

'You mean you've Googled him?'

'More than that, a lot more, but there's nothing. I like to know who I'm dealing with before I break bread.'

'His parents brought him here from Serbia in the late nineties to escape the Balkan war. He went to UCL to study Russian where he met Sofie, whose parents are from Albania. He works for the Foreign Office and she is in some sort of security job.'

'How do you know all this?'

'I was showing a flat to a would-be purchaser near St James's and bumped into Sofie. We went for coffee and she asked me to forget what I'd seen.'

'What had you seen?'

'She was kissing an older man. Very handsome.'

'They're having an affair?'

'I'm not sure. She told me, he saved her life.'

'Saved her life, how?'

'She wouldn't say.'

'So, both Miroslav and Sofie work for our Government?'

'They are both British and speak several lingos.'

'Well done, sweetheart. I'm impressed. Invite them to

dinner. I've a few questions I'd like to ask. Give them a little interrogation.'

'And that's why you and I will always dine alone.'

# 2

Audrey Cadwallader glanced at her watch and compared the time with the Honda's clock.

'Can you put your foot down a bit, darling?'

'I'm in my eightieth year and they would like nothing more than to rob me of my licence. But for you, my sweet, it is a piddling sacrifice.'

Audrey felt a surge of power as her husband roared down Hawksmead High Street, surprisingly busy for a Sunday.

'We should've gone to Undermere,' Malcolm said, crossing the centre line. 'If you miss it, make sure you blame me. It will take the sting out of your father's rebuke.'

'I should never have agreed to travel on the weekend,' Audrey replied. 'The train service is always so unreliable.'

'Well, let's hope it's reliably late this morning.' Malcolm indicated left and swung the little car into Hawksmead station forecourt.

*'I've something to tell you.'*

*Tina sat up in bed and saw Gary's eyes drop down to her boobs. 'What is it?' Her heart thumped. Every day she feared bad news until he walked back through the door.*

*'I've been asked to…' He hesitated.*

'If we have to move, we have to move. It's just rented.'

He took a breath. 'They've offered me a job. I can turn it down, of course.'

'You want to do it, otherwise you would've turned it down already.'

'It's a challenge. There'll be training. But, it could have its risks.'

She felt her mouth go dry. He reached for her but she was too quick. Her lithe limbs slipped out from under the duvet and she stood by the bed, naked and afraid. 'Tell me what it is.'

'They want me to...'

'No!' She held up her hand. 'Don't tell me. I don't want to know. It's bad enough praying every day that you come home, safe.' She gave him a hard look. 'I'm going to take a shower.'

'Tina. Wait. Please. You have to know one thing.'

She stood with her hands resting lightly on her slender hips.

'I'll be assuming a new identity and going undercover.'

'What happens if we're seen together? Won't your cover be blown?'

'The operation is outside the capital and... and I won't be coming home for three months, possibly six.'

'Six months!'

'It might only be six days. I need time to earn their trust.'

'Whose trust?' She stared at him.

No response.

She reached for her dressing gown hanging on the back of the bedroom door. 'When do you leave?'

'In about ten days.'

'Then I'd better make the most of you while you're here.' She dropped the gown and flung her light frame *on top of him.*

The train squeaked and clanked to a grinding halt as Tina hauled her yellow suitcase off the rack. She extended the handle and wheeled it to the carriage door.

*'Why yellow?' she had asked her policeman husband.*

*'It's easy to spot on airport conveyor belts, people won't take it by mistake, and it's a very unattractive colour to thieves.'* Gary's wise words echoed around her head as tears flooded her eyes. She had to clear them with the heel of her hand to locate the illuminated button. The door hissed as it sprang into life and slid open.

She stepped down from the carriage. The first difference she noticed was the air. How she had missed its earthy smell. The second, after the train had pulled out of the station and she was standing alone on the platform, was the silence.

The quiet.

The loneliness.

She sank to her knees and wept.

'Are you okay?' spoke the voice of an elderly woman. She felt an arm slide around her shoulder.

'I'm all right. Leave me alone, please.'

'It's Audrey, Tina.'

She looked into the kindly face of the woman squatting down bedside her. 'Audrey?'

'I'm here for you. We all are.'

'I look a mess.' She roughly wiped away her tears and stood.

Audrey held out her hand. 'Can you help me up? It's my knees. Too much ballet in my youth.'

Tina managed a small smile and gripped the woman's hand. More than forty years apart in age, they looked at each other, then hugged.

*'The next train to arrive at platform one is the twelve*

*forty-five for London King's Cross.'*

A long intercity train ground to a noisy halt. Tina pulled apart from Audrey and saw a blue wheeled suitcase abandoned a few feet away. 'Your train! You'll miss it.' She heard the guard's strident whistle.

Audrey brushed aside her concern with a small backwards wave of her hand. 'I'll call Malcolm and he can join us for a coffee at the Olde Tea Shoppe.'

'Isn't it closed on Sundays?'

'Not anymore. Eleanor says it's one of her busiest days.'

Tina opened her mouth to speak but the air was filled with sharp blasts from the guard's whistle, followed by the carriage wheels gathering speed as the long train pulled out of the station.

*She was flicking through the latest offerings on Netflix when her phone buzzed. Most evenings sitting alone in their London flat, Tina binged her way through big dramas. Her favourite was a Spanish series set in the late 1950s called Velvet. She liked seeing haute couture mixed with high drama and romance. Her phone had buzzed just as Alberto had swept Ana off her feet and carried her to their luxury bed. When was Gary going to ever do that? She pressed pause. A few moments later, Sofie was in her flat. The two couples shared a terraced, Edwardian house, split in two on Southfields grid. It was a popular area for families with good transport links, good schools, and a great park where children could play. Tina wanted a baby, but that was definitely on hold until Gary was home.*

*She looked at Sofie who was a little above average height, athletic, with brown hair and eyes, and a Slavic nose above a generous mouth. When not smiling she could look very serious. She was not smiling now.*

'Is everything all right?' Tina asked.

'No.'

'What is it? Tell me.'

'Have you heard from Gary?'

'I told you, he's away on a job. He should be back soon.' Tina did her best to disguise her true emotion.

'But, have you heard from him?'

'No.'

'Gary and I work together. At the Met.'

Tina stared at her friend. 'You're a police officer?' That explained why her clothes were always so practical.

'Sort of.'

'Why didn't you tell me?'

Sofie smiled. 'Need to know... I hope you understand.'

Tina unscrewed the metal cap from a bottle of red wine and poured it into a tumbler. She took a long pull and threw the glass into the sink where it shattered. 'Well? What have you got to say, my lying friend?'

'We've lost contact with Gary.'

Tina stopped breathing.

'There are many ways he could let us know he's okay, but he's made no sign for over a month.'

'What are you going to do?' Tina could barely mouth the words.

'Monitor, as best we can. But, I think we must prepare for the worst.'

'The worst! What are you saying?'

'We will not give up searching for him, but he was mixing with dangerous people.'

'How could you let him, Sofie? How could you? I thought you were my friend.'

Towing their wheeled suitcases side-by-side, the old and the young strolled up Hawksmead High Street.

'It all looks the same,' Tina said, as they passed bow-fronted shops, some closed, some open.

'What time are your parents expecting you?' Audrey asked.

'They've given up on me. They want me to move on, but I can't. I can only move back.'

'They miss you. We all do.'

'I know. I've had so many cards, emails, texts. I'm sorry. I couldn't reply. I had nothing to say.'

'What about your job?'

'They were great. Everyone's been lovely. I was sad to say goodbye.'

Audrey stopped pulling her case and looked at the young woman who had married the man of her dreams in Hawksmead's memorial garden attended by what had felt like the whole town.

Tears filled Tina's eyes. 'They've given up looking. It's been almost two years but they still won't tell me what the job was or who he was spying on. They've abandoned Gary and just want me to go away. And now I have abandoned him, too.'

Audrey gripped Tina's arms. 'You saved me when I needed your help the most. Now it's my turn.'

# 3

Malcolm had heard his phone ring whilst driving home and then heard it buzz as a text came through. It would be Audrey letting him know that she was safely on the train bound for the big smoke. Since their marriage three years ago, every day had been one of pure pleasure. Both had been widowed and both had nearly died in accidents before realising they had a second chance of happiness, if they would only grasp it.

As he walked up the path to Mint Cottage, he pulled a few brown leaves off the rose bushes and stopped to breathe in the petals' heady scent. He had a quick look at his bedding plants and saw that his choice of fuchsias, petunias and geraniums were still competing to offer bees brightly coloured blooms, before the weather changed.

His phone buzzed again as he slid a key into the front door. He was looking forward to settling down to the preamble before the next round in the Formula One racing calendar. The text message cancelled his plan and within a minute the sole of his shoe was pressing down on the Honda's accelerator pedal.

Eleanor placed two buck rarebits on the table in front of Tina and Audrey, beside two glasses of orange juice and two cappuccinos. The Olde Tea Shoppe was her livelihood but music was in her bones. Despite being a non-believer, she enjoyed playing the pipe organ in the Methodist church every other Sunday and at various recitals. A professional opera singer, now retired, and a divorcee with no children, she'd given up all hope of finding a man to accompany her through her dotage.

'I hope I've got the egg right,' she said. 'Perhaps I should take it off the menu and just cook Welsh rarebit – a lot easier.'

'But you could lose your buck rarebit clientele,' Audrey smiled.

'True, but every time I cook a poached egg I'm walking on egg shells – literally!' Eleanor turned to Audrey's companion whose face was hidden behind her lank blonde hair. 'It's lovely to see you, Tina. I am so sorry.'

Tina scooped her hair behind her ear and looked at Eleanor. 'It's why I've come back. I need...' Fat tears filled her eyes and spilled down her cheeks. She roughly wiped them away. 'He's missing, presumed dead, but he's not dead to me. I know Gary. He would never leave me without a fight.'

'What's the latest from the police?' Eleanor glanced at Audrey who gave an almost imperceptible shake of her head.

'They think he's dead,' Tina said. 'But until they find his body I won't give up.' She picked up her knife and fork and stabbed the poached egg, spilling yolk over melted cheese and toast.

In the halcyon days of the 1950s when Malcolm had learned to drive and owners of cars were but few, it was possible to simply pull up and park almost anywhere at any time. Hawksmead had so far resisted the march of traffic wardens and the scourge of yellow lines, but following the Sunday service exodus from St. Michael's

Church, parking spaces near the Olde Tea Shoppe were as rare as a vegetarian with a shotgun on a grouse moor.

Malcolm parked his Honda in the short drive leading to the memorial garden. Through the windscreen he could see the remaining low, uneven walls of the former school boarding house, now home to a variety of young trees, shrubs and late summer blooms. He opened the car door and eased his way out. Although still sprightly at seventy-nine, if seated too long in one position his pinned bones gave him jip. He yearned to walk around the high perimeter wall encircling the garden and to say a little prayer in front of the memorial, but he was anxious about Audrey and, especially, Tina. He owed that beautiful young woman more than he could ever repay, and it saddened him greatly to think of the cruel blow that had robbed her of happiness. Her husband was dead, of that he was sure. But, without a body, it was impossible for the young widow to start the grieving process.

Tina looked at her plate and was surprised to see that she had eaten all the buck rarebit. The quaint tea shop was full of happy chatty people and Eleanor was busy sliding her ample hips between wooden chairs as she dealt with the Sunday rush. Three years ago when Tina and her newlywed husband, Gary, had departed for London, Eleanor had worked alone, but word of mouth had clearly increased footfall and she now had a young waitress to help her, and a trainee chef in the kitchen.

Slim fingers picked up the dirty plate. 'Would you like to see menu?'

Tina looked into a pretty but unsmiling face. 'Are you Polish?'

'Yes.'

'My name's Tina. Have you worked here long?'

'I bring you bill.' She turned away, snaked through the chairs, and pushed open the swing door into the kitchen. Audrey emerged from the lavatory and worked her way back to the table.

'Thank you for bringing me here,' Tina said. 'I wish we'd never left Hawksmead. This is home.'

Audrey placed her hand over Tina's. 'Let Hawksmead help you build a new life. We can't turn the clock back but we can help you make your days more bearable. Four years ago I came here as a widow looking for an answer to a question that had all but destroyed my family. I found more than an answer. I found friendship and love. The internet brought me here, it brought you and me together – not in a swipe right sort of way, of course.'

Tina couldn't help but smile.

'But, without the internet,' Audrey continued, 'I would never have made the leap from Sevenoaks to Hawksmead, and changed my life from that of an aging widow to a happy and fulfilled aging wife.'

'You think I should try a dating app?'

'Hawksmead is teeming with people who really care about you, especially your dear parents, but until you find that someone who tightens your stomach, who makes your heart pound with excitement, it's going to be almost impossible for friends and work ever to be enough for you to build a new, happy life.'

Tina looked around at the people filling up tables in the tea shop. There were a few men, but they were clearly all taken, although at least a couple kept casting their eyes in her direction.

'That's my point.' Audrey squeezed her hand. 'You can't fish in this pond. Gary is too tough an act for the young bucks of Hawksmead to follow.'

Tina picked up her glass of orange juice. 'I know you're right.' She took a sip and put it down. 'I started drinking too much. It was the only way to dull the pain.' She looked down at her left hand. Could she really take off her engagement and wedding rings, given to her by the man she loved, and would continue to love to her dying breath? She looked at Audrey. 'You were on your way to London. I've spoiled your plans.'

'I called my father when I was in the loo and as soon as I explained, he was absolutely categorical that I should not consider visiting him until you were sorted out. His words.'

'Do you really think dating again will sort me out?'

'Gary wouldn't want you to pine your life away.'

*Breakfast in the big man's impressive home was invariably excellent. The house was set in fifty acres of lush countryside northeast of London. The grounds were patrolled twenty-four hours a day by a private security firm mostly made-up of ex-army and so-called reformed criminals. The perimeter fence was razor wire fitted with sensors to alert security if there was a breach, and was patrolled by dogs on running leads. The house itself was tastefully designed with a mock-Tudor facade, but with large bullet-proof picture windows instead of classic, single-glazed leaded lights. The entrance was grand and equally impregnable with two black-steel doors set in a secured metal frame. In effect, the house was a charming fortress built to withstand attacks from burglars and, more importantly, the police.*

*'If the bastards ever do get in,' Frank Cottee snarled to Gary, 'there's a secret room where we can hole up for days, weeks if necessary.'*

*Gary digested that fact. 'The police always get archi-*

tect plans before making a raid.'

'That's why the architect knows nothing about it. What kind of fool do you take me for?' Frank was a charming host but the criminal in him regularly bubbled to the surface.

'May I take your order, sir?'

Gary looked up at the plump, middle-aged Spanish maid, decked out in full livery with an embroidered FC. Showing-off was Frank's Achilles heel. Every summer, he hosted a charity fete in his fifty-acre garden and would often hold extravagant balls, peopled by local dignitaries and politicians. He wanted everyone to see what his power and money had bought him and few would've been unimpressed by the Italian marble floors, the vast interior reception rooms and bedroom-suites, many with triple aspect views; the sumptuous spa, steam room and gym by a magnificent indoor swimming pool; and an underground garage with turntable and car lift.

'Mr Gary? What would you like?'

He was dragged back from his thoughts. 'The Full Monty, please, Marta.'

'Thank you, sir.' Marta looked at Frank's strikingly beautiful daughter. 'And for you, Miss Stacy?'

'Coffee and pomegranate juice.' Stacy was still in riding gear from an early morning gallop around the estate. Her father had built an equestrian centre for his only child and, for a short while, she had entertained the idea of becoming an Olympic three-day eventer. Her usual day clothes were high-end designer and mostly chic, although the flash-Essex in her would occasionally break through the careful facade.

Gary was always wary, especially in her father's presence, but Stacy, when she smiled, totally disarmed him. The night before he had slipped-up in her company and called her Tina. He feared he'd wrecked the whole under-cover operation, but the conversation over breakfast was light and free-flowing so he felt confident that he'd got away with his error. He hoped so. Criminals such as Frank Cottee did not get rich by playing nice. He got rich by smelting smuggled gold, distributing cocaine, money laundering, internet scams, protection, a few legitimate property deals, and bumping-off anyone who got in his way. Gary's cover job was that of a luxury car dealer and fixer. He and Frank had hit it off, immediately, but Stacy was a different story.

Frank's driver and minder, Keith Hardman, was seated at the far end of the dining table. He rarely spoke unless directly addressed.

'Keith,' Gary called. 'Stacy told me that you used to box. I don't believe her – you're way too handsome.' He hoped his joke would help him get back in the fold.

Keith stopped eating his scrambled eggs and put down his knife and fork. He looked at Gary. 'Thank you. You're too kind.'

'By the way, I love your name.' Gary felt encouraged.

'What's special about Keith?' He picked up his knife and fork and shovelled a large slab of toast, egg and bacon into his mouth.

'Hardman. It's a perfect name for a minder. It's the same as a vicar being called Shepherd.'

'Or someone being called Large when they're little,' interjected Stacy. 'Or Small when they're tall, as in Tina Small.'

The thud in Gary's gut was like a punch from Keith Hardman. He fought to remain calm, normal, to not panic. He forced a smile and looked into Stacy's flint-hard eyes.

'All I had to do,' Stacy continued, 'was Google Gary and

*Tina and up popped a photo on the Hawksmead Chronicle website celebrating the marriage of Police Constable Gary Burton to Tina Small, estate agent. Does your wife know what her policeman husband has been doing of late?'*

*The game was up. He shook his head. 'She knows nothing.'*

*Frank sat back in his chair and spoke from the end of the long table. 'Ignorance ain't always bliss 'cause she's gonna know nothin' of what's about to happen to you. It will be her punishment for making the wrong choice of husband. But, one day, she will fully appreciate your betrayal.'*

*Gary tried to control his breathing, but his heart was a sledgehammer under his ribs. 'My superiors know I am investigating you. If I don't check-in, they'll tear this place apart. You can't make me disappear.'*

*'I assure you, son, I can. I'm a very creative wizard.' He picked up a glass of freshly squeezed orange juice and swilled it around his mouth.*

*'Daddy, I don't want him to disappear.' Stacy's voice cracked on the last word. She took a breath. 'I want to see him suffer, every day. I need to know he is suffering.'*

*Hardman got up from the table.*

Rise House was a detached, double-fronted, 1920s' property in Woodland Rise, a secluded and select leafy lane off Hawksmead High Street. To the left was a short drive and double garage. To the centre were solid oak gates and a wide York-stone path leading to a terracotta tiled step and an open porch. Curtains were drawn across a first-floor bedroom window.

Malcolm enveloped Tina within his long arms. 'Dinner, lunch… anytime, anywhere. Or we could walk the high ridge before winter sets in.'

She prised herself free and looked into his faded blue eyes, framed by crinkled skin. 'Thank you.' She kissed him on his cheek.

Audrey held Tina at arms' length. 'Whenever it gets too much – and it will – don't be a martyr. You have to give yourself a break.'

She nodded and reached for her wheeled suitcase.

'Are your parents expecting you?' Malcolm asked.

'I sent them messages but I've not heard back. It's not a problem, I have a key. I just hope they haven't changed the alarm code.'

'If there's any problem,' Audrey said, 'come and stay with us.'

'Any problem,' echoed Malcolm.

'And, I know it can't be,' Audrey paused, 'but happy birthday.'

Tina smiled. 'Thank you for my card. You never forget.' She blew a kiss to them both and they watched the forlorn young woman wheel her suitcase down the path towards the porch and front door.

'Come on,' Audrey said. 'I think we need to stretch our legs.'

Malcolm offered his left arm and gripped the extended handle of her suitcase. With the wheels clattering behind them, they shared the pleasure of a gentle stroll on the warm, late September day.

'Where is everyone?' Malcolm asked.

'They've fallen asleep on the sofa whilst watching Formula One.' She squeezed his arm.

'Tina worries me.'

'Yes, but all we can do is be there for her.'

# 4

Tina rang the bell instead of searching the depths of her handbag for the door key. Her mother had once let slip that she and her father were still sexually active. She sincerely hoped this was not one of their more energetic moments. She rang the bell again and waited.

Nothing.

She dug deep for the door keys and slid a solid brass key into the mortise lock. It was unlocked. She pulled it out and slid the Yale key into the top lock and turned. The door opened. She pushed it back and saw a pile of mail, leaflets and a copy of the local Hawksmead Chronicle newspaper, strewn on the floor.

'Mum! Dad!' She wrinkled her nose and closed the door. 'It's me. There's a terrible smell coming from somewhere.' She walked through the hallway into the large reception room. The first thing to strike her was the elaborately framed, wall-mounted portrait of Tina and Gary on their wedding day. She closed her eyes and took a few deep breaths to steady herself. But it had the opposite effect and dizziness forced her to seek out the sofa. She sat down and put her head between her knees to try and stop it from spinning. Hot, she peeled off her jacket.

'Mum!' she called. Exhausted, she closed her eyes and was quickly asleep.

Audrey was deep in thought as she and Malcolm wandered along Woodland Rise, her case clattering behind them.

'There's still plenty of daylight,' he said. 'We could drive up to the Rorty Crankle, have a brisk walk on the moor and earn ourselves a light late lunch, courtesy of Harry and Cathy.'

She squeezed her husband's arm. 'Mr Cadwallader, you are full of very good ideas.'

He stopped and looked down at his wife. 'What's that mosquito buzzing in your ear telling you?'

'Her parents might be away and I hate to think of her all alone in that big house. She needs to be with people. She's had more than enough loneliness waiting for Gary to return.' Audrey dipped her long fingers into her handbag and removed her phone. She swiped the screen, scrolled down her contacts and put the phone to her ear. 'It's ringing. Damn. Voicemail.' She cut the connection and slipped her arm through Malcolm's. 'I'll try again later.'

Tina stirred. Her head, pulsed. She took a few deep breaths and pushed herself onto her feet. She swayed and staggered as she made her way back into the hallway. Grabbing the handrail she placed a foot on the bottom step of the carpeted tread and lurched her way up to the first floor. Sweating from heat, she saw that her parents' bedroom door was shut. She sucked more air into her heaving lungs as she zigzagged her way across the landing, knocking over a Chinese vase precariously positioned on top of a pine, Doric column. It fell on the carpet and broke in two.

'Oh no!' She almost fell to her knees and reached for the broken pieces. Could they be glued? Her head was pounding as she forced herself back on her feet and banged with her palm on her parents' closed bedroom door.

'Mummy.'

Her knees buckled, her elbow caught the handle and the door sprung open. She could just make out her parents lying on the king-sized bed before she vomited on the thick-pile carpet.

Arm in arm, Audrey and Malcolm strolled along the leafy lane towards Hawksmead High Street, their unspoken thoughts accompanied by the rattling suitcase wheels.

'What about your father?' Malcolm asked. 'Are you going to set another date to visit?'

'Hang on. I'll try Tina again.' She stopped and retrieved her phone from her handbag. She tapped the screen and put it to her ear. She sighed. 'Tina, it's Audrey. Please call me back ASAP.' She dropped the phone into her bag and continued walking. 'Come on.'

Malcolm looked at his wife. 'You're going the wrong way.'

'I have to know her parents are home.'

'You want me to drag this suitcase all the way back to Rise House?'

'If you would be so kind.'

'I tell you what. I'll drag this heavy weight back to the motor and I'll pick you up from the house.'

'Perfect. See you shortly.' Audrey marched off down Woodland Rise and almost broke into a jog. But, aged nearly seventy, power-walking was the best she could do. Anyway, there was no hurry. She just had to be sure that Tina was safely restored to her parents' care.

Twenty minutes later, she stood at the end of the short drive leading to Rise House and liked what she saw. In Sevenoaks, the house she'd shared with her late husband, Duncan, and where their two sons had grown-up, was rented out. Although she loved Malcolm's two-up, two-down cottage, there were times when she missed the space. The double-fronted house owned by Tina's parents met with her approval. The tended beds with their shrubs and flowers were still vibrant and although the lawn could do with a bit of a trim, it was uniformly green without any dead patches or moss. She particularly liked the symmetry of the bow windows to the left and right of the portico entrance. She and Malcolm had run into Tina's parents a few times since her marriage to Gary and although Audrey would not class them as close friends, they had a mutual love for Tina and a shared history going back decades.

She took a deep breath and strode down the path to the front door. To the right was a porcelain bell push with the word PRESS. She obliged and heard the answering ring.

Someone was at the front door. Tina had to get help. She had to save her parents. She gripped the bedroom door frame to try and lever herself up but her head would not stop spinning. Using her last reserves of grit and determination, she dragged her body across the wool carpet to the top of the stairs, ignoring the shards of broken vase and the vomit on her hand. She tried to push herself up, but the handrail was too high for her to reach. Floral wallpaper turned grey and she tumbled down the carpeted stairs to the half-landing.

Audrey was puzzled. Tina had not answered her phone and now nobody was answering the front door. She was not naturally nosey but something was not right.

She looked back to the road. There were no passers-by and no Malcolm. She bent down and lifted the flap to the letterbox. There was another flap on the inside of the door so she couldn't see in. But she didn't need to. The smell of death told her all she needed to know. She reached for her phone and dialled 999.

'Emergency. Which service?'

'Police, oh and ambulance. Actually, fire service, too.'

'What is the nature of the problem?'

'I'm standing outside a friend's house and I think something bad has happened. Very bad.'

A few more questions and responses were concluded with Audrey giving the call handler the address.

'A police vehicle has been dispatched. Please wait until it arrives.'

Audrey terminated the call and checked the windows to left and right of the front door, but they were all sealed shut. Worse, they were leaded and double-glazed with fifteen small panes per window. Great for keeping out burglars. To the far left was an up-and-over double garage door and to the far right a solid wooden gate which Audrey presumed led around the side of the house to the rear garden. She tried it but, of course, it was locked and had sharp spikes at the top, designed to keep out the most gymnastic of burglar. Even if she got around the back, it was sure to be equally tough to break in.

'Have you rung the doorbell?'

Audrey looked at Malcolm.

'I didn't hear you come. I've called the police.'

'Why?'

'Put your nose to the letterbox. There's a terrible smell.'

'Have you tried calling Tina again?'

Audrey reached for her phone as Malcolm bent down and pushed open the letterbox flap. 'Good God!' He recoiled and let the flap snap down.

'Lift the flap again. I think I heard her phone.'

Malcolm did as she suggested. 'Yes. I can hear it ringing. She's definitely in the house.'

'Malcolm. We have to get in.'

'The police may have one of those battering rams. It's not the kind of door you can simply shoulder open.'

'We cannot wait for the police. By the time they arrive it could be too late. Do you have anything in your car we could use?'

'You mean like a jemmy?'

'Yes! That would be perfect.'

Audrey watched Malcolm hurry as best he could up the path and with growing frustration, observed him painstakingly hook back each wooden gate to a short wooden post.

'What are you doing?' called Audrey.

Malcolm acknowledged her entreaty with a brief wave and hurried around the nose of the Honda to the driver's door. The car was almost four years old but it still looked shiny and new. One of the great joys being married to Malcolm was that he rarely lazed around. He was always busy, always looking for another job to do – in the house, in the garden or sprucing up the car. It seemed his sole aim was to try and make Audrey's world as perfect as possible.

The Honda's engine sparked into life. Much to Audrey's surprise, Malcolm mounted the pavement and drove slowly down the footpath leading to the front door. He lowered the driver's window.

'What on earth...?' Audrey asked.

'I don't have a jemmy, but I have a battering ram.'

25

'Your car?'

'Stand back. Stand right away.' Malcolm did up his seat belt.

Audrey watched as he eased the Honda's front wheels up the step until the nose of the car was under the porch. 'It's a pity it's an automatic,' he shouted. 'But I'll do what I can. We may have to cancel our trip to Florida to pay for the damage.' He raised the window.

Audrey held her breath. The engine roared and she smelt the burning clutch as Malcolm held the car on the brake. Suddenly, the front wheels spun on the terracotta tiles and the car lurched forward, smashing into the front door and frame.

It held.

He reversed and rammed again.

The side window lowered.

Audrey bent down. 'What's the problem?'

'I can't get enough momentum.'

'Keep trying.'

The *whoop-whoop* of a police siren attracted both their attentions as a marked patrol car came to a halt. Its doors opened and two young police officers hurried down the path towards them.

'Don't speak. Listen,' Audrey commanded. 'There's a young woman in the house not answering her phone or the door, accompanied by a stench that can only mean one thing. We have to get in.'

The two policemen looked at each other. 'Get the big red,' said the older man. The younger police officer hurried back to the patrol car.

'Sir. Would you mind backing up?'

Malcolm nodded and reversed the Honda. The front of the car banged down on the edge of the step and broken glass from the headlights fell onto the path. He turned off the engine and got out. 'I think we'll need a taxi home,' he said to Audrey.

The younger policeman arrived carrying in two gloved hands a heavy red tube with a handle at the top and another at the rear.

'That should do it,' commented Malcolm.

'It weighs sixteen kilos,' said the older policeman, 'and if my young colleague here operates it right, it can exert an impact equivalent to three tonnes.'

'Shall I get on?' asked the younger man.

'One moment.' The older policemen rang the door-bell then banged on the door. He squatted and opened the flap to the letterbox, recoiled, and almost staggered as he stepped back. 'Get it open.'

The young police officer carefully targeted the head of the ram and swung it back like a mediaeval log hanging from a trapeze. The door opened immediately.

'Geeezus!' said the young policeman.

The senior officer turned to Audrey and Malcolm. 'Wait here.'

He entered the hallway, followed closely by Audrey.

'I said wait outside, madam!'

'Tina!' Audrey shouted.

'She's on the stairs,' said the senior officer.

Audrey rushed to the half landing and put her face close to Tina's head, which was lying on the carpet.

Malcolm sidled past the two police officers and entered the sitting room.

'Sir!' shouted the senior officer. 'I order you to get out of the house.'

'We need to open windows at the rear,' Malcolm called back.

The senior officer spoke into his radio by his left lapel. 'We're attending Rise House, Woodland Rise. We require ambulance assistance. Lights and siren.' He turned to his colleague. 'Check upstairs.'

'I don't know about you, boss, but I feel a bit woozy.'

Malcolm re-entered the hallway. 'Carbon monoxide, I'm sure of it.'

'Audrey?' Tina's eyes blinked several times.

Audrey smiled. 'You're going to be okay.'

'My parents.'

'I'll check on them.' She turned to her husband. 'Malcolm?'

He climbed the first short flight of stairs and eased his tall frame down. He put his arm around Tina as Audrey stepped up to the landing.

'Madam. Don't touch anything,' ordered the senior officer. 'Do you hear me?'

Audrey felt sick as she stood at the top of the stairs. The stink of death was overwhelming. She forced herself to cross the landing, avoiding the pieces of broken vase, and stopped by the pool of vomit. She peered into the master bedroom. The stench was beyond any smell she had ever experienced. As her eyes adjusted to the dim light seeping through the closed curtains, she saw two semi-naked bloated bodies entwined on the bed.

# 5

'Did you see the ANPR camera?' Malcolm asked as he pulled on the handbrake and turned off the engine. 'They really are determined to squeeze us dry.'

Audrey released her seat belt.

'I like this Daewoo,' continued Malcolm. 'I feel unfaithful to my beloved Honda, but this little beauty has a lot to offer.'

Audrey opened her door and looked at the grey hospital edifice. 'I had hoped I'd never darken those corridors again. I feel breathless just thinking about it.'

'The last time I walked or rather limped out of there was when Tina came to collect me after my accident.'

'I've not given this place a moment's thought for four years and now it feels like I never left.'

'They did a good job for us – let's hope they're still on their game.'

Tina was awake. The air she was breathing tasted strangely good. She was comfortable apart from the mask covering her nose and mouth. Nothing hurt. But she was frightened of opening her eyes. She didn't know why she was scared but she knew that something bad had happened. She just didn't know what.

'Hello, I'm Dr Manson. Are you a relative?' The young woman was talking quietly and Tina had to strain to hear her voice.

'I owe her my life, so we are more than connected.' Tina recognised the refined voice of the older woman, but couldn't place it.

'We knew her late parents,' said another voice. This time a man and quite elderly. Late parents? What was he saying? She strained to hear their conversation.

'Her brother lives in New Zealand,' the older woman said. 'I understand that the police are getting in touch. But, that's all by the by. Our sole concern is Tina. Please tell us how she is.'

Tina tried to move her arm but her whole body felt paralysed. All she could do was lie there and listen.

'As I am sure you are aware, carbon monoxide is lethal. We are giving her oxygen to try and flush it out of her system.' The doctor was talking quietly and Tina couldn't be sure she was hearing her right. 'Even if CO poisoning doesn't kill a patient, the damage it can do is often irreversible.'

'What kind of damage?' interjected the elderly man.

'We need to do tests to determine the extent but, from what we know, Tina was exposed to a high level of carbon monoxide. The effect can be tremors, stiffness in the joints and, generally, slowness in thought and movement. In extreme cases, impaired vision and hearing.'

She can't be talking about me? I can hear, perfectly.

'How long before you know?' the older woman, asked.

Audrey?

'The length of time it takes to recover from carbon monoxide poisoning varies with the individual. Is Tina a smoker?'

'Would that have an effect?' Of course – dear Malcolm.

'Smokers often have higher than normal carboxyhaemoglobin in their blood, which makes it hard for us to determine what the level would have been prior to the CO poisoning.'

'I'm sure she wasn't a smoker,' Audrey said.

'I see. Well, the level of carboxyhaemoglobin in Tina's blood was very high. The lack of oxygen will, most likely, have caused some damage, especially to the nervous system and brain, how much we can only tell when she wakes.'

'I think losing both parents will have the greater effect,' Audrey said.

Tina forced her eyes to open. Her hand flopped onto the oxygen mask and she dragged it clear of her mouth. 'What are you saying?' She didn't recognise her own hoarse voice.

Audrey was the first to react and went to the side of the bed. 'Tina, it's Audrey.'

'Long time no see.'

'You've had an accident, but you're going to be okay. Malcolm and I are here to help you get well.'

'I feel fine. Just a bit groggy.'

From the other side of the bed, Dr Manson carefully replaced the oxygen mask. 'Hello Tina. You're suffering from the effects of carbon monoxide poisoning. Oxygen will help flush it out of your bloodstream. So no talking. Rest and give your body a chance to get better.' She looked at Audrey. 'Would you come and find me before you go?'

'Of course.'

Tina watched the doctor leave the side ward.

'Shall I get us a cup of tea?' Malcolm asked. His voice sounded far, far away as Tina slipped back into blissful oblivion.

Dr Manson was finishing a phone conversation when Audrey and Malcolm approached. She handed the receiver back to the receptionist and looked with tired eyes at the elderly couple.

'Leaving already?'

Audrey smiled. 'She's fallen asleep. We'll come back tomorrow. Hopefully, you'll be able to tell us a bit more by then.'

'She very nearly died,' Dr Manson said. 'I've spoken to a senior consultant and in his opinion, Tina will inevitably suffer memory loss, problems with her balance, and there could be a change to her character, her personality.'

'Will the effects be permanent?' Malcolm asked. 'Or will she get better over time?'

Audrey made a half-step towards the young doctor. 'Or could she get worse, like people who've had a stroke?'

Malcolm touched his wife's arm. 'That's a bit gloomy, darling.'

Dr Manson looked from one pair of ageing eyes to the other, and took a tired breath. 'CO poisoning is not like a stroke where the symptoms in severe cases can get worse, but carbon monoxide deprives the blood of oxygen, and lack of oxygen for a prolonged period does cause damage. How much, we don't know yet.'

# 6

Tina pressed the red Help button she hoped would summon a nurse. It was morning, the early October sun was nearly up and there was already a bustle around the side ward.

Nobody answered her call.

She pulled off her oxygen mask and gently eased her legs out of bed and planted her feet on the cold floor. She looked down and saw a tube coming out from under her gown that was plugged into a plastic bottle hanging on the side of her bed. She unhooked it and shuffled in bare feet out of the side ward.

Amy, one of the receptionists, looked up from her screen and got to her feet. 'Please go back to bed. A nurse will be along, soon.'

'I need the loo, *now*.'

'Okay, let me help you.' Amy came out from behind the curved reception desk and took Tina's arm.

'Your face looks familiar,' Tina said.

'You and your friend... was it Tony? ...were almost permanent fixtures here when that lovely elderly couple were guests in this establishment a few years ago.'

Tina almost laughed but it hurt too much.

'I went to your wedding,' Amy said. 'I am so sorry about Gary.'

'I have to go to the loo, *now*,' responded Tina.

'It's just along here. If you have any problem, there's a red string pull. I'll come straightaway.'

Tina entered the loo, parted her gown at the back and sat down.

Amy had forgotten all about her one-time friend and current patient when Tina suddenly appeared in front of the reception desk holding her gown closed at the rear. In her free hand was the bottle of urine.

'Can someone please remove this? I'd like to take a shower.'

'When the doctor sees you later this morning, you can ask her.'

'Do you know where my things are?'

'The clothes you came in are stored in your bedside cabinet. They've been laundered. I have a key.'

'What about my phone?'

'All you had were your clothes. You can use this phone.' Amy pushed a landline phone towards her.

'I don't know the number.'

Amy moved her mouse and looked at the computer screen. 'We do have a contact number for you. I'll write it down.' She copied the number onto a small pad with *Undermere General Hospital* printed at the top and peeled off the sheet.

'Thank you.' Tina stared at the piece of paper. 'Could you dial it for me? My eyes are a bit blurred.'

'Of course.' Amy stood and pulled the phone's base towards her. She looked at the number she'd just written and tapped the keypad.

'Mum, it's me,' Tina said. 'I'm in hospital. I don't know what's happened but can you come and get me?' She listened. 'Audrey?' She listened some more and then looked at Amy. 'When can I see the doctor?'

'She does her round at about eleven.'

Tina spoke into the phone. 'Can you come late morning?' She listened. 'Thank you. Bye.' She placed the receiver back on its base and focused her eyes on Amy. 'What's going on? Please tell me.'

'I wish I could. I'm sorry.'

'Why won't anyone tell me?' It was more of a wail than a question.

# 7

'We really would like you to stay for another day,' Dr Manson said. 'Especially as you're still a bit foggy.'

Tina stood by the bed in the side ward, trying her best to keep her mind focused on what the petite doctor was saying. The door was open and many noises were coming from the communal acute wards.

'I want to see my parents. I don't understand why they've not visited.'

'When the police came, you were asleep. Let me call them and they can explain what happened to you. It's not for me.'

'I want this out.' She pointed to the bottle half-full of urine hooked to the side of the bed.

'Okay.'

'Thank you for what you have done for me, Dr Manson. I am really grateful.' She admired the young woman, who conveyed confidence, knowledge and authority with such ease.

'Is anyone coming to collect you?'

'My friend, Audrey.'

'Do not hesitate to come back if you feel unwell.'

'I will. I promise.'

'Okay, lie down.' Dr Manson snatched a couple of latex gloves from a wall-mounted dispenser and closed the door.

Malcolm was going to make chicken Elizabeth. He didn't know how long Audrey would be, so had decided to prepare a meal that was not time sensitive and could be eaten hot or cold. Before Audrey left for the hospital, they had prepared the spare bedroom. The days ahead were going to be even tougher for Tina than they had been since Gary went missing. But, he and Audrey were determined to do all they could to support the beautiful young woman, especially through the inevitable post mortem and double funeral.

Tina sat down on an upright chair by her hospital bed and waited. She was wearing the clothes she'd had on when she was brought into hospital by the ambulance, freshly laundered but creased. She had nothing else. No phone, no purse, no keys.

A face appeared around the door.

'Audrey!' She leapt to her feet, lost her balance, and had to use the bed to recover. 'Still a bit shaky.' She gave Audrey a hug. 'Have you spoken to my parents?'

'Let's get out of here. We can talk in the car.'

'Yes of course.'

'Do you have everything?'

'Yes, apart from my parents. I don't understand what's going on. It's most unlike them.'

Audrey walked with Tina across the hospital car park and tapped her debit card on the machine reader to validate her ticket.

'The cost has almost doubled in four years,' Tina observed as they approached the Daewoo. 'New car?'

'Rental. The Honda is in for a bit of surgery.'

Tina laughed. 'Malcolm's heavy right foot?'

'He's really looking forward to seeing you.'

'I'm sorry for being such a poor friend. I'm not myself, these days.'

Audrey drove Tina straight to the cottage. The young woman was very tense and, at times, it had been difficult to deflect questions about her parents. Audrey's aim was to get her safely inside before breaking the devastating news. She parked and switched off the engine.

'Audrey, may I ask you a question?'

'Why don't we have a nice cup of tea, first?' Audrey released her seatbelt. 'Malcolm's always got cake.'

'Wait. Please. It's about Malcolm and you.'

'Malcolm?'

'Are you happy?'

'Happy?'

'Is it possible to find true love... as a widow?'

Audrey took Tina's hand in hers. 'This is a very, very tough time for you. But, you will meet another man and you will fall in love. Every relationship is unique. I have found a man in Malcolm who makes me laugh and feel loved every day. I treasure the many happy memories I have of my life with Duncan but, as a friend of my mother often said, we're a long time dead. So, we need to live in the present, smell the crumpets and eat Malcolm's homemade jam.'

He heard the front door open and hurried through to the narrow hallway. Two days ago, Tina had looked thin and strained but Malcolm was still surprised by her emaciated appearance and lack of vivacity.

'Darling Malcolm,' Tina said. 'I'm just popping in for a quick cuppa and then I must go to my parents. They'll be wondering what's happening.'

His heart flipped. 'Is there time for a hug?' For a brief second as her face brightened, he saw the Tina who had helped save Audrey's life, and helped him recover after a bone-shattering fall.

'I'm a bit smelly,' she laughed. 'I've not had a shower for goodness knows how long.'

He wrapped his arms around the young woman who felt as frail as she looked.

# 8

Tina was puzzled. She was sitting on the sofa in Malcolm's front room sipping a cup of tea but there was no chit-chat. Sunday was the first time she had seen Audrey and Malcolm since Gary had disappeared. She hadn't even been back for Christmas or Easter. They both looked a bit older, a bit plumper and a whole lot more content than when estate agent Tina had first sold Audrey the old school boarding house at the north end of Hawksmead. Flames flickered through her mind as she remembered the fire that had destroyed the Victorian building and nearly killed Audrey. She thought about the high-speed car chase when she'd rushed Audrey to hospital pursued by flashing blue lights, driven by a police officer who continued to chase her all the way to the altar.

*Gary. Such a cocky young man. How she missed him.*

'Lovely tea, Malcolm. I like the blend.' Tina smiled as she returned the cup to its saucer. 'Your cottage looks lovely, too. It's quite a while since I was last here, but I hope you know how much you two mean to me. Whatever is on your mind, whatever you have to say, won't change that.'

She watched the elderly couple look at each other and felt a lump of lead drop into her stomach.

Audrey got up and sat beside her on the sofa.

She took Tina's hand in hers. 'Darling.' She swallowed. 'Your parents have died. It was a terrible accident which the authorities are investigating. We are so sorry.'

Tina pulled her hand away. 'No. You're wrong. I saw them. They were in bed, having a nap. They're fine.' She pushed herself up onto her feet. 'I have to talk to them. I have to go home.' She looked at Malcolm. 'Will you drive me?'

'We'll all go,' Audrey said.

The elderly couple's cottage was on a quiet road about halfway between the bustling centre of Undermere and the former mill town of Hawksmead, where Tina's parents lived. Malcolm took the Old Military Road across the moor, driving cautiously. If Tina were at the wheel she would've really put her foot down, but she had to be patient. It would only be a few more minutes before she saw her folks.

'Slow down for the bridge,' Audrey ordered from the rear seat.

'As if I wouldn't,' responded Malcolm. They approached an old stone humpback bridge which was only wide enough for a single vehicle. He tooted his horn and Tina felt her stomach flip as the car came down on the town side.

'Watch the speed camera,' she warned. 'I got done a few years ago.'

They all looked to their left as they passed the entrance to the memorial garden where the old school boarding house had once stood.

'You must visit the garden, Tina,' Audrey said. 'It's looking glorious.'

'I would like that.'

Malcolm turned off the High Street and into Woodland Rise. He drove the Daewoo slowly along the winding, tree-lined road and came to a gentle stop by Rise House.

Something wasn't right. Tina released her seat belt and opened the passenger door. She hurried down the pathway and came to a wooden box that had been constructed around the entrance. Stapled to the plywood was a laminated sheet.

POLICE NOTICE

Do Not Enter

This building is deemed unsafe for persons and animals owing to toxic air.

By Order of the Magistrate's Court, Undermere, entrance is prohibited until work is completed to obviate the danger.

There was more but Tina couldn't read it as her vision was blurred by tears. She felt Audrey's arm around her shoulders as she sank to her knees and sobbed. Everyone she loved was spinning down a never-ending tunnel as the pain of loss enveloped her. She thought her heart would seize and her brain would melt. Her stomach retched and she vomited a pathetic stream of tea and cake. Tears poured down her cheeks as her whole body convulsed in grief.

'Everything all right?'

Kneeling on the path with her arm around Tina, Audrey looked up at a man wearing blue overalls, a white hard hat and carrying a grey case. Hanging around his neck was a gas mask designed to cover his whole face, with a black tube over his shoulder to a bright orange tank strapped to his back.

'This is her parents' house.'

The man nodded. 'I have written instructions from

the coroner to determine the source of poisoning.'

'Could she go into the house? It might help.'

'I'm afraid not.'

'I brought her here three days ago. When she got taken to hospital, her handbag and bright yellow suitcase were left in the sitting room. Could I pop in and retrieve them?'

'I'll get them. Please do not follow me in.'

'I won't.'

The engineer unlocked the narrow door fitted at the front of the temporary construction and pulled on his mask. He turned on a tap, checked that Audrey was not about to follow him, and entered the building.

Audrey looked up the path to Malcolm who was standing by the Daewoo. Parked behind was a white van with blue wording on the side panel, but Audrey needed her glasses to read it.

'Madam.' The gas engineer put down Tina's suitcase and placed her handbag on top.

'Is there gas?'

'There's quite a process to go through before I can declare the house safe. I'd better get on.' He re-entered the temporary structure and made sure that the door was closed and locked.

Malcolm picked up Tina's handbag and pulled her case along the path to the Daewoo.

Audrey kept her arm tight around Tina's shoulders as she tried to absorb every twitch and spasm of overwhelming loss and grief.

# 9

He hated the heat, he hated the sickly smell. The Heath Robinson network of air conditioning units and pipes, cobbled together to disguise the growing of marijuana on the floor below, was impressive. Dermot O'Hanlon, the apparent leader of the travelling family, seemed inordinately proud of their illegal achievements and, when Gary had first arrived, insisted on demonstrating to him every aspect of his ingenuity.

'Yer see, Gary, we may be stupid spud pickers to Britain but, given a chance, we rule the world. It amuses the hell out of me that we are farming this wonderful cash crop right under the noses of the boys in blue.' He laughed, but Gary did not see the joke. 'I know this game inside out. It's in my DNA. You reckon your police helicopters will stumble across this cannabis farm because we're thick Irish itinerants. Dream on. There are no telltale heat sources for their infrared cameras to detect, even in winter.'

The ground floor was taken up with a large refectory, changing and shower rooms, and staff accommodation and offices. The first floor was untouched by the travellers and was all classrooms, the top floor was given over to dormitories and shower rooms where Gary and the migrants slept, but the second floor was where all the illegal activity took place. Windows were blacked out by original wooden shutters and men, mostly young of East Asian origin, worked silently tending the plants.

'Heat from all these lamps,' Dermot insisted on explaining, 'usually give the game away but this middle floor is cocooned. Of course, heat has to go somewhere and the dormitories above would get so hot, no frost or snow would settle on the school roof. One of your police whirlybirds would be sure to take a closer look.'

Dermot took him up to the top floor and proudly showed how the air conditioning units in the dormitories, which Gary would discover hummed and squeaked day and night, extracted the hot air.

'We're Irish, Gary, and we're smart. Hot air is expelled along these flexible pipes, via the back stairs. Now, I know what you're thinking. You think we're so simple as to release hot, pungent, cannabis vapour into the air around the school, for visitors to inhale.' Dermot tapped his head. 'But God gave me the solution. Five hundred years ago, monks from the monastery redirected the brook to turn a water wheel for grinding their corn.' He laughed and once again Gary could not see the joke. 'Yer see, the hot, stinking air is pumped into the fast-flowing brook and although it bubbles to the surface, it is cold and the stink is dissipated.' He slapped Gary's back. 'Clever eh? You've gotta admit it.'

'Thank you for the tour. Very illuminating.' Gary had witnessed much low level criminal activity since being held captive in various locations, but this cannabis farm was a major leap.

'We're not done, yet,' Dermot insisted. 'Power needed for the UVA and LED lamps that speed the growth of our marijuana plants, and turn the fans in the air-conditioning units, draws high levels of electricity from the grid.'

That was the straw Gary was grasping. He had hoped the excessive demand of power, even if cables were diverted around an electricity meter, would attract the attention of the authorities.

'I can see your wheels turning.' Dermot almost winked conspiratorially. 'In the early 1970s, Gary, power workers and coal miners were on strike and caused frequent power cuts.' He guided Gary down to the top of the back stairs that led to the basement, the chains linking his hand and ankle cuffs clinking as they walked.

Dermot pulled open the door and Gary could hear a slight hum coming from somewhere in the darkness below. 'To solve the problem of power being cut off,' Dermot said, continuing his lecture, 'this remote school out on the moor installed its own electricity generator and, if you listen carefully, you can hear it still works. But how is it fuelled, I hear you ask. I agree with you, buying diesel in cans to run the generator could attract unwelcome interest. Rather than fill cans with diesel at the nearest service station, we fill our vans and trucks in the usual way and then the fuel is simply siphoned off. Nobody is any the wiser.' Dermot slapped Gary on the back again. 'And that, my friend, concludes our tour.'

Gary smiled to himself. Hawksmead College really was a seat of learning, an education. It was a pity he was chained to it.

'She's asleep,' Audrey said in a quiet voice as Malcolm poured boiling water into a floral teapot. She looked through the kitchen window, not appreciating the brightly-coloured blooms, trimmed verges, and perfectly shaped bushes, all benefitting from the early autumn's warm weather.

'I have never witnessed such pain,' Malcolm said as he put the lid on the pot and placed it on a tray.

'No.'

He looked at Audrey. 'What can we do?'

'You can make sure she eats.'

He nodded and briefly smiled. 'We should contact her brother.'

'His number will be in her phone, I presume. I'll put it on charge.'

'We'll have to figure out the pass code.'

'It'll be the date of her wedding,' Audrey said. 'I know Tina.'

'Gary's parents? Did you meet them at the wedding?'

'His mother was there. His father died a long while ago.'

'She must be so wretched.'

Audrey took in a deep breath. Her wheeze, since being trapped by fire, would always be with her. 'She ended her life.'

Malcolm stared at her. 'I didn't know.'

'I ran into Tina's father in the memorial garden. We spent a little while sitting and talking. He told me the sad news.'

'Why didn't you tell me?'

Audrey took another wheezy breath. 'Okay. John and I often meet – or rather met – in your beautiful memorial garden. Sometimes we talked about the loss of his brother and sometimes we talked about mine. Sometimes, we just talked. And, sometimes, we just sat on the bench and looked at their names carved in the memorial stone.'

Malcolm nodded. 'I didn't know.'

'I was John's connection to a brother he barely knew. I never met Mark but you know how close he and my brother were.'

Malcolm swiped away an escaping tear.

She touched his arm. 'Not for one second did John blame you for what happened. You know that.'

'Black ice… not my fault but I'll never forgive myself.'

'I know. Do you understand why I didn't tell you?'

Malcolm nodded.

She kissed his cheek.

'Thank you.' He pulled back his shoulders. 'Cake?'

Audrey nodded and smiled.

Malcolm reached for a tin and pulled the roof off Buckingham Palace. 'Shop-bought Battenberg or home-made jam sponge?'

'I think I need a slice of your homemade jam sponge more than ever.'

Tina opened her eyes. The room was dark. Not even weak rays from a streetlight. For a moment, she had no idea where she was. But, she needed the lavatory and she needed it fast. She got out of the comfortable single bed and ricocheted off a chest of drawers into a side table which fell over onto the thick carpet, which she could feel under her bare feet.

She really needed a pee. Her knees pressed against the side of the bed as she eased her way around the base and headed for what she thought was the window. She felt fabric in her hand and pulled a curtain back along its track. Weak, yellow rays from a sodium street light brought a little definition to the furniture and she was able to locate the door. She turned the porcelain knob and pulled.

Darkness.

Where was she?

That could wait. She had to find a loo or she'd wet her pyjamas. How did *they* get on? She felt along the wall and found a switch. A hanging light with a floral shade lit a narrow landing. She tip-toed across to an open door and the cool linoleum told her feet she was in the right place. She arced her hand and it came into contact with a string pull. At the end was a large ceramic toggle. She pulled and was almost blinded by ceiling lights. She didn't mind as she could see well enough the object of her desire. Leaving the door open, she hurried to the lavatory, pulled down her pyjamas and let go almost before she felt the cold plastic of the seat.

Once the pressure was off, her estate-agent eye was able to take in her surroundings. The bathroom was pretty and well-appointed with a period-style enamelled bath that looked very tempting.

Audrey was on a beach, a massive wave crashed over her and she spun round and round as if in her mother's Bendix washing machine. She didn't know which way was up. She clawed the water but it held her in its suffocating embrace. She opened her mouth to scream.

'Audrey! Audrey!' whispered a man's voice.

She was being shaken and gradually she surfaced. A shaft of dawn light found a gap in the curtains.

Her lungs hurt.

'I was drowning.'

'You were dreaming, my darling.'

'Water. There's water! I can hear it.'

Malcolm hugged her to him. 'It's Tina. She's running a bath.'

'I was on a beach, searching for my little brother. I couldn't find him. And then I was drowning.'

'You're safe, now.'

'Yes.' Audrey kissed her husband. 'We have a special someone to take care of. How are we going to do that?'

'Perhaps a cup of tea will help.' He eased away from her.

'Or coffee. Better for joining the dots.'

Tina lay in the bath, cocooned in the comforting warmth and bubbles. She tried to quell the voices in her head but one came through, as he always did.

*'Mrs Burton... we cannot find him. As you know, he was working undercover to expose a criminal family. We lost contact and despite all our efforts he's disappeared. We are doing what we can, Mrs Burton. We will never give up looking for Gary.'*

She closed her eyes and submerged her head in the water. They did give up. When the Detective Chief Inspector retired his words were seared in her memory. *'It's time for you to start living again. It's been more than two years. If Gary were still alive, he would have found a way to make contact.'*

Only her parents' positivity had kept her hopes alive. Her parents...

The Irishman yanked his chain and the policeman was immediately awake. Not that Gary ever slept well in the hand and ankle cuffs he had to wear, whether he was working outside, nurturing marijuana plants, eating, washing or sleeping.

It was always hard to tell whether it was day or night in the long dormitory as the windowpanes were blacked out and the shutters closed. There were thirty metal beds with thin mattresses, of which about half were occupied. He was the only one chained.

On a metal tray was a bowl of porridge and a cup of

tea. He could not fault the quality of the food. It was nutritious if basic, but not nearly enough for the work he was forced to do, by day picking potatoes and at night tending marijuana plants.

'Breakfast in bed, Dermot,' Gary said. 'You're clearly going for a Michelin star.'

'We have a visitor, later.'

'Who?'

'Don't get excited. Just some old geezer to do with the building's trustees. He's not about to break you free.'

Despite his youth and training, the opportunities to escape his captors had been few. Frankly, Gary was impressed. At times, he felt crushed by his situation despite being assured by the Irishman that there would come a time when he and his co-workers would be released.

He didn't believe him. He knew that the former outward-bound school had its own cesspit. But he played along, waiting, watching... hoping for an opportunity. But, after more than two years being moved around the country and almost suffocating more than once in the confines of a lorry trailer, now being so near to where he grew up was acutely painful. He missed his wife. He missed his life. He went over and over how he got it so badly wrong. How he'd managed to make a massive rookie mistake. He was the only one to blame. But the price he had to pay was pretty damned high.

The October weather was good, and the thought of another twelve-hour shift in the tropical heat of the enclosed building, lit with LED lamps, sickened him. But the Vietnamese workers seemed to thrive in the heavy, dense air. Many had travelled from the poorest regions of Vietnam, at great financial cost, only to find that the promised land was forced labour growing grass. Born in the tropics, they preferred the pungent smell of marijuana to the mud of the potato field. Marijuana was the gang's staple crop but the home-grown potatoes were a useful cover and helped to feed the twenty-five or so Vietnamese workers.

Gary was impressed by the travellers' simple and yet effective working practices. Mostly, the migrants were passive – everyone loved someone and that someone's continued good health relied on the migrants co-operating. Gary knew that the danger to Tina from Frank Cottee was all too real. There were times when he could have tried to escape, but that would have put her life at risk.

# 10

Malcolm showered and shaved in the small cloakroom off the hallway on the ground floor. He didn't much like the face with its white stubble staring back at him but he was approaching eighty so he knew he had to be grateful.

Since marrying Audrey three years ago, he had enjoyed life more than he had thought possible. His remarkable wife had come to Hawksmead as a new widow on a quest to learn the truth behind her little brother's tragic death. And now Tina, who had been his friend and saviour during the dark days when it looked as though he and Audrey would be apart for good, was suffering the loss of her young husband, compounded by the sudden deaths of her parents. Somehow, he and Audrey had to help her build a new life.

'Not easy,' he said as he lathered his chin. 'Not easy at all.'

Audrey heard Tina leave the bathroom and hurried in to have a quick wash. She hoped the smell of crispy bacon wafting up from the kitchen would lure Tina to have some breakfast. The young woman was underweight whereas Audrey, examining her naked form in a full-length mirror fixed to the wall, was definitely looking a little rounded. She blamed Malcolm and smiled. His homemade scones and damson jam, topped by Cornish clotted cream, were pure heaven. Throw in Sunday lunches at the Rorty Crankle out on the moor and her 1970s' frame, once Twiggy-like when she was a photographic model, was now, as Malcolm put it, perfectly plump and a comfortable cushion. She laughed and immediately felt guilty. It would be a long time before their guest would laugh again.

Tina lifted the lid of her suitcase and looked at her neatly folded clothes. The Oxfam shop in Southfields had done very well. She'd had to be brutal; not just about clothes she couldn't fit in her case but about personal knick-knacks and gifts... and all Gary's clothes.

'If you return to London,' said Iain, her team leader, 'do not think about working anywhere else but here.'

She would not return. For all its charms, London would never be home. Where was home? She thought it was with her parents... she screwed her eyes shut and slammed the door on her grief. 'Breathe in to one and out to three,' she said to herself. It took a few deep breaths to restore her composure.

Almost exhausted by the effort, she riffled through her case. What should she put on? The early October weather was still quite warm so she slipped on a pair of comfortable joggers with a drawstring waist, blue socks, a white camisole and a casual shirt. She looked in the mirror. Her eyes were red, her cheeks hollow and her blonde hair needed shaping. She was a pale shadow of the young estate agent who had had such big dreams when she first worked for Harper Dennis, aged eighteen. Now, she had no dreams, no hope, no future. There was nothing left. Just a brother who had chosen to live on the other side of the world.

*No!*

She had more than that. She had friends who cared for her, and she had Audrey and Malcolm. They had written to her both jointly and individually. Although she had rarely replied, they had never given up on her. She felt the tears coming and quickly wiped them away.

The aroma of cooked bacon wafting up the stairs made her tummy rumble and for the first time since Gary had disappeared, she felt real hunger. She grabbed a brush and quickly pulled it through her hair. For a short while she was determined to take a break from the tsunami of grief. She still felt a bit odd – there were blanks in her mind – it was hard to think straight – images would appear uninvited.

She pulled open the bedroom door. All the times she had visited Malcolm's home when he and Audrey were apart, she had never been up to the first floor. She tiptoed in her socks across the landing and quietly walked down the steep stairs. From the hallway, she entered the sitting room and looked at its gilt-framed paintings, antique furniture, chintz covered sofa, and assorted *objets* on the mantelpiece. It was as if she were seeing them for the first time. Double doors were open to the dining room where the rosewood table was laid for breakfast with decorative place mats, strawberry patterned china, matching pots for jam and marmalade, silver cutlery and an incongruous bottle of HP brown sauce.

Audrey carried a matching strawberry-patterned pot of coffee into the dining room and placed it on a heat-proof coaster. She looked at her.

'It's the smell of bacon,' Tina said.

Audrey nodded and smiled. 'Malcolm likes to bake it in the oven so that it's extra crispy. He's also cooked tomatoes from his garden, and scrambled eggs in his own special way. Secret recipe.'

'Thank you.'

'Tea or coffee?'

'The coffee pot winked at me.'

Audrey laughed. 'A lot of things wink at you in Malcolm's cottage, hence my larger dress size. Come and sit down.' She pulled out a rosewood chair with a woven padded seat. Tina sat down facing the French windows and the neat garden with its raised beds and wooden pergola.

Malcolm entered from the kitchen carrying a rack of carefully balanced toast.

'Your garden looks so pretty, Malcolm.'

'It's been a good summer.'

'You should see the memorial garden,' Audrey said. 'It's truly beautiful. There are benches now, so visitors can sit and have a picnic, or read, or do what I do.'

Tina waited for her to expand. She saw Audrey and Malcolm exchange looks. 'Please don't walk on egg shells. It's lovely to see you. To be here.'

'Let's get down to business,' Malcolm said. 'The full works, Tina?'

She smiled. 'The full works.'

He slipped away into the kitchen and Audrey poured coffee into Tina's cup.

'We want you to stay here,' Audrey said. 'I mean, live with us. Use this as your base. No ties. Just, until you want to move on.'

Tina took a few deep breaths. 'I may not be that easy to live with. I'm a bit of a basket case. I'm not the person I was.'

'Life changes us all.' Audrey put her hand on Tina's. 'We are here for when you need us.' They both looked up as Malcolm placed a plate with crispy bacon rashers, grilled tomatoes, mushrooms and scrambled eggs in front of Tina.

'The Mint Cottage special,' he said, and hurried back to the kitchen.

Audrey stage-whispered towards Tina's ear. 'The old man's a great cook but he always caters for the five thousand. There are only so many times one wants to eat leftovers.'

Malcolm returned with two more steaming plates. He placed one in front of Audrey and one at a place set opposite Tina. 'Toast?' He indicated the toast rack.

Tina's head began to spin; she gripped the table edge and took several deep breaths to steady herself. Once her vision had settled, she dared to turn her head and look at Audrey. 'Thank you for welcoming me into your home. You have both been incredibly kind.' She looked up at Malcolm who was still standing. 'And thank you for your more than generous offer.' Tears filled her eyes and she had to blink several times to push them back. 'I accept.'

'Excellent,' Malcolm said and he pulled out his chair. 'But it is only toast, albeit from a home-baked loaf.'

Tina grinned and used her linen napkin to wipe away an escapee.

# 11

The uniformed police officer escorted Tina to the double garage situated to the side of Rise House.

'Do you have the remote?'

She looked at the policeman. 'I have a key for the house. The car keys will be in a metal dish on a side table in the hallway.'

'I'm very sorry, miss, but the house is still under investigation. It's not been released yet. It's why I'm here. You can't go in.'

'How long have you been with the Undermere force?'

'About six years. I've been offered promotion but I like being in uniform, out on the road.'

'Did you ever work with Gary Burton?'

'Gary!' He looked intently at the young woman. 'I am so sorry. It's Tina, isn't it?'

She nodded.

'We are all devastated about Gary. And then to have this on top. We all feel for you down at the station. Gary was very popular. There's a framed photo of your wedding in the gents' toilet.'

Tina gasped.

'I mean, it's there because it's the only place the brass would permit us to hang it.' He paused. When he spoke again his voice was thick with emotion. 'They will find him, Tina. They will bring him home. They will.'

'Thank you.' She turned and walked up the drive away from the house.

'Don't you want your car?' called the copper.

Tina looked back at him. 'I don't have the garage fob or car key.'

'Then, I'd better get them.'

She watched as he used a key to open the door in the temporary wooden structure.

'Hold your breath!' she shouted. 'I mean it.'

'It's all been shut off; should be okay.' He vanished from view and a few seconds later he emerged with an electronic garage door fob attached to a VW Golf key. He pressed the fob and the garage door lifted and slid over two parked cars – a teal blue Mercedes 220 SE two-door, and a white VW Golf, four-door.

'That is a beauty.' The police officer approached the Mercedes. 'A true classic. It has to be mid 1960s.'

'1965. Dad bought it in honour of his brother who died that year. Uncle Mark had a die-cast model he and my dad used to play with together.'

The policeman touched the metal with his finger-tips. 'Phenomenal condition.'

'Yes. Dad kept it polished. It's almost too precious to drive.'

'And the Golf is yours?'

'It was mine. Dad bought it off me for an inflated price when Gary and I moved to London. Gary said I shouldn't drive in the city as there were too many ways for me to get a ticket – yellow junction boxes, bus lanes, speed cameras. In reality, I sold it because we needed the money. Mum uses it as a runaround.' She paused. 'At least she did.'

'Here's the key.' He handed the VW key and fob to her.

'Insurance?'

She nodded. 'Thank you, yes. What's your name?'

'Hett. PC Hett. Matthew.'

Tina leaned forward and kissed him on the cheek. 'Thank you, Matthew.'

She opened the driver's door and slipped into the familiar seat of the white VW Golf. The interior had a comforting aroma – a mix of leather and cleaning spray.

She smiled.

She was home.

# 12

Trevor Harper rubbed his eyes. His estate agency business was ticking over but increasing levels of regulation were complicating both sales and lettings. His main problem was the turnover of staff. As soon as negotiators got any good, they left him for one of the chains. Or, got married and moved down south. He heard the door open and Max, a negotiator who he wouldn't mind getting rid of, leapt to his feet.

'What are you doing here?' Max almost shouted. 'You're not coming back?'

Trevor looked at the person standing by the door. 'Tina?' His beautiful and talented young negotiator was now a gaunt figure. He pushed back his chair and wrapped his arms around her. He didn't know what to say. He turned to Max. 'Brew us some coffee, then pop out for pain au raisin and pain au chocolat.'

'What? Why? She's not a client?'

Trevor pulled apart from Tina and removed his wallet from his jacket pocket. 'Here's some cash.' He handed Max a note. 'The prodigal has returned.'

'The what?'

'Go get the pastries. I'll make the coffee.'

Max snatched the money and Tina held the door open for him. He stomped out.

'You're his nemesis,' Trevor said with a big grin.

Tina closed the door. 'I'm surprised he's still here.'

'Do you know how hard it is to get rid of dead wood?'

She laughed. Trevor saw her face light up, but not like it used to. 'Come and sit down.' He gestured to a sitting area.

'Can we sit at your desk?'

'Yes. Of course. I'll grab you a seat.' He pulled over a chair on castors from another desk and Tina sat down. 'It's so good to see you, Tina. We've missed you. I heard about your husband. Terrible.'

'My parents' house will be for sale, soon. I'll make sure you get the business.'

'Are they moving? Downsizing?'

She told him in sparse words what had happened.

Silence.

Trevor looked at his former negotiator. At one time the world was at her feet, now it was crushing her. The door opened and Max sauntered in carrying a paper bag. 'Thank you Max. Get a couple of plates, make the coffee then take an early lunch – on me.'

'What's going on?' Max looked both pleased at the free lunch but annoyed at being ordered around.

'Tell you what, Max. Forget the coffee. Go now.'

Max examined the cash in his hand. 'Don't expect any change.' He threw the bag of pastries on Trevor's desk, pulled the door open and banged it shut behind him.

'Where is everyone?' Tina asked, looking around the agency.

'One is on maternity leave. One has a dental appointment. One is on holiday in Morocco. That leaves Max and me. I would get rid of him but he's been here too long and can be useful.' He swallowed and stood. 'Tina, I'm so sorry.'

She half-smiled and shrugged. 'It never rains but it

pours?'

He picked up the bag of pastries. 'I'll make us some coffee.'

She followed him into the tiny kitchen where he put a pod in the Nespresso machine and a cup under the spout. Without thinking, she opened a cupboard and removed a couple of plates. 'How's the family?' she asked.

'Olivia kicked me out. I'm in rental accommodation above Merlin's hardware store on Hawksmead High Street.'

'Trevor, I remember that flat. It's a dump. There's mould on the walls and last time I looked it was infested with moths.'

'Yes it is a dump, but it's a cheap dump.'

'What happened?'

He put another pod in the machine. 'I made a stupid decision.'

'We all have history.'

They waited for the coffee to finish then Trevor placed both cups and plates on a tray together with a small jug of milk.

'I had access to a chunk of cash. A friend of mine who had made quite a bit out of property advised me to buy some cheap houses in Hull.' He carried the tray to his desk.

Tina picked up the bag of pastries and followed. 'Hull?'

'Kingston upon Hull.'

'Why there?'

'There was supposedly a lot of investment and re-generation. I stupidly listened to my friend. In the three years since I bought the houses they've halved in value. I can't even sell them. They're rented out to the local authority who use them as temporary housing. At least once a month there's a police raid – usually for drugs or to recover stolen goods.'

'But why did you and Olivia break up?'

'I used her inheritance to buy the houses. Bad decision.'

'She'll come round, I'm sure.'

'Tina. I mucked up my family and I mucked up my business. I should've made you a partner. If I had, you might not have left for London.' Immediately, he regretted his words. 'How can I help?' He placed a cup of coffee in front of her and slid across the milk jug. 'Is there anything I can do for you?'

Tina stood and wandered around the empty agency. 'I presume your online presence is better than your kerb appeal?'

Trevor forced a laugh. 'It's not bad. Max is in charge of that. With everything that's going on, I've not given it the attention I should. Pain au raisin or pain au chocolat?'

'Au raisin, thank you.'

'Come back.'

Tina looked momentarily confused.

Trevor pushed on. 'It's why you're here, isn't it?'

She slumped down on the wheeled chair. 'For a few minutes I wanted to wind back the clock.'

'To when you sold the old school boarding house?'

She smiled. 'That changed a lot of lives. At the moment I'm staying with Audrey and Malcolm Cadwallader. They've been really good to me.'

'They owe you a lot.'

She looked down at her hands.

'Do you have any plans?' he asked.

'My parents' funeral. Clearing the house. Selling it.'

'Don't you have a brother?'

She nodded. 'As soon as he can get away from work, he'll fly back to help with the funeral and stuff. He's married, now.'

'I thought he was gay.'

'He is. New Zealand was one of the first countries to allow gay weddings.'

Trevor took a bite of pain au chocolat followed by a sip of coffee. 'The school on the moor could do with your magic touch.'

'Has it not sold?'

'Who would buy it? The old monastery is Grade I, the land is designated National Park and the school buildings look like Dartmoor Prison... not a lot of charm. Although it's not all doom and gloom. We did manage to let it out to a charity that finds work for migrant labour. The rent is minimal but the trustees are happy as it covers a few costs. In an ideal world, they would like to be shot of it.'

'You could sell it to Disney and turn it into a medieval theme park.'

'You know, if it sold, I think some aspects of planning would be relaxed.'

Tina looked at her Swatch.

'Have you somewhere to be?' Trevor asked.

'I came here because I have nowhere to go apart from back to Malcolm's cottage.'

'You have friends, Tina. Many friends.'

'Friends I have neglected.'

'Nobody blames you for keeping vigil for Gary. And now with your parents... let your friends be your friends.'

'It's good to see you, Trevor.' She stood to leave.

'Commission only. You don't even need to come in,

unless you want to.' He looked up at his former star ne-gotiator. 'I need your help, Tina.'

'I can't come back.'

'No. I understand. How about just this one special project? Use your skills to find a buyer.'

'But it's let.'

'One month's notice. No problem.'

'Commission?'

'Ten percent.'

'Wow.'

'I can still negotiate.'

'What will I get?'

'I should've made you a partner years ago. Fifty-fifty. Five per cent.'

'Where do I begin?'

'I have no idea.'

'I'm not a miracle worker.'

'Yes you are. Get in your car. Go see the place and spin your gold.'

'Keys?'

'All out. You'll have to knock.'

# 13

Industrial potato picking is usually undertaken by two machines that harvest the crop in tandem. No such luxury for Gary. He squatted down in the mud and picked each tuber individually and then chucked it into an old plastic bucket. It was a warm, clear day out in the potato field and for a few moments he imagined being a free man, despite being chained hand and foot. The school was remote, set in a beautiful but forbidding landscape. His captors had two drones with cameras they used to survey the area for uninvited attention. He had to admit, it was a neat set up from which all manner of crimes were probably being committed, including the growing of marijuana, exploiting illegal migrants, and no doubt much more yet to be discovered.

One day, soon, bad weather would prevent the flying of drones and he would make his escape. But he had to be patient and choose his moment, carefully. He would not buy his freedom at Tina's expense.

Hawksmead High Street looked little changed from when Tina had last driven her pride and joy. Every bow-fronted shop window triggered memories of a time when she thought she was sophisticated, but now realised she'd been ignorant and naive.

She was a twenty-one-year-old estate agent when she had sold the old school boarding house at the top of Hawksmead High Street to Audrey. More than forty years apart in age, the two women had immediately clicked, pricking Tina's conscience for selling the gloomy house with a sad history to such a lovely and vibrant woman. But it was the history of the house that had brought Audrey and Malcolm together, and its later destruction by fire that introduced Tina to her policeman.

Over the following spring months and through much of the summer, Malcolm and friends had created a beautiful garden with a memorial stone engraved with the names of five boys who had attended Hawksmead College in the 1960s and who had all tragically died. On a glorious September afternoon in the memorial garden, Reverend William Longden had married Christina Louise Small to Gary Simon Burton. It was the happiest day of her life. Three years later, the October sun was shining but there was a deep ache in her heart.

She focused on the road and came to the humpback bridge spanning the River Hawk. Through tear-filled eyes she negotiated the stone-built bridge with its single-lane and felt her stomach flip as the VW Golf thumped down on the north side. She used the heel of her hand to try and clear her eyes but she was going too fast. Fortunately, the Old Military Road was clear of traffic and she got away with her erratic driving.

A rusting sign pointed to the right and she turned into the school's mile-long drive. Bordered by hawthorn hedges and deep ditches, the winding road could be hazardous, especially in the wet at night, but it invited Tina to open up her carburettor and stretch the rubber on her tyres. In a little over a minute, she rounded a final bend and swept onto the oval apron in front of the former boarding school. She skidded to a halt on the loose gravel, turned off her engine, released her seatbelt and climbed out. Several vehicles were parked near the main entrance towards one end of the long building; big old cars whose glory days were far behind, and classic white tradesmen's vans, rust showing through muddy wheel arches.

Ivy grew unchecked up the mighty Victorian facade, blocking out most of the windows. To the far left were the ruins of an old monastery, torn down by King Henry VIII in the mid sixteenth century. Across the fields to the right, were ramshackle barns and sheds. Much work needed to be done if she had any hope of finding a buyer. A tiny buzz attracted her attention, she looked up at the sky and spotted the small dot of a drone flying high overhead.

The crunch of large feet on gravel startled her but she stood her ground as a tall man approached. In his hand was a controller with a screen, two stubby aerials and two joysticks. He stopped about ten feet from her.

'And who might you be?'

His few words told her he was from the Republic of Ireland, endorsed by his dark wavy hair, deep blue eyes, and white teeth that almost shone from his tanned face. He had to be late thirties but his clothes were out of an old movie. He wore battered suede boots, heavy cotton trousers that looked like buckskin, a check shirt, floral waistcoat and an almost matching neckerchief.

'I'm a consultant for the estate agency selling this property,' Tina said.

'Well, you're not doing a very good job. If it wasn't

for us, this place would be overrun with rats.'

'That's why I'm here, to see what needs to be done.'

'Forget it. There's no market for a place like this.'

She smiled as she flexed her selling muscles. 'There's always a market if sold in the right way.'

'Look, sweetheart, we're helping people here. We're making a bit of money so can pay more rent, if that's what it's all about.' He moved closer to her, touching distance. 'We're here to help people. Not just those seeking to make England their new home, but the local community. Perhaps we could help you, too?'

She felt a strange conflict inside her. The man was handsome, goddamned sexy, and was cocooning her with his silky Irish lilt. It was intoxicating.

'Mr O'Hanlon?'

'Dermot. And who might you be?'

'Tina. Tina Small.' Why hadn't she used her married name? She waited for him to offer his hand but he reached for a pocket in his waistcoat and offered her his phone.

'Put your number in here, please.'

'Why?'

'Do it.'

She took his phone and thumbed in her number.

'Now call it,' he ordered.

It took a few seconds before they heard her phone ringing in the car.

'Next time, Tina...' He came right up to her so she could feel the warmth of his breath. '...make an appointment.'

She reached out her hand and gently pushed him away. 'Next time, I'll come with a team.'

'A team? A team of what?'

She handed back the phone and opened her car door.

'I'm serious about selling this place. But, before I can do that, it has to be spruced up.' She got in the car.

O'Hanlon held the top of the door. 'Look. I have people scraping around picking potatoes. Let me get them to clear the weeds and the ivy. As you say, spruce the place up and, if you're happy, you pay a fair price for their effort.'

She looked up at him and was infuriated by the hot feeling creeping up her chest and neck. 'If you do the job well, I'm sure the trustees would be happy to forego the rent for a week or two.'

'A month... at the very least.'

'Well let's see the result first. I must go.'

He continued to hold the door. 'I take it you're married, Tina?'

She was momentarily flustered and looked at the rings on her left hand. 'Yes. No. I'm not sure.'

'Perhaps we could discuss your marital status over a drink? What are you doing this evening?' His direct approach and unblinking eyes fringed by dark lashes, rekindled her dormant desires. He pushed on. 'Do you know the Falcon pub?'

'Yes.'

'I'll be there at seven. It would be grand to see you.' He stepped away from the car and closed the door.

She felt him watching her through the side window as she clicked-in her seatbelt and started the engine. From the corner of her eye she saw him give a little wave. Heat burned her cheeks. She pushed the gear lever into first and released the clutch. The Golf lurched forward but was held by the handbrake. The engine stalled. She took a breath, restarted the engine and swiftly pulled away. As she swung around the large oval apron she sneaked a peek.

He waved again.

Gary looked up from his muddy furrow and caught a glimpse of a white car.

Another dealer picking up his stash. In broad daylight. When was somebody going to get suspicious?

In the pale blue sky, he saw a hawk circling above, its beautiful wings and wide tail perfectly designed for swooping to the ground and catching an unwary rabbit in its talons.

The black dot of a drone attracted his attention. It was also perfectly designed to survey the landscape through its high-definition camera lens. For the price of a few quid on Amazon, it was easy for his captors to keep watch.

Roll on winter. Roll on freezing fog.

# 14

Tina decided to take the scenic route back to Malcolm's cottage along the Old Military Road. She wouldn't go that way at night. Even in daylight the road carved a dangerously curved route through a beautiful but bleak rolling landscape with treacherous bogs, deep gorges, sharp-edged escarpments, and rapid water courses in a vast area where mobile phone coverage was patchy at best.

Dermot O'Hanlon's handsome, smiling face flashed before her eyes. Her friend, Audrey, had come to Hawksmead, newly widowed, and had found love in a truly unexpected way. Could the same happen to Tina? Or was it simply a sexual awakening after more than two years sleeping in a lonely bed?

*Please forgive me, Gary.*

She looked at the car clock and planned her afternoon.

Malcolm heard the front door open and smiled. He'd insisted on giving Tina a key, so she could come and go as she pleased. It was part of his strategy to help her settle in and feel at home rather than a guest.

'Is that you, Tina?'

'Yes. I thought I'd pop back for a while before going out again.'

'There's a little lunch if you're feeling peckish.'

'I am, thank you. I'll just wash my hands.'

Malcolm heard her enter the cloakroom off the hallway as his wife came down the stairs.

'Did you mention lunch?' Audrey asked, as she approached the kitchen. 'Not that I've earned it and we did have a very good breakfast.'

'It's only a few bits and pieces from the farmers' market, aided and abetted by Waitrose.'

'Sounds delicious.'

'I'll be back in a minute.' Malcolm went into the hallway and took his time climbing the stairs.

Tina opened the cloakroom door and stood in the entrance to the kitchen.

'I see you've been reacquainted with your car,' Audrey said.

Tina smiled. 'Yes. I met a kindly policeman who knew Gary. The house is still sealed.'

'They have to be sure. It must've been horrible for you.'

Tina paused. 'I went to Harper Dennis.'

'I didn't expect that.'

'Nor I. The car took me there. I've been offered a job, or rather a project.'

'Are you sure that's a good idea?'

'I have to do something.'

'If you're worried about money, it's not a problem. We can help.'

Tina felt the resurgence of her tears. 'That is so kind. The Met is still paying Gary's salary, so I'm fine. I'm just not fine in my head. I have to do something or else I'll go mad.'

'Yes. You're right to keep busy. Malcolm often says that doing nothing is the fast track to dementia. Although, I quite enjoy doing nothing.'

Audrey removed a bottle of sparkling elderflower from the fridge and took three glasses out of a cupboard. 'It's just a light lunch before an afternoon snooze.' She carried the bottle and glasses to the dining table.

Tina heard Malcolm come down the stairs and smiled when he entered the kitchen. 'I've been to your old haunt,' she said.

He looked a bit puzzled. 'Not Paddy Power the bookie on Hawksmead High Street?'

She laughed. 'Almost. Well he is Irish. I drove up to the old school and met a guy who runs a charity helping migrants.'

'That'll be O'Hanlon.' Malcolm ushered Tina into the dining room.

'You know him?' she asked.

'We have met. His name is on the contract. I'm one of the school's trustees. When I was Mayor of Hawksmead they invited me onto the board.' He turned to the dining table. 'You sit there, Tina, facing the garden.'

She pulled out her chair and admired the lovely spread. 'A light lunch?'

'What were you doing up at the old school?' Audrey asked as she sat down.

'I've been tasked with finding a buyer.'

'For the school?'

'I'm delighted,' Malcolm interjected. 'Once it's sold, it will free up cash to provide a myriad of activities for young people. At the moment, it's of no use to anyone.'

'Apart from helping migrants.'

Malcolm looked intently at Tina. 'What do you make of O'Hanlon?'

'He's clearly a bit of a rogue but seems okay.'

'I hope you're right. I was against him taking over the old school building. I felt, and still do, that he's up to no good, and that getting him and his travelling companions out could be a problem. But, my fellow trustees were keen to take any money going, so I was outvoted.'

'I'll let you know more after my meeting tonight,' Tina said.

Malcolm exchanged a glance with Audrey seated at the end of the table.

'It's just a drink,' she explained, emphatically.

'You *should* go out,' Audrey said placing her napkin on her lap. 'Just take care.'

'Don't worry. I learned my lesson after the Russian.' She thought back to another encounter four years ago with a crooked property developer whose sculpted features and rough charm had more than turned her head.

'Yes, he was also a bit of a rogue,' Audrey responded, 'but very handsome.'

Malcolm cleared his throat. 'Why do women always go for bad boys?'

'Because, Malcolm,' Audrey said, 'I find you impossible to resist!'

He burst out laughing.

Tina smiled. 'I promise it won't happen again.'

# 15

Magdalena Jablonski was an opportunist. She was barely out of her teens when Britain opened its doors to new members of the European Union. She was tall, handsome, athletic, and used her physical might to good effect as a professional cleaner, eventually running her own company, specialising in end of tenancy cleans for lettings agencies, including Harper Dennis.

She had decided not to live in London and chose the town of Undermere as it was big enough to find work but not so big that she would feel like an ant. Almost fifteen years later, she had married a fellow Pole but divorced him within a year for sleeping with Paulina, her prettiest cleaner. It was the jolt she had needed. She sold her cleaning business and used the money to train as a beautician. It didn't take long before she was visiting homes providing manicures and pedicures, facials, make-up tips, eyebrow threading, and all forms of waxing.

'I am aesthetician,' she would say. 'I go where hairs should fear to grow.' Her big problem had been managing all her clients. Her solution was to open a salon and train staff the way she had trained her cleaners. A newsagents had recently closed in Hawksmead High Street and although the rent was quite high, compounded by rates, she felt that a salon was the only way to make real money. But what to call it? She spoke to her English clients but none of their ideas worked for her.

'I think I have name for salon,' she said to Maureen, a woman in the autumn of her life who was always perfectly groomed and liked everything just so.

'I hope it's not one of those dreadful puns that hairdressers love so much like Curl-up and Dye.'

'No pun. Straight to point. Can you guess?' She guided Maureen's hand under a curved LED lamp to harden the nail gel.

'Let me see. File Away?'

'File Away? No. It should be File *Here* not File *Away*.'

Maureen laughed. 'Let's try again. House of Nails?'

'You make me sound like hardware store.'

'It's not just nails, is it?'

'I give total package, but not cut hair on head.'

'Oh, this is a good pun.' Maureen looked very excited.

'You said no puns.'

'Ignore what I said. This is so good… Mag Wax.'

'Mag Wax?' Magdalena was totally perplexed. 'What pun is that?'

'Mag Wax as in Mad Max! You know, the 1980s film with Mel Gibson.'

'I not heard of such thing. Customer think I crazy, mad woman. No I have name. Change hand.'

'*Change hand*? That's terrible.'

'Put left hand under lamp.'

Maureen laughed and changed hands. 'Tell me. What's it going to be?'

'Wax Polish.'

Maureen burst out laughing. 'That's the best pun yet.'

'No pun. I wax and I Polish.' Magdalena watched

Maureen as she tried to contain her giggles.

Without fail, every time Magdalena said *Wax Polish* her clients fell about laughing but all thought the name, brilliant.

'Why it funny? Why you laugh?' But what did please her was that every client promised to visit her salon.

A new business is always a risk but Magdalena had thought it through and was confident that the salon would be a success. She wanted to still supply a personal service, but she knew she couldn't handle all the work on her own. She'd heard that her ex-husband and Paulina had broken up and so she contacted the young woman.

They spoke in Polish and it was to the point. 'You finish with husband?'

'He no good,' Paulina retorted. 'Why you marry him?'

'He ask me. Big mistake. You come back. Work for me.'

'I am happy in job.'

'Nobody is happy as cleaner. Only boss happy. I train you to be beautician. Plenty money.'

A few doors down from the salon was the office for The Hawksmead Chronicle. The bell pinged when Magdalena entered and she was met by a tall man, late fifties, with sandy greying hair and a welcoming smile revealing crossed front teeth. 'You are the famous Magdalena,' he said.

Magdalena was not usually lost for words but this charming man had taken the wind out of her sails. 'Yes. Are you psychic?'

He held out his hand. 'Andy Blake. My daughter-in-law told me she's delighted you're opening a beauty salon in Hawksmead. It saves her driving to Undermere. With three children, nothing's easy.'

She shook his hand. 'Thank you. I have opening in two weeks. I want to put in advertisement.'

'There'll be no charge if you agree to my son, Tony, taking photographs of the event. Perhaps he could also write a feature story about you, your history and your hopes for the future?'

'He is good photographer. I see his photos.' She held out her hand. 'We have deal.'

Andy shook her hand again. 'How about an Ad that the reader can cut out to get a discount on treatment, say for a month after opening? Just to get you going.'

A tall, gangly young man entered the office from the street. Over his shoulder was a large bag Magdalena knew contained his photographic equipment.

'Hi Dad.'

'Tony, I would like you to meet Magdalena, she owns the new beauty salon up the road.'

'Magdalena!' Tony's face broke into a big smile. 'How wonderful to see you. It's been way too long.'

'Not since Tina's wedding, I think.'

'Eden is thrilled you're opening a salon in Hawk-smead.'

'I should have called her. Given home visit.'

'In truth, she likes to go out and get her beauty treatments, to have a rest away from the little ones.'

'Tony.'

Andy's son turned to his father.

'Magdalena's agreed to our coverage of her grand opening.'

'Brilliant!' Tony smiled at Magdalena. 'I'm sure Wax Polish is going to be a big success.'

'Thank you. It's Wax *Polish*.'

'That's what I said!'

'It's his northern accent,' Andy laughed.

# 16

Magdalena had enjoyed a busy morning that had gone through lunch into mid afternoon. Paulina had worked for eight hours straight so the young assistant had left for home when Magdalena heard the bell tinkle above the door. She looked up from her work station and her mouth fell open. She leapt to her feet. The young woman standing by the open door had excellent posture, and blonde hair that shone with conditioner. But her clothes looked a size too big for a frame that was short of her famed, natural curves. More than anything, her eyes lacked their former spirit.

'Tina!'

The young woman looked directly at Magdalena and her smile lit up her face, the way Magdalena remembered when she had first started to clean for Harper Dennis.

'Hello Mags.'

A great wave of emotion washed over Magdalena. She knew Tina had lost her husband and the news that her parents had died in tragic circumstances had spread throughout the little town. Without another word, she walked over to Tina and wrapped her arms around her, feeling her bones as they hugged. 'We have missed you so much.' She cupped Tina's chin in her large hands and kissed each cheek twice.

'It is wonderful to see you, Mags.'

'I won't ask how you are. I imagine.' She released Tina's face. 'Would you like tea or something stronger? I still have drink from grand opening.'

'I wish I hadn't waited so long to come home.'

'You had to wait. You had to be sure he no come back.'

'I'll never be sure.' Tina walked into the salon and Magdalena shut the door.

'No. That is truth. But Gary would not want you to waste precious life.'

'Wow, Mags, I cannot believe this was the old newsagent. Look at it.' She continued in a deliberately seductive sales voice. 'Bright yet soft lighting, delicate decor with floating shelves displaying gorgeous-looking products, vibrantly coloured abstract art, all-white workstations, easy-clean padded chairs, a sofa and coffee table in the waiting area, and a chevron-patterned tiled floor that is pure drama.'

Magdalena laughed. 'I didn't know it was so good 'til you tell me!'

Tina gripped her arms. 'Mags, it's fantastic. You've got everything here. I'm so impressed.'

'I'm now impressed with self, too.'

They both laughed.

'You want treatment?' Magdalena looked Tina up and down. 'What you really need is good meal. You are too thin, my darling.'

'I don't think I can put on weight between now and seven this evening. I have a date.'

Magdalena felt a twinge of disappointment. 'A date?'

'Well, sort of. He's Irish. He runs a charity helping migrants. They're based up at the old school.'

Magdalena took Tina's hands in hers. 'Be careful, my

sweet. They are travelling people. I don't trust them.'

'It's just a drink. I managed to get my hair shaped but I am worried about the rest of me.'

'I give facial, do make-up. You look like movie star.'

Tina laughed. 'If only. But I would love to have my legs waxed. I have neglected my personal grooming.'

'You blondes don't know what hair is.'

'I want to feel good. He won't know, of course, but I will.'

Magdalena put the closed sign up and locked the door.

'You mustn't turn away customers,' Tina said.

'End of day. No customers. Come into my house of wax.' She guided Tina to a secluded section of the salon and pulled a curtain around a padded treatment table, with a headrest at one end and a roll of paper at the base 'You like music? Lady Gaga?'

'I love her.'

Magdalena fiddled with her phone and Lady Gaga's distinctive voice filled the air through white Sonos speakers. She placed the phone on a white plastic treatment station with sections and shelves for wooden spatulas, talcum powder, pots of wax, assorted creams and lotions, and a wax heater.

'Take off trouser and lie down. Have you had wax before?'

'A few times. But never with Lady Gaga for company.' Tina unlaced her trainers and peeled off her jeans. She draped them over a chair.

Magadalena pulled the paper from the roll over the entire length of the table and smoothed it flat. 'Hop on.' She slipped on a pair of ultra thin silicone gloves whilst Tina made herself comfortable. 'You, lucky. I strip off hairs in next to no time.' She ran her hands up Tina's legs. 'Bikini?'

'I was thinking of having the Full Monty.'

'What's that?'

'You know... smooth all over.'

'It's very fashionable. Take brief off.'

Tina rolled down her briefs and Magdalena placed them on the chair. She felt her mouth go dry and didn't trust herself to speak. From the moment they first met at Harper Dennis, she had fallen for Tina, who was eighteen and just out of school at the time, but did her best to always hide it.

'You've gone very quiet,' Tina said.

Magdalena looked into her eyes and swallowed. 'Would you like legs or bun first?'

Tina laughed. 'Bun! That's a new one on me.'

'If I do privates first, you have longer recovery time before drink with gypsy.'

'I think *traveller* is what they prefer.'

'Yes. You right. I no like Polack so I understand. Right. Let's get going. The wax is warm not hot and I will quickly strip your bun bare, my pretty. First I sprinkle powder to absorb body lotion.'

Magdalena worked fast to make the process as comfortable as possible. She used a wooden spatula to paste on narrow strips of thick green wax, before ripping each one off. As soon as she did, she pressed her free hand against the tender bare skin to ease the painful shock.

'Usually, it takes three times as long to clear foliage but God kind to you.'

Tina did not respond.

Magdalena looked up from her task and saw a tear trickle from the corner of her eye.

'I don't think God's been that kind to me,' Tina said,

in little more than a whisper.

Magdalena was angry with herself. 'No. He has not.' She reached for a tub of cream that was ultra expensive and saved for special clients. 'This will wipe away pain of wax.' She unscrewed the lid and felt overwhelming desire for the exceptionally pretty but vulnerable young woman lying on the couch. 'It's a bit cool,' she said as she scooped up a wad of cream and smoothed it over Tina's pink skin in gentle, circling motions.

'That feels nice.'

Magdalena glanced at Tina's face and saw that her eyes were closed. 'You have beautiful shape.'

'Shame I can't show it off!'

'Shame I can't put photo in window like barber shop.'

Tina burst out laughing.

Magdalena continued to work the cream with her fingertips.

'Mmm, that feels really good. You have a magic touch. No wonder your clients love you.'

Magdalena pulled her hand away as her eyes filled. 'Tina, I am not good person.'

'What do you mean?' She sat up on her elbows.

Magdalena took a deep breath. 'I like you wrong way. I always have. I so sorry.' Tears coursed down her cheeks.

'I don't understand. You're married. Were married.'

'Yes. I Catholic. My thoughts are a sin. I never confess to priest. Please don't hate me.'

Tina lay back down on the padded table. 'Mags... finish what you started. Legs please.'

Later, they shared the white faux-leather sofa in the waiting area as they worked their way through a bottle of Sauvignon Blanc. Magdalena was back to her old self, the self she projected when Tina was starting out as an estate agent.

'My husband seduced Paulina who worked for me in cleaning company. I break with him 'cause I like *her* ... and I jealous. She now works here, as beautician.' Her eyes sparkled as a bright smile lit up her face.

'Has she had the wax treatment?'

Magdalena choked on her wine and some splashed on the sofa.

# 17

It was gone seven in the evening when Tina left Wax Polish and headed down to The Falcon. She felt good and slightly shocked by how much she had enjoyed the delicate touch of Magdalena's fingers.

She pulled open the door to The Falcon and walked up to the bar. It was a traditional, old-style pub with dark wood tables and chairs, padded benches in wood-panelled booths, and rosewood-framed black and white photographs of school plays, cricket matches, fetes and picnics.

'Hello Ted.'

The once-handsome barman, now stout and florid but with a massive smile of welcome looked at her through the row of metal tankards hanging above the darkly-stained counter. 'Good grief. Heather!' he boomed. 'Kill the fatted calf.'

A petite, pretty, blonde popped up from behind the bar. 'I wouldn't call you a calf, Ted, more of an old bull.'

'Look who's here.'

Heather stared at Tina open-mouthed. 'Ted. Gin, tonic, zest of lemon. I'll make the pork sandwiches. She looks half-starved.'

'May I have a hug first?' Tina asked.

Ted leaned across the bar and gave Tina an all embracing hug.

Heather opened the bar door and came into the public area to greet her. 'We're so happy to see you… and so sorry.'

'I thought I'd be forgotten.' She gave Heather a hug.

'Never. Never my darling.'

'I wanted to come home. But I couldn't face returning without Gary.'

'There's no news?'

Tina shook her head.

'Take a seat. Ted'll bring you your drink and I'll be back in a few mins.'

'Hello.' The voice had an enticing come-hither tone.

Tina looked behind her into smiling Irish eyes. All her dark and depressing thoughts evaporated.

'My name's Dermot,' he continued in his gorgeous accent. 'In case you had forgotten.'

'I hadn't forgotten.' She held out her hand.

His smile cocooned her in a teenage world of fantasy. 'These two lovely people got a hug.' He indicated Heather and Ted with his eyes.

'They've more than earned it.' She pulled her hand back but kept out of hugging range.

'I have a booth,' he said. 'Would you care to join me?'

Heather lightly touched Tina's arm. 'I'll bring your food over.'

'Food? Whatever you're making, could it be for two?' Dermot asked.

'Of course.'

Tina felt his hand gently rest on her upper arm as he guided her to a booth where there was a tall glass of black liquid. She slid onto a padded bench seat and he sat opposite her.

'I love these old pubs,' he said. 'Full of character. Reminds me of a nice little establishment in Mullingar.'

'Is that where you're from?'

'From there and everywhere. Travellers see the whole world as their home.'

'Well you can keep your thieving hands out of mine!' The voice was rough, intoxicated.

Tina and Dermot looked up at the red, bloated face of a man in his early seventies.

'I don't believe we've been introduced,' Dermot said, holding out his hand.

The man ignored the peace offering and looked down at Tina. 'Watch your step, girlie. He'll have those rings off your fingers to give to one of his gypsy tarts.' He laughed and took a swig from his tankard.

Tina glanced down at her wedding and engagement rings.

'Listen, old man,' Dermot said. 'You don't know me and I don't know you. So, be off.'

'Ten years ago your type broke into my home, but I got him with my old school cricket bat. I knocked him for six.'

Tina saw Dermot's face, flush. 'We've mended our ways since then.'

'Vincent,' called Ted from the bar. 'Leave the young couple alone.'

'Couple… I like the sound of that.' Dermot turned to Ted standing with his hands planted on the counter top. 'Another drink for my friend, kind sir.' He reached into a pocket and pulled out a wad of well-handled notes. He peeled one off. 'This should cover it.'

Vincent snatched the cash. 'It cost a lot more than that to fix my window.' He looked down at Tina. 'Gary forgotten, already?' He turned his back and meandered to the bar.

Dermot looked at Tina. 'I take it, Gary's your husband?'

She felt a large lump of guilt in her gut. 'Yes.'

'What time would he be expecting you back?'

She was pleased to see his disappointment. 'I'm...' She hesitated saying the words. 'I'm a widow.'

Relief, even joy swept over his handsome face. 'I'm sorry to hear that, and for one so young.'

Ted placed a gin and tonic on the table in front of Tina. 'My apologies for Vincent,' he said to Dermot. 'He's a troubled man. His head says one thing and his heart says another.'

Dermot watched Ted return to the bar then picked up his tall glass and looked into her eyes. 'To *your* good health.'

'I must go.' She slid across the booth.

Dermot put down his glass and reached for her wrist. 'Don't go, my darlin'. How does it help Gary for you to go now?'

The touch of his hand ignited a fizz, she knew would be hard to ignore, especially if it grew stronger. 'It's not just Gary. My parents died a few days ago. I should be wearing black, lighting candles, praying, wailing.'

'Jesus! I had no idea you were Roman Catholic.'

'Oh I'm not. But I *should* be doing all those things. Shouldn't I?'

'They will come later. Right now you're in shock. It's devastating what's happened to you.'

Heather placed two tempting plates of pork and apple sandwiches in front of them. 'There's napkins over there.' She indicated a paper napkin dispenser on the table.

Tina smiled. 'Thank you, Heather.'

The older woman rested her hand gently on Tina's shoulder. 'It's so lovely to see you.' She turned away and hurried back to the kitchen.

'They like you here,' Dermot said, picking up a sandwich quarter.

Tina relaxed. 'What is that dark brew? Guinness?'

'Guinness without a head? No, it's Cola. Guinness doesn't travel well to England.'

'I've never drunk Guinness.'

'It's a hard drink to like but an even harder drink to give up.' He bit into his sandwich.

She mirrored him and picked up a sandwich quarter.

'What's your story, Tina?' His Adam's apple bobbed as he swallowed. 'Putting aside the obvious, why are you the belle of the ball?'

She put down her sandwich and took a sip of her gin and tonic, intoxicated by his blue eyes which she could now see had flecks of green.

'Did something happen?' Dermot pressed. 'I think so. It's not just your natural charm that has made you so popular with these folks.'

She took another sip of her drink. 'Four years ago, Audrey, the woman I'm staying with, came to Hawksmead to find out what happened to her little brother in the 1960s. I had sold her the school boarding house which used to stand at the top of the High Street. It's now a memorial garden in memory of her brother, Robert, and his best friend, my Uncle Mark – both died in tragic accidents. Ted, the landlord, knew her brother as they had acted in the same school play along with our drunken friend, Vincent, who had fallen in love with Robert.'

'In love?'

'Vincent played Cyrano de Bergerac and Audrey's brother was Roxane.'

'I can see how the wires could get crossed.'

'There's a cast photo from the play over there.' She indicated a clutch of old framed photos hanging on a far wall. 'Anyway, you can see how we're all linked.'

'There's more than that,' he pushed.

She sipped her drink and fought to suppress her awakened desire. 'Audrey's house caught fire and she only just managed to escape. I drove her to hospital. It's how I met my husband. He was in the patrol car chasing me.'

She saw Dermot take a deep breath as he leaned back away from her. 'Your husband was a policeman?'

'Yes. Anyway, the remains of the boarding house were removed and Audrey's husband created a beautiful memorial garden to honour the memory of Audrey's brother, my Uncle Mark, and three other boys who died whilst attending the school. It's where Gary and I were married.'

Dermot picked up his glass and took a long pull of cola. He placed the glass gently on the old, stained table. 'I'm beginning to get a sense as to why you are held in such high esteem.'

She laughed. 'I don't know about that!'

'To be serious. What family do you have, Tina?'

'When the coroner releases my parents' bodies and we can lay them to rest, my brother will fly back.' She felt a tear trickle down her cheek and roughly swiped it away. 'He lives in New Zealand with his husband.'

'Husband? What a modern world it is.'

'Not everywhere.'

'True. In my community, certain things are acceptable and certain things are not.'

'Tell me about your community.'

'Honour. Code. Secrecy. They are what we live by. It protects us from outsiders.'

'People like me?'

'The police, the authorities, those who would hurt us.' A pint of Guinness was slopped down in front of him.

'Drink your poison then get out.'

'Please Vincent.' Tina touched the elderly man's hand and he immediately softened.

'You mean much to me, Tina,' Vincent slurred. 'I didn't know your Uncle Mark but I knew Roxane, Audrey's little brother.' He looked at Dermot. 'Have a care with this gentleman. "Traveller" is a catch-all phrase for tax dodger, sponger, fly-tipper, confidence trickster, burglar, and all-round nuisance.'

Dermot stiffened as Vincent lurched away.

'Thank you for not retaliating,' she said. 'He's led a sad life.'

'I couldn't argue with the guy. Travellers are all those things... and more.'

'More?'

'He forgot to mention loyalty and big loving hearts. I hope I can prove that to you in the coming weeks.'

She bit into her sandwich as the fizz got stronger.

# 18

Magdalena was overwhelmed with guilt and kept crying as she prepared her salon for the following morning's rush, ensuring that all implements were in their correct place and all surfaces clean. Her final job before going upstairs to her little flat was to mop the floor. A clean floor was a must in her eyes and often she would ask Paulina to give it another mop during quiet periods.

Her business really was booming. Customers were prepared to give up buying magazines and eating out, but they regarded personal grooming as a necessity, and word-of-mouth was bringing in new clients every week.

*Why did I not have control of self? Why am I not normal?*

She trudged upstairs to her flat and tried to answer her question. She had waxed so many legs and given some beautiful women the *Full Monty* but had never succumbed to touch anyone inappropriately. Was she really a lesbian? Did she really like women more than men?

She removed a bottle of white wine from the fridge and broke her own golden rule by drinking alone. Two easily-acquired habits affect women's skin – smoking and drinking. Many Poles smoked but Magdalena had resisted. She was big-boned with full breasts and a curvy figure so eating the right food was essential. And she was determined not to put on the kilos her dear mother had done, before a botched operation to clear a blood vessel had triggered a massive and fatal stroke.

She took a plate with smoked mackerel, tomatoes, cucumber, grated carrot and lettuce to her small pine dining table and considered turning on the television. Her thoughts were a complete jumble. She was Roman Catholic and sex outside marriage was a sin. Sex with a woman was inexcusable.

She had to get a grip on her emotions.

Was she straight or was she gay? She had been married and had enjoyed sleeping with her husband but she had thoughts about women that were not normal, as she put it. When she first met Tina, she had fought hard to quell the feelings she had for the young estate agent. Tina was blonde with a heart-shaped face, a straight nose and a generous mouth. Neither too tall nor too short, she had the kind of body that wore clothes to perfection. More than that, unlike many British girls who stomped, Tina walked with a natural grace that was a joy to watch. Paulina, her assistant, was similar in many ways to Tina although she had the annoying habit of regularly going outside for a smoke. When her husband walked out on Magdalena and started a relationship with Paulina, the jealousy she felt she knew was the wrong way round.

What was she? Google told her she may be bicurious. Or gynesexual – attracted to femininity. And yet, she wasn't turned on by men dressed in women's clothes. Yes, she was happy to go to a drag night at the Hope and Anchor pub in Undermere, but the men she had slept with, and there were only a few, had been, as far as she knew, happily straight. Why couldn't she be happily straight? She'd managed to keep a lid on her desires until Tina walked into her salon. Now, all she could think about was kissing every inch of her body.

That was the truth.

She could sleep with a man and enjoy making love but the person she wanted to share her bed, share her world, share her life with was Tina.

Magdalena took a slug of wine and laughed. 'Well, that ain't gonna happen!' She spoke in English as she thought about herself as a young girl, who knew barely a word of English when she left Poland, so long ago.

Her phone buzzed. The clock told her it was nearly midnight. She swiped the screen and saw that it was a text from Tina.

*I'm too drunk to drive to Audrey's cottage. May I stay with you?*

Magdalena's heart went thump. The feeling that rippled through her body would dictate her actions. She was out of control. Her hands shook as her thumbs moved quickly over the screen.

*Of course, my sweet. Coming down.*

She put her untouched plate of food in the fridge, grabbed her keys and hurried down the stairs to the salon flicking on lights as she went. She could see Tina's outline through the semi-opaque glass door. Consumed with excitement, she inserted a key in the lock and pulled it open.

'Come in. Come in.'

Tina entered the salon and Magdalena relocked the door. 'Come up to the flat and tell me how you got on.'

'It's late. I feel bad. I just need your sofa for a few hours.'

'You shall sleep in my bed and I will sleep on bed of

nails to atone for my sins.'

Tina laughed and Magdalena followed her up the stairs into her flat.

'Wow. It's lovely, Mags. A real home. Not like I imagined at all. The decor is really pretty. I love it.'

'Wine or coffee?'

'Wine. I'm buzzing enough, already.'

Magdalena poured Tina a glass of wine and placed it on a coffee table in front of a two-seater sofa. She reached for her own glass on the dining table and managed to splash some of the wine. 'Look at me. I'm too excited to hear.' She grabbed a tea towel from the small kitchen, wiped the base of the glass and stared at Tina. 'To you, my sweet.'

Tina smiled and raised her glass. 'To the success of Wax Polish.'

'Sit down.' Magdalena indicated the sofa and sat down beside her. 'I can see you're all fired up. Tell all.'

'When I first met Gary, I wasn't completely bowled over until we met again for a drink and I saw the man not the uniform. This morning, when I first met Dermot, I was instantly attracted to him but wary of my reaction. This evening, when we met again, I felt the same churn in my gut I'd felt for Gary on our first date. Mags, he is so attractive; I can't even begin to describe how much he lights my fire.'

'He's a gypsy. A traveller.'

'I think that's part of it, but he's also incredibly handsome. Not in an obvious way but his soul seems to penetrate right through to my heart. The more we talked, the more I wanted to give my whole being to him. If he'd taken me round to the back alley, I would've happily gone.'

'But you resisted?'

'Only just. More than two years without sex has taken its toll.'

'What's next? Do you have any plans to see him again?'

'I said I'd be up at the old school tomorrow to have a proper look around. I need good photos so that I can create a decent prospectus.'

'And Gary?' It was cruel of her to mention him but her inner voice had lost control.

'He's gone, Mags. He's gone. I have to accept that, now.'

# 19

Gary couldn't sleep. Snoring, like a baton in a relay race, reverberated around the long dormitory room to a constant background of whirring from the air-conditioning units. He envied the unfortunate Vietnamese men and teenage boys who tossed and turned on thin, lumpy mattresses. At least they had each other, and could speak in a language that their jailers did not understand. They kept their distance from him as his hand and ankle cuffs marked him out as doomed. He was on his own, that was for sure, and had to dig very deep just to get through each day.

The aged wooden floorboards were warmed by heat rising from the grow lamps above the marijuana forest in the room directly below. Although the air in the dormitory was kept fairly cool, the air-conditioning units did not remove the ever-pungent smell that overwhelmed the natural odours of the former boarding school.

He had tried all the usual tricks to win round individual captors but, he had to admit, the travellers were too well-bonded for him to drive a wedge between them. There had been moments when violence may have enabled him to escape, but the threat to Tina's safety, he knew, was not an idle one. In more than two years held captive travelling around the country and for over six months at the old school, the only friend he'd managed to make was Hector, a bullmastiff. For some reason, the ugly hound liked him.

Why couldn't he get to sleep? He was exhausted but his brain refused to take him into another world. He loved dreaming. Sometimes Tina would appear and the glow would help him through another interminable day.

He squeezed his eyes shut and forced himself to relax. Just as he was nodding-off, a hand shook his shoulder. He opened his eyes and looked up at an annoyingly handsome face.

'I have news,' Dermot said.

His lilting, friendly tone reminded Gary of a famous TV presenter, but he'd learned early on that Dermot's surface charm betrayed a ruthless determination.

'Your in-laws. They're dead.'

Gary felt a sick thud in his gut.

'Faulty boiler, it would appear.' Dermot sat down on the side of the bed. 'CO poisoning – the silent killer. Deeply tragic, but wholly avoidable. It just goes to show how important it is to fit a modern carbon monoxide alarm.'

If Gary had been in any doubt about the risk to Tina if he escaped, the deaths of her parents, whether accidental or not, shattered all hope that he could break free and not endanger the person he loved more than anyone in the world.

'You'll be relieved to know Tina's okay. She was in hospital for a short time but is tickety-boo, now.'

The white car he saw... it must've been Tina's. He squeezed his eyes shut and fought the tears that came every time he thought about his sweet and courageous wife.

'Come to bed, Mags.'

Magdalena looked up from her prostrate position on the small sofa to the exquisite young woman, too small for her borrowed pyjamas.

'Are you sure?'

'One hundred per cent. Tonight of all nights, I do not want to sleep alone.'

Magdalena threw off the blanket and carried it into the bedroom.

'Which side do you usually sleep?' Tina asked.

Magdalena smiled. 'The left.' She placed the blanket on a chair.

Tina slipped into bed and folded the duvet back.

Magdalena switched off the bedside light and got in beside her. 'I have done soul searching,' she said, 'and I have concluded that I am bad person. Very bad.'

'You are a beautiful person, Mags.'

'But, could you love me?'

'I love you already.'

'But, you're not... gay.'

'That's true. I don't want to live with a woman but I enjoy the company of women.'

Magdalena couldn't see Tina but she luxuriated in her warmth. Moments later, she pushed her away. 'Forgive me, my darling. I cannot be this close to you. I lose control. I sleep on sofa.'

'No, stay. I'll put my pillow between us.'

Magdalena tried to sleep, to think of her accounts, anything that could distract her from the little beauty lying so near. She whispered, 'I love you, my sweet. We all do in Hawksmead. Good night. Sleep tight.'

# 20

'Shall I lay the table for three?' Malcolm asked as he pulled open the cutlery drawer.

Audrey checked her phone. 'Yes. Depending on traffic, she should be back in a few minutes.'

'I don't remember ever meeting Magdalena.'

'She was at Tina's wedding. She's tall, very striking, even beautiful. And has a lovely way with words.'

'I'm so pleased Tina had the sense not to drink and drive.' He selected an assortment of knives, forks and spoons, and closed the sideboard drawer.

'That girl has a lot of sense,' Audrey responded as she placed mats on the dining table. 'But with all she's going through, don't be surprised if she's a little unbalanced at times.'

Malcolm nodded. He placed the cutlery in a bunch on the table and entered the kitchen.

Audrey heard the front door open. 'Tina?' She hurried to the hallway via the sitting room.

'I can smell bacon.' Tina hung up her jacket and kicked off her shoes. 'I missed you.' She gave Audrey a kiss and a hug.

'We missed you, too,' Malcolm declared from the kitchen.

Audrey followed Tina through the sitting room into the dining room as Malcolm carried in a plate with scrambled eggs on toast, grilled mushrooms, tomatoes and crispy bacon.

'Ooh that looks tasty. I'll be back in a minute.' Tina scooted off to the cloakroom.

Malcolm put the plate on a tablemat and returned to the kitchen. Audrey trailed after him. 'Isn't it delightful sharing your cottage with Tina?'

He picked up two more plates, piled with food. 'It's not *my* cottage, it's our home. And yes it is.'

She followed him back into the dining room.

'She was there for us,' he said, 'when we really needed her.' He put the plates on the table and returned to the kitchen.

The cloakroom door opened and a few seconds later Audrey delighted in seeing Tina's smiling face. 'You look surprisingly fresh,' Audrey said as she pulled out a chair for their special friend.

'I had a good evening and it was a treat to catch up with Magdalena again. Her beauty salon's doing really well.'

'I was sorry to hear her marriage broke down.'

'She took revenge on her husband by hiring the woman he ran off with. Needless to say, that relationship is over.'

Malcolm placed a pot of fresh coffee on a mat. 'Please sit.'

'I feel you're both waiting on me,' Tina said with a smile as she and Audrey sat down. She looked at the plate of food. 'You're a master chef, Malcolm. I can't tell you enough how much it means to me to stay with you.'

He leaned across the table and put his hand on hers. 'Tina, sweetheart. We would love you to treat this as your home for as long as you want. Without your courage and devotion, Audrey and I would have nothing like the life we relish each day.'

'But come and go as you please,' Audrey added resting her fingers on Tina's other hand. 'We don't want you to feel beholden.'

Tina looked from Audrey to Malcolm. 'Thank you. I do have one request.'

Audrey squeezed her hand.

'Would you mind releasing my hands so that we can all eat this lovely breakfast?'

# 21

Rain hammered down on Tina's VW Golf as she drove at a leisurely pace along the winding Old Military Road. She loved the moors but on a dull, wet day, with its subdued green and brown hues, forbidding ridges, and flash floods, the bright lights of London's West End were much more appealing. She saw the sign warning drivers that they were approaching a school, now bent and rusting, and turned left into the long, twisting drive, lined with hawthorn hedges and rather menacing-looking ditches. She pressed the accelerator and in little more than a minute was at the former outward-bound boarding school. As she circled the large gravelled apron in front of the ivy-clad edifice, the rain came down so hard she decided to sit it out in the comfort of her Golf, which she parked away from a large white van, and an assortment of trucks and cars.

She picked up her phone from its hands-free rest and checked her messages. There was one text. *Sweetie. Thank you for being so kind. I am here for you whenever you need wax or bed for night. I am your friend.*

Tina thumbed in a brief reply. *You are much more than my friend.*

Another text came through. *xx.*

***ROFF! ROFF!***

She jumped and looked through the rain-soaked

side window at a snarling, tan, bullmastiff with a scarred pelt over solid muscle.

She lowered her window an inch and rain spattered her face as she looked up into a void, shrouded by a dripping waterproof hood.

'I'm here to take some photos, once the rain stops.'

'There'll be no photos done here.' He had an accent similar to Dermot's, but without the lyricism or charm.

'Kind sir, would you call your lord and master and tell him Tina's here?'

'Tina?'

'Yes. The one who had supper with him last night. He knows I'm coming today.'

'Okay, follow me, but no photos.'

'Not today, I fear. Of course, it might brighten up. It often does in these parts. Have you got a firm grip of your dog?'

'He won't harm you, unless I tell him to.' He pulled open the door and the rain lashed her.

She reached for a golf umbrella and climbed out, closing the car door behind her. She pressed a button and the large umbrella sprung open, startling the dog, who barked and snarled.

The man pulled on the lead and the heavy chain cinched the dog's neck. 'Don't you know it's dangerous to open an umbrella in an electric storm?' Below his dripping hood, she could just discern his ravaged face, deeply lined and furrowed with a patchy beard and bushy brows.

'What's your name?' Tina asked, deciding to ignore his advice. She was not going to look like a drowned rat when she saw Dermot again.

'My name's Eamonn. Follow me.'

A bolt of lightning was swiftly proceeded by a deafening crash of thunder. The dog cowered at the man's feet and was rewarded by a heavy kick in its ribs. It yelped in pain and lurched away from Eamonn, who lost grip of the wet leather lead.

Tina looked at the safety of her car. Maybe it wasn't a good idea to come to such a remote place alone.

*'Get back here!'* The ferocity of the man's command made her jump. But he was directing his ire towards the dog who stood his ground, baring his teeth. The rain continued to bucket down. 'Get back here.' He had real menace in his voice and Tina hoped the dog would teach him a lesson.

*FLASH! CRASH! CRACK! FLASH! Rolling boulders of thunder...* The terrified dog sank down onto his haunches as Tina, reluctantly, closed the umbrella. Within seconds her hair was soaked. The man went to grab the trailing lead but the dog jumped away and snarled. There was another flash and an immediate deep rumble of thunder. The dog cowed. Eamonn bent down again to pick up the trailing lead but the dog leapt back and galloped away across the gravelled apron towards the field and distant farm buildings.

'Are you coming?' His voice matched the dog's growl.

Tina duly followed the man to an entrance on the far side of the former school. She was surprised to see at least half a dozen grubby-looking caravans parked in an over-grown sports field, with rugby posts standing at precarious angles. An old sheep pen was home to a variety of large dogs, all tethered and all looking miserable in the torrential rain.

Gary was soaked. His worn boots were clogged with mud as he trudged through the downpour, made harder by the ankle cuffs linked by the steel chain.

He entered a barn, a former milking parlour, and settled down on some rotting hessian sacks. The rain pounded the rusting metal roof and he was surrounded by pools of water. From his low position he had a perfect view of the former school. Through the downpour he could just make out the ruins of the old abbey tacked to the side of the Victorian hellhole. In a store room he had found a prospectus detailing the school's history. *Isolated on the moor, the former workhouse was once a residence for impoverished families, orphans, cripples, lunatics, fallen women, unmarried mothers, and the decrepit. In 1901, following the death of Queen Victoria, the workhouse closed and the building was converted into a hospital for infectious diseases. In the 1920s, it was sold to a philanthropist who saw it as a perfect fit for a new style of educational establishment. It had everything an outward-bound school required: kitchens, chapel, bakery, laundry, plenty of farmland to supply vegetables and milk, and wards that were converted into a refectory, dormitories, and classrooms. Troubled boys were sent to the school to be straightened-out through rigorous work, discipline and physical activities.*

Gary could easily imagine what those activities entailed; he was experiencing them for himself. Five boys did not make it home to their parents and their tragic deaths were commemorated in a beautiful, walled garden created by Malcolm Cadwallader from land donated by Audrey. The memorial garden had been an emotional setting for Gary's marriage to Tina three years back. What a glorious day that had been. He would never have met her if she hadn't driven like a racing driver to Undermere hospital with a badly burned Audrey.

Police Constable Gary Burton, fresh from a hot-pursuit training course, had given chase with his blue lights flashing and his siren wailing. When he had finally caught up with her outside Accident & Emergency, he was spellbound by the determined and beautiful young woman.

*Grrrrr…*

'Come here, Hector.' Gary watched as the bedraggled dog approached. He looked as cold, wet and miserable as Gary. 'Come here, boy.' The scarred and brutalised beast came within arm's length and Gary gently stroked his muzzle and ears. The dog came closer and Gary hugged the beast to him. 'Good boy. I'll get you out of here. I promise. One day, soon.'

The rain continued to pound the muddy potato field. There would be no drones flying today. Perhaps he and Hector should just make a run for it? The nearest help was in Hawksmead. If they managed to get across the boggy moor they would come to the River Hawk. At this time of year, especially after all the rain, it would be in full flood and way too powerful to swim across, especially with hand and ankle cuffs. But, if they followed the bank downstream they would eventually reach the humpback bridge – and freedom.

'Tina's here.'

Gary woke from his reverie and looked up at Dermot, dripping wet in his rain-proof windcheater with hood. He considered begging the handsome bastard not to hurt her but behind his Irish charm, he doubted there was a shred of empathy.

'She has many friends in Hawksmead.' Gary tried to shore up his weakened voice. 'Hurt her and they will come for you.'

Deep from within Hector came the low rumble of a growl. Gary hugged the dog closer to him.

Dermot squatted. 'No harm will come to her, of that I give you my word. Just as long as you are a good little boy.'

Tina was so near to him he could almost smell the beautiful scent of her hair. But, if she saw Gary and realised he was alive, Dermot would have no choice but to keep her quiet, one way or another. 'Why is she here?'

'She wants to sell the school, but that's not going to happen.'

If anyone could find a buyer for the school, Tina could, but Gary was not about to tell that to Dermot.

'Stay in here,' Dermot commanded. 'I'll let you know when she's safely gone.'

'I'm soaked through and cold. I have a fever coming on.'

Dermot reached for Hector's lead and stood up. 'The school has its own chapel and mortuary. We'd give you a good Irish send-off.'

Gary watched Dermot battle the rain as he and Hector trudged back across the field towards the pen where other dogs were huddled.

# 22

'Tina me darlin'!'

She looked up from her cup of coffee at Dermot. She was seated on a stool at a long refectory table in a large, antiquated kitchen. Through grubby window panes she could see the vast expanse of rain-soaked farmland and, beyond, the moor with its brutal beauty.

'Where is everyone?' There was a slight tremor in her voice. Eamonn and his big dog had unnerved her. She felt vulnerable.

Dermot poured a mug of coffee and sat down at the end of the table, a few feet from her. 'Our main site is on common land south of Undermere. That's where the children and women are. As for the migrants, some are resting up in the dorm or playing cards in a day room, but most are out working on construction sites in Undermere or attending private jobs – decorating or gardening.'

'Gardening? In this weather?'

'They're tough. Just travelling to the UK in the pitch black of a refrigerated lorry is pretty bad. Some don't make it. A little rain is nothing to them. I know they miss the warmth of Southeast Asia, but they would rather be here where they can earn a lot more money, which they send home to support their loved ones. To them, Britain is a land of bounty, but they came here illegally, some were trafficked, so it's not as straight-forward as they expected. Most of my time is taken up fighting Government deportation orders.'

Tina nodded. It was funny seeing Dermot the day after their intimate chat the night before. She felt his rough hand on hers. 'Not good weather for photos, I fear.'

'I hoped it would clear, but it looks set in.'

'Another day.' He took a slurp of his coffee.

'I can still look around and see what's best to shoot.'

'And I'd be honoured to escort you. Some parts have been closed off by the trustees for being too dangerous, rotten floorboards and the like. Whoever buys this place will have to spend a fortune just to make it safe.'

'There are buyers out there. Not many, but I will find one. I'm sorry.'

'That's your job. But don't be too good at it. We like it here.' He smiled and she felt a surprising rush of heat.

Neon lights hummed into life revealing a long, dismal corridor, half wood panelled and half cracked and scarred yellowed plaster walls. The windows to the left were cloaked in ivy to the exterior and the doors to the right were all closed.

'This is a safe floor,' Dermot said. 'Although I've yet to explore it.'

Tina walked ahead of him along the corridor on cracked linoleum, and opened the first door. Weak daylight from windows at the back of the building exposed a traditional school science lab with aged wooden workbenches sporting an array of old equipment including microscopes, assorted glass bottles with rubber bungs, weighing scales, racks with test tubes, and Bunsen burners joined by rubber tubes to blue cylinders marked GAS.

They approached a schoolmaster's desk, standing on a raised plinth. Behind was a large blackboard with just discernible words written in chalk: *ARBEIT MACHT FREI.*

'Poor taste.' Dermot undid his neckerchief. 'About a million Jewish souls died in Auschwitz.' He used the cloth to rub away the words. 'And about twenty thousand Roma and Sinti. Gypsies.'

'It's probably just a schoolboy likening the college to a concentration camp. Not really understanding the insult. It would've been written long before you arrived.'

'I'm not surprised this place closed.' He stepped down from the plinth and came up close to her. 'It's like turning back the clock.'

'I don't think they spent much time in classrooms. It was an outward-bound school. A regime of hard physical exercise. Sometimes, too hard.'

'Nothing much to photograph here.'

She heard a scraping sound above her. 'What was that?'

'Rats. As soon as we get rid of them they're back.'

She sighed. 'I think you're right. The interior isn't worth photographing. A developer will completely gut it, anyway. I'll focus on the exterior. I know I can get some great shots of the old abbey ruins.' She weaved her way past acid-stained workbenches to the rain-spattered windows on the far side of the classroom. Through a grimy pane she looked down on a muddy field and scattered barns, barely standing. Beyond was the vast expanse of moorland with its rolling hills, high ridges and scattered clumps of trees. 'I won't bother with the farm buildings as they're bound to be demolished. Most important of all is getting decent shots of this view. It must be even more amazing from the top floor. Yes, I think I can make it work for a buyer.' Her last few words were more to herself than to Dermot.

She looked round and saw that he was still standing near the desk. She smiled. Day or night, he looked good. 'Imagine this room,' she continued, 'converted into a hotel suite.' Her natural enthusiasm enriched her words as she turned back to the window. 'How wonderful it would be to wake up to this view. In summer, the setting sun must be beyond stunning.' She spotted a hunched figure emerging from the largest barn. 'There's a man out there getting soaked. Is he one of your migrants?'

Dermot came up behind her. 'No, he's one of my guys. Lazy bastard. The charity works damned hard to find employment for struggling migrants, and all my cousin can do is skive.'

Tina faced him and before she knew what she was doing, her hand was on his arm. 'Don't worry. It's not likely to be a quick sale and it could take another year before development begins.'

Dermot gently broke away as rain continued to hammer the window panes. 'I love this old school,' he said, 'surrounded by all this ancient moorland. It's uniquely beautiful. I don't want to see the potato field concreted over, or the bog turned into a housing estate with paved drives and box-like units.'

'They won't build houses on this land,' Tina said, standing close enough to feel the heat from his body. 'Maybe a golf course or two. Indoor tennis courts, a gym. Any construction would be in and around where there are buildings already.'

'I hope you're right.'

She looked up at Dermot and felt a ripple as their eyes

connected. 'I would like to see the abbey ruins.' The husk in her voice brought a flush to her cheeks. She was sure Dermot had noticed. What was going on? She was in mourning.

'Why not come back when it's not raining? You'll get soaked out there.'

'I'm an estate agent. We go where others fear to tread.'

The entrance hall to the old school was enormous and dark. Its walls were part oak-panelled and part lath and plaster, deeply scuffed from decades of human traffic, as was the uneven stone floor. Dermot located a switch and old, stained lights flickered on.

'Follow me.' He led Tina down a long corridor to a door marked *Headmaster* in faded gold leaf. He pushed it open and reached for a switch. A neon strip, hanging in the centre, blinked on. 'This is my home.' He unhooked his still-wet windcheater from a freestanding coat and umbrella stand and slipped it on.

Tina looked around the study. To one side was a large oak desk and an old fashioned computer and monitor. Hung on a wall were black and white photographs of mountains and mountaineers from a bygone era, and lying scattered across the threadbare carpeted floor were yellowed newspapers and text books, and stained ordnance survey maps.

Discarded newspapers fluttered as she crossed the room to the window, where rain continued its assault. 'My uncle went to this school.'

'Your uncle? When was that?'

'In the 1960s. He didn't survive.' She looked through the blurred glass across a vegetable patch to dilapidated outbuildings.

'Oh, that's calamitous.' Dermot sounded sincere.

'What happened to him?' He came up behind her.

She glanced at him over her shoulder. 'Black ice on the humpback bridge leading to Hawksmead. He was riding his bike to school and a car, driven by a young schoolmaster, crushed him. Not the driver's fault.'

'I'm sorry to hear that.'

'That same term, two boys drowned in the river, also by the humpback bridge.'

'It seems that old stone bridge has a lot to answer for.'

She looked into his blue eyes, fringed by dark lashes and heavy brows. 'Do you believe in life after death?'

'That's a big question which deserves a considered answer.' He placed his hands at the tops of her arms. 'I've not known you long and you've suffered great personal loss. But, could you find it in your heart to join me for a late lunch? It's such a miserable day. I feel we need cheering up.'

Sheltering from the persistent rain under an old bicycle shelter, Gary kept himself concealed as he watched two figures cross the apron, sharing a golfing umbrella. He was sure it was Tina with Dermot but was still shocked when he saw Dermot get in the front passenger seat of her VW Golf.

Jealousy was quickly replaced with joy. Surely this was his chance to escape? It could be hours before Dermot discovered he was gone. By then, Gary should have alerted his mates in Undermere police and ensured Dermot was arrested. Tina could be secreted away to a safe house until Stacy and her father, Frank, were in custody.

He looked up at the sky and was thrilled to see that the rain did not look like letting up anytime soon. His ankle cuffs linked by the toughened steel chain to handcuffs would slow him down, but at least they weren't the kind of heavy irons that slaves in the colonies were forced to wear.

Forked lightning cut through the blackened clouds, followed by an almighty crack and a growling rumble of thunder. By road the school was about two miles from the humpback bridge that traversed the River Hawk, but the risk of being seen by one of the travellers coming or going was considerable.

He hobbled through the pounding rain away from the old school across the gravelled apron. When he was a police patrol officer, he knew the roads all around Hawksmead and Undermere but had totally ignored the countryside. On a day like today, the vast expanse looked formidable. His vision blurred by rain, he still managed to make out the peat bogs and hillocks he knew hid deep gullies. In the distance he could just see the famous Ridgeway – a high hill with a twisting ridge he'd been meaning to traverse but had never quite got round to tackling. Luckily, the Ridgeway was to the southeast and his trajectory was southwest. But, without the sun to guide him, there was a risk of walking around in circles and eventually dying from hypothermia.

He hobbled on. Not quite running but going faster than a walk, despite the ankle cuffs. He was cold and very wet but he hoped the rain would continue, preventing search by the dreaded drone. Tina, his gorgeous wife, would spin her natural web of charm around the Irishman and Gary was confident that he had at least two to three hours before anyone would come looking for him.

*'If you ever try to escape, Tina's last thoughts will be of you and how much you betrayed her.'* Stacy's threat

echoed around his head as he scrambled over a dry stone wall. His old boots were clogged with mud as he drove himself forward, seeking firm ground.

This was it. He had gone beyond the bounds of the former boarding school.

# 23

It felt odd but quite nice to have a handsome stranger sitting in the front passenger seat of her Golf. His clothes had an old worldly smell that charmed her. She drove especially carefully along the country road as the surface was awash with torrents of water that filled the deep ditches to each side.

She glanced at Dermot. 'At least there won't be a problem getting a table. People are tough around here but this rain is too much.'

'Climate change. It's like watching a train wreck in slow motion.'

'I have to be honest. For the last couple of years, the climate has not been at the top of my worries.' She eased the car around a sharp bend and pressed the accelerator as they began to climb a long hill.

'I get that. It's hard to worry about the environment when you're worried sick about someone you love.'

She glanced at Dermot with his strong nose balanced by an equally strong chin. 'What's your story, Dermot?'

'Traveller. There's not much more to tell.'

'Any children?'

'None that I know of.'

They crested the brow of the hill and were presented with a vast landscape of soft green and brown hues, with peaks and ridges shrouded in rain and mist. Tina didn't bother to indicate left as she swerved into the walled car park of the Rorty Crankle – deserted, save for two cars that probably belonged to the owners of the seventeenth-century coaching inn. She pulled on her handbrake and cut the engine. Rain continued to pound the car's roof.

'I thought it would let up,' Dermot said, 'but it looks set in.' He released her seat belt and then his own.

Tina looked through the blurred windscreen. 'When I was growing up, I took this beautiful space for granted. Walking on the moor was for tourists, not me. I see it differently now. My parents loved to come up here for Sunday lunch, then walk off the excess before driving home.'

'But not on a day like today. The colours look soft but I know the landscape is treacherous. You wouldn't get me out there.' He turned to her, and smiled. 'Ready to run the gauntlet?'

Dermot did his best to shield them both from the rain as they ran to the pub's main entrance. They burst through the double doors and laughed with relief as water puddles formed on the aged wooden floor.

A deep voice boomed from the bar. 'Cathy! Look who's here.' He was a tall man, with a grey mop of curly hair and a ruddy complexion. He came out from behind the bar and approached them with open arms. He engulfed Tina and hugged her into his solid girth. 'It is beyond wonderful to see you, my darling. We are so sorry. So very sorry.' He kissed her damp hair.

Tina looked up at the big man, raindrops on her shiny cheeks. 'It's wonderful to see you, too, Harry. I should've come home much sooner.'

'We are all so sorry. And now your dear parents...'

That was too much for Tina, and Dermot stood back as she buried her face in Harry's chest. Her shoulders convulsed as she sobbed. Harry held her while Dermot watched and waited, wishing that she were in his arms. She looked so beautiful, so fragile. The policeman's wife had tapped an emotion deep within his heart. He wanted her; unfortunately, there was someone else – the daughter of an Essex crime lord. What kind of revenge would she wreak if she found out his true feelings for Tina?

He knew.

He knew Stacy Cottee all too well.

The rain was biting. Gary was bone cold. The spongy earth seemed to suck at his feet with every stride. He was exhausted. The stark outline of the former workhouse taunted him.

Was there no escape?

He forced himself to keep going, but two years of captivity had flayed the fat from his bones. The desire to crawl into a hole was almost overwhelming.

He had already lost one boot, stuck in the cloying mud. It didn't matter. His whole frame was soaked, his white skin tinged blue.

*Keep going. Keep going.*

Distant barking carried on the north-easterly wind.

He kept pushing.

More barking. Louder. Fiercer. This time he turned to look. There were at least five men, each holding back a dog, no more than one hundred metres behind him.

He found a stone path and although he was able to get a better purchase, the sharp stones tore at the sole of his bare foot. He tried running with his booted foot on the path and the other foot on softer ground.

The barking was much closer now. What would the

dogs do to him? Was he a man, or red raw meat? He hobbled over another small brow, lost his balance and rolled down a short bank. He clawed at the sodden earth as he fell into the swollen torrent of the River Hawk. The bubbling, fast-flowing, freezing water took him into its fatal embrace. Ahead was the humpback bridge with its stone arches. He had no strength. No fight. At least the love of his life would have his body to kiss goodbye.

Harry handed menus to Tina and Dermot. 'Everything is on the house. This is my treat.'

'Thank you, Harry,' Tina said. 'It's so lovely to see you, and a feast as well, but I insist we pay.'

'Let me tell you, my dear. Those old lovebirds you brought together have more than filled my coffers every week, and my heart with their joy and laughter. As for your dear parents...' He sniffed and hurried away.

'That is beyond generous.' Dermot opened his menu. 'People really respond to you.'

'There's a lot of shared history.'

'It's more than that. It's something within you that touches their souls.'

She laughed. 'I cannot imagine what that is.'

'I feel it too.'

She looked into his eyes and felt again the fizz of an electrical charge. She had no control over it and it often came when not wanted. But, at that moment, sitting in the pub's comforting warmth, opposite a man who was powerfully attractive, she didn't mind.

*Gary.*

Everyone said he had to be dead. But short of a body how could she be sure?

'What are you thinking? I can see those pretty cogs,

turning.'

She smiled and picked up her glass of sparkling cranberry juice. 'I was thinking about... you.'

'Me?'

'Yes. I was thinking about your life and wondering what your big dream may be.'

'My dream? My dream is... sitting in front of me.'

Her vessels opened and hot blood pulsed into her cheeks. It happened so quickly, she didn't have a chance to fight the blushing by contracting her buttocks, her usual technique.

'I didn't mean to embarrass you.'

She picked up her napkin and placed it on her lap, resisting the desire to cover her face. 'It's a while since a man complimented me that way.'

'Words are cheap but I mean it. I like you Tina.' He reached across the table and took her hand. She didn't resist.

Gary hugged the stone bridge as the gushing, icy water tried to suck him away. His fingers were beyond numb. He had nothing left to give. He was shattered. His eyes closed and his grip relaxed. The torrent grabbed him and tossed him over and over. He was spun around until a metal eye for tying barges snagged the chain linking his handcuffs. He gasped and water filled his mouth as his head banged the stone arch. The broken branch of a tree tore him free and he was swept out from under the bridge into strong hands.

He felt himself being dragged out of the water onto the river bank. He tried to open his eyes but he was spinning round and round down a long tunnel.

'Coffee?'

Tina tore her eyes away from Dermot and looked up

into Harry's jovial face.

'I'd love a mint tea if you have it.'

'Cathy loves a mint tea,' Harry replied. 'Even I sometimes drink it. We all have our moments of madness.' He looked at Dermot who laughed. 'And you, good sir. May I tempt you to an infusion?'

'There's nothing in this pub that I don't find tempting.'

'Even me?' Harry winked.

'You look tip-top from where I'm sitting,' Dermot declared.

Harry guffawed.

'If you have builder's tea,' Dermot continued, 'that would go down very well.'

The white VW Golf swerved around a Land Rover Discovery and roared straight through traffic lights on red. Gary gave chase, his siren wailing. He saw the Golf slide across oncoming traffic and skid to a halt outside Accident & Emergency. The driver's door opened and an angel emerged.

*'Tina!'*

He tried to reach her but he was sinking deeper and deeper into the sucking, swirling torrent…

Harry held the door open for Tina and Dermot and they stepped out into the dwindling light. The rain had let up. Dermot placed his arm around her shoulder and guided her back to the car park. She pressed her remote and the indicator lights on her beloved Golf flashed. They slipped into the front seats and she slotted the key into the ignition.

Dermot touched her arm. 'Don't start it yet.'

She turned to look at him and, once again, felt a rush of heat spread throughout her entire body. Something about the man rendered her helpless. She touched his face with her palm and he kissed it.

Heavy slaps pounded his numb cheeks as hands shook him. His whole body shivered and convulsed with spasms. He didn't try to open his eyes. He knew he was on the floor of a van, back on the road to hell.

Tina clicked-in her seatbelt and started the engine, switched on the lights and reversed the car out of its slot. They turned onto the Old Military Road and in the fading light of day, she drove with haste along the deserted, meandering scar.

They didn't speak. She focused on her driving, knowing she was going too fast for the conditions.

Ahead, pin pricks of light grew bigger and she slowed as they came to the junction for the former boarding school. Headlights on full beam blinded her as a van cut across their path.

'That's odd,' Dermot said.

Tina accelerated up the mile-long drive and saw the white van coming to a halt on the far side of the gravelled apron.

'Stop here.' He held up his hand. 'Don't go near.'

She halted the Golf some way from the van. Lit by her headlights, she saw two men get out and go to the rear doors. They stood by them, waiting, looking towards her car.

'I'd better see what they're up to.' He kissed her tenderly on the lips. 'Go home to your elderly friends. They are clearly good people.' He opened his door and almost ran to the van. She waited and watched as he talked to the men.

Surprisingly disappointed, she swung the car around the apron, her tyres spitting grit. But, something flashed in the corner of her eye and she slammed on her brakes. She thrust the gear lever into reverse and quickly backed up, flicking her headlights onto full beam.

*What is that? A Porsche Spyder? Here?*

She was tempted to get out of her car and take a closer look but the rain had returned. Could it be Dermot's? She hoped so and smiled at the prospect of giving it a spin, as she roared-off down the long drive.

Gary felt himself being hauled out of the back of the van and carried without due care into the school and down to the basement. He was numb with cold; his whole body shook with spasms. They dumped him onto a concrete floor and water cascaded over him, gradually getting warmer. He lost track of time as he relished the hot water pounding down until chilblains set in and his ankles and feet burned, and became excruciatingly itchy.

Rough hands pulled him out of the shower and he opened his eyes. Eamonn O'Hanlon, Dermot's less attractive older brother, shouted in his face. 'Take your clothes off.'

Gary saw that his ankle and handcuffs had been removed, exposing scarred and raw skin. It took massive effort to get to his feet in the former school changing room, and his hands shook as he peeled off his clothes, leaving them in a pile on the floor. His swollen feet looked a mess and were beyond itchy.

'You've a cut on your head,' Eamonn said. 'We've someone here to fix it. Dry yourself.' He handed Gary a used towel with baked-on mud stains.

Gary looked down at his intensely white skin. Two years in captivity had weakened his once muscular physique. He used the towel to dry his hair and noticed splashes of dark red blood. He walked over to a row of washbasins and cleared condensation from a wall mirror, heavily silvering at its edges. There was a large gash just below his hairline.

'You're a bit shrivelled for my taste,' spoke a voice from Essex.

He didn't bother to cover himself as hatred coursed through his veins.

'Sit down, Gary. I'll fix yer 'ead.'

He stared at Stacy and imagined wrapping his towel around her neck. Eamonn had gone so he could do it.

'Relax.' Stacy held out a first aid box with a red cross.

'Come near me, and I promise you'll regret it.'

'Oh come on Gary. Put aside your hard feelings. We had something, once.'

'We had nothing. It was all pretence.'

He had seen Stacy come and go over the summer as her romance with Dermot had blossomed, but this was the first time she'd spoken to him since that fatal breakfast in her father's house. He put the towel on a wooden bench and sat on it, picking up another towel to cover himself.

Stacy looked at his head. 'You want to be careful. This is nasty.' She put the box down beside him and opened a pack of gauze. 'It should be stitched properly,' she said dabbing his head. 'But I've got butterfly stitches. They'll bind the wound. It will leave a bit of a scar, though.'

He was surprised by how tenderly she administered the wound, pulling it together and using the narrow sticky strips to hold the skin in place.

'How've you been, Stacy?'

She continued to work. 'I've been fine, thank you, Gary.'

'And your dad?'

'All well. Tip top.'

'How's business?'

'Surprisingly good. And you? Are you enjoying your sabbatical from the Met?'

'Absolutely. It's wonderful. Thank you so much for the opportunity.'

'You're welcome.' She put the pack of strips back in the box and took out a small canister. Using her left hand to shield his eyes, she sprayed the wound. 'A bit of antiseptic.' She returned the canister to the box. 'Try to keep it clean.'

'How's your love life? Are you still open to all comers?'

'Don't push it Gary, or I'll rip the strips off.'

He paused before continuing. 'I didn't mean it to happen, Stacy. I apologise. I am genuinely sorry.'

*'Are you doing anything tonight, Gary?'*

*He had found himself alone with Stacy in the small flat he was renting in Chigwell. She only had to look at him and he felt a stirring in a part of his anatomy that should be entirely reserved for his wife. She was twenty-eight, brunette, crystal-blue eyes, straight nose, generous mouth, breasts worthy of attention, and legs that promised heaven.*

"Remember, Gary. Sleeping with the enemy is not an option. Keep your night stick, zipped. It will cost us a conviction and we could end up paying compensation."

*He knew it was not acceptable for an undercover police officer to form an intimate sexual relationship with a target, but Stacy was beyond beautiful. She was unbelievably alluring. She was also Frank Cottee's only daughter and should be entirely off limits; but the two men, thirty years or more apart in age, got along better than Gary had with his own late father.*

*In the written guidance he had received during train-ing it stated:* When a police officer deems it neces-sary and proportionate to achieve operational objectives, communications of a sexual nature may be authorised.

*Gary had not been authorised and he could not claim an immediate and credible threat to himself or others, but surely this was a chance for him to break into the Cottee inner circle? To crack a criminal syndicate that was running rings around the authorities.*

*'What are you thinking?' Stacy asked.*

*He looked into her eyes and knew he was a goner. 'I was just running through all the women I've met...'*

*'You mean, slept with.'*

*'Not one, and I've dated some beauties, comes close to you.' It was a lie. There was one and her name was Tina.*

*'What are you gonna do about it?' Her voice sounded breathy. Were they her pheromones at work – or his?*

*She moved in close and he could feel the hardening tips of her breasts through his shirt. She was a criminal with a criminal gene running from head to toe through her sculpted body. Blood surged through his veins. Her head tilted up and he cushioned his lips against hers. Their tongues met and they kissed like teenagers.*

*Within seconds she had removed her top and bra and the promise of exquisite breasts was fulfilled. She kicked off her pleated, Victoria Beckham miniskirt and peeled off her tights and thong at a speed Gary felt sure had broken all records. Within moments, they were lying naked on the plush carpet and he was covering her slim, smooth, skin with butterfly kisses.*

*He and Stacy were more sexually compatible than any woman he'd ever slept with – including Tina. He really fancied her beyond the stuff of dreams, but he loved*

*Tina, he loved his wife and knew he was doing wrong.*

*One night, following a great meal out in Southend, and after more than a few glasses of Prosecco, he and Stacy were in bed and building to yet another amazing crescendo. He could not believe how incredible she was. They were a perfect, physical fit and she drove all reason from his mind.*

*'Oh my God, Tina!' He could not hold himself back and the explosion blasted his mind. His whole body pulsed. Twenty seconds later and panting hard, he was finally able to look at Stacy and did not like the expression in her eyes.*

*'Are you cheatin' on me?'*

*'Of course not. I love you. When have I had the opportunity to cheat? We're together all the time. Did you not come?'*

*'So who is she, then?'*

*'Who? What are you talking about?'*

*'Tina.'*

*'Tina? I don't understand.'*

*'You shouted, Tina, when you blew your rocks.'*

*'No I didn't. I don't know anyone called Tina.'*

*'Well it either came out of your mouth or your dick, but I definitely heard it.'*

*Gary eased himself away from her and grabbed a fistful of tissues, which she reluctantly accepted.*

*'She's a girl I broke up with about a year ago. We were together for quite a long time.'*

*'Tina what?'*

*'What's it matter?'*

*'What the fuck's her name?'*

*'It's Turner.'*

*'Tina Turner? Don't take me for a fool.'*

*'Stacy. I'm not telling you her name because I don't*

want you to hurt her.'

'Now why would I do that?'

'Jealousy?'

'She does have a great singing voice, I grant you that.'

'Tina gave me the elbow which is why I moved to Essex. I had to get away. Make a change.'

'But you still love her. Wish she was here instead of me.' She threw back the bed covers and retrieved her clothes from the floor.

'Please Stacy, don't go. I've got something for you. I was waiting for the right moment but this may be my only moment.'

It was Gary's escape chute. "When all else fails, get down on your knees." Wise words from an old police hand with many years working undercover. He grabbed a pair of boxer shorts from the floor and pulled them on, opened his sock drawer and removed a small, velvet-covered box.

He looked at Stacy.

She stared back at him.

'Stacy, my darling.' He went down on one knee. 'Would you do me the great honour of becoming my wife?' He opened the box to reveal a gold band with a diamond centrepiece, surrounded by sapphires.

'Gary and Stacy. Sounds more like a comedy show than a married couple.' She took the ring out of the box and slipped it on her wedding finger. 'The band is too big.'

'I misjudged it.'

She took the box out of his hand and used her enamelled thumb nail to remove the recessed base. Inside was a folded receipt.

'Jewellers always hide them there just in case the proposal is rejected. Okay, let's see how much I am worth.' She unfolded the piece of paper and held it under the bedside light. 'Mmm, Hatton Garden. Quality assured. My dad considered getting involved in that bonkers raid – but he was too young.' She laughed at her own joke – all the raiders had been pensioners. 'Is this Tina's reject ring?'

'Of course not. I bought it to match your crystal-blue eyes.'

'Well you must have second sight. This receipt is dated before you even knew me.' The last few words were spat at him followed by the hurling of the velvet box. 'I'll keep the ring. It's gotta be worth a few quid.'

Gary got to his feet. 'It's Gavin and Stacy, the comedy show. Yes, I bought it before I met you but not before I'd seen your photo. Of course, I wanted to work for your dad but it was you I fantasised about. It was you I fell in love with. And then I met you and I knew my feelings were for real.'

'Nice try. Good effort. I'll see you in the morning. Come for breakfast.'

*Come for breakfast.* He would always remember those fatal words.

Stacy packed up the first-aid box and replaced the lid.

'Wait here. I'll find you some clothes.'

He reached for her hand. 'I am sorry for hurting you. I mean it.'

'Save it.' She pulled her hand free.

He called after her. 'He doesn't love you.'

She turned and stared at him. 'What are you talking about?'

'Dermot. He has a wandering eye.'

She didn't have a ready response.

He decided to push the point. 'Ask him where he's been this afternoon. More importantly, who he's been with.' He was taking a calculated risk but he had to sow dissent and he was confident that Tina would be protected by Dermot.

'Piss off, Gary.' She marched out of the changing room.

Tina parked her car behind Malcolm's repaired Honda and took a few deep breaths. Sodium-coloured street lamps cast the world she now called home in a strange yellow light. A large pool of water from the recent heavy rain had gathered by a blocked drain.

What was she doing?

She took another breath and released her seatbelt.

Her phone buzzed in her handbag. It was a call via WhatsApp.

'Sam! Where are you?'

'They won't let me in. Some tosser on the door said it's a crime scene.'

'Samuel… be polite. The police are just doing their job.'

'Their job?'

'They have to make sure.'

'Of what? You said they were gassed.'

'Yes. Carbon monoxide poisoning.'

'Where am I going to stay?'

'Walk back to the High Street, turn right and a little way down on the left is the Falcon. They have rooms.'

'Is it still run by Heather and Ted?'

'Yes; remind them who you are.'

'When will I see you?'

'In a couple of hours. We can either eat at the pub or have a bite in The Old Forge.'

'Put 'em on.' Stacy threw a few items of clothing at Gary.

'Charity shop?'

'You know how much I care about the third world.'

'Developing world.'

'Get dressed.'

Gary looked at the clothes. 'Mmm… not bad.'

'So tell me, where was Dermot?'

He looked at her. 'Why not ask him yourself?'

'No. You tell me.'

He took a moment to deliberate his response. 'Listen Stacy. The police already assume I am buried in ready-mix concrete. My wife thinks she is a widow. I'm sure Dermot was one hundred per cent discrete when they went out.'

Her eyes turned to flint. 'When was that?'

'Last night and again today. He seems to like her.'

'Bollocks. You're full of it. I don't believe a word.'

'I saw them kiss.'

Had he blown it? Said too much? Her whole frame looked rigid.

'Stacy, I got involved with you despite orders not to. I couldn't help myself. You're beautiful. It's not Tina's fault. Her parents have just died and Dermot offered a shoulder.'

She stormed out.

He reached for the clothes she'd brought and as he put them on, wondered whether he'd been a complete and utter fool.

A minute later, the door opened and Dermot strode in. Following was Eamonn carrying the chains and cuffs, which he threw on the floor at Gary's feet.

He ignored them and looked at Dermot. 'Did you talk to her?'

'Who?'

'Stacy. She's going after Tina.'

Dermot was momentarily silent. 'What did you say to her?'

'The truth.'

'You fool!' He looked as though he was about to punch him.

Through high windows with their toughened glass came the faint throaty roar of a car engine sparking into life. Dermot almost ran from the room.

'Put the cuffs on,' Eamonn snarled.

Gary sat on the bench and picked up the cuffs. 'You'll have to help me.' He slumped into himself, keeping his eyes slightly open.

Eamonn knelt down on one knee in front of him and Gary took his chance. He whipped the chain joining the hand and ankle cuffs around the leathery man's throat and pulled with all his remaining strength.

# 24

Tina pushed open the door to the Falcon and looked around the pub. Ted was serving behind the bar.

'Tina!' he called.

She walked over to him.

'You'll be looking for your brother,' he smiled.

'Thank you for finding him a room.'

'We are here to help you both. It's a very tough time.'

'Thank you.'

'G & T?'

'Diet Coke, please.' She opened her bag.

'Put that away.'

'You can't keep giving me free drinks.'

'I can and I will.' He opened a bottle and poured the bubbling liquid into a tall, iced glass. 'Gavin's over there.' He indicated an alcove near the rear of the pub.

'He uses Samuel, his middle name, these days. Well, since he met his husband, Luke.'

'What's wrong with Gavin?'

'He says it's too common. Not classy enough.'

'But, it means white hawk, perfect for a man of Hawksmead. And don't forget Sir Gawain, he was one of King Arthur's Knights of the Round Table, and a mighty warrior. On the other hand there was St. Gavinus, a noble Christian, who ended up dying as a martyr.'

'Gavin was also the name of an ex of mine who my brother never liked.'

Ted laughed. 'Samuel, good choice. I'll try to remember.'

She blew him a kiss and picked up her coke. 'Thank you.'

Sam was thumbing a message on his phone as Tina approached.

'How's my big brother?' She put her drink on the stained and scarred oak table.

He stood and hugged her. 'You're thin. I need to fatten you up.'

'For the kill?'

He laughed and let her go. 'I've booked us a table at The Old Forge.'

'Thank you.' She slid onto the bench opposite him and they sat in silence for a few moments. 'It's just you and me, now,' she said.

'Don't make your big brother cry. I'm already a girl's blouse.'

'It's so stupid.'

'Dad was always cautious. It won't be his fault.'

'It doesn't matter. Whatever the cause – they're dead.'

Sam took a deep breath. 'Are you going to be okay?' He used his hand to wipe his eyes.

'Are you?'

'I don't know. It didn't feel real in New Zealand. It still doesn't.'

'How's Luke?'

Sam blew his nose into a paper napkin. 'He's well, thank you. But, I can't leave him on his own for too long. You know what men are like.'

Tina almost smiled. 'I've met someone.'

'Whilst all this is going on you've found time to meet someone?' Sam looked intently at his sister.

'He's been gone nearly two and a half years and missing for over two.'

'You've accepted... he's not coming back?'

She nodded.

'I'm so sorry.'

'It's not been easy. I've been like a robot. Working, drinking, sleeping.'

'Sex?' Sam cocked an eyebrow.

She looked at him sharply. 'No. Not yet.'

'Who's the guy?'

'His name's Dermot O'Hanlon.'

'Ah, the luck of the Irish.' He looked at his watch. 'We'd better head off. You can tell me all about him over a classic prawn cocktail, assuming it's still on The Old Forge menu.'

Below ground level it was very dark as Gary felt his way along a corridor. There were lights, but he didn't dare turn them on. He bashed into several abandoned tables, chairs and boxes as he hurried past open doors that led to a former bakery, laundry facility and various empty rooms.

What drove Gary crazy was the knowledge that he was so close to civilisation, to freedom. But the Irish travellers were canny. They were used to living outside society, taking what they needed to survive. He was surprised they'd risked attracting the attention of the police by linking up with a ruthless criminal family that had all but destroyed his life. He constantly thought about Tina and the danger he had put her in.

Had he been a fool telling Stacy about Dermot's interest in her?

Had he put her needlessly at risk?

He had seen in Dermot's eye that Tina was more than just another girl. Surely, that gave her some protection?

Eamonn's hands and ankles were chained to a cast-iron water pipe, and a soiled rugby sock had been stuffed in his mouth. He knew Gary could easily have throttled him, but he still had the principles of a police officer.

*Fool.*

He spat out the sock and continued to spit to get rid of the taste.

Sam leaned back in his chair in the Old Forge; a traditional, country restaurant with dying embers in an inglenook fireplace and low beams ready to catch the heads of tall diners of which there were only a few at the brandy and coffee stage. 'Do you plan to see her again?'

'Of course I plan to see her again.' Tina smiled. 'When I need another wax. And for the occasional drink or coffee. We're friends.'

'Friends? She wants to be your lesbian lover!'

Tina was aware of a couple at a neighbouring table turning their heads towards them. 'She knows I am *not* a lesbian,' she whispered.

'I think you're playing with fire, my darling.'

'She *knows* I like men. Dermot in particular.'

Sam leaned across the table and spoke like an investigating detective in a TV drama. 'Despite knowing Magdalena's proclivities, after seeing Dermot, you went back and stayed the night.'

'I couldn't drive. I'd had too much to drink.'

'You could have taken a taxi. Instead, you decided to share a bed with your lesbian friend.'

Tina licked her lips. 'I needed company.'

'You needed company,' he echoed. 'What about her feelings?' He dabbed his mouth with a napkin. 'It must've been torture for her.'

Tina blew out her cheeks and sighed. 'Yes, you're right. It was wrong of me.' Fat tears rolled down her cheeks. 'I don't know what I'm doing. I'm not myself.'

Sam reached across the table and squeezed her hand.

Gary came to a pantry off a scullery that had clearly not been used since the school closed nearly a decade earlier. Behind built-in shelving was a space, large enough to sit upright, with a vent Gary had been working to remove over the past few weeks. With a bit more chipping, he was sure he could push it out and crawl through the gap in the bricks. He'd checked its location from the outside and although there was a bit of a drop, the landing was on grass which, thanks to the rain, would be soft. He would hide for two or three days and then in the dead hours of night he would make a run for it, down the long drive rather than across the moor.

He risked switching on a light and the old bulb's yellowed glow revealed a disturbing handwritten sign: *To whom it may concern. We are aware of you squirreling away tins of food and have removed them. There is no escape.*

Gary checked his hideaway and saw that his tool for chipping at the bricks, and his stash of food had gone. Once again, he had underestimated the travellers. He turned off the light and slumped down on the floor, exhausted. Eamonn would be found soon and then they would come for him.

He heard a bark. A few seconds later, lights flickered on in the corridor and Hector ran into the pantry, all excited to see him.

'Don't lie to me, Dermot.'

They were standing in the Headmaster's study. He looked at Stacy and saw flecks of danger in her eyes. 'I admit. I like her but it's all part of the job. Keep your friends close and your enemies closer.'

'How close do you intend to keep her?'

Dermot risked touching her arms. 'Close enough to hear what's happenin' in Hawksmead, nothin' more than that.'

'We agreed that if Gary tried to escape, we'd take away his most prized possession.'

'All the while there is a threat to Tina, we can keep him in check. We hurt her, or worse, who knows what he might do.'

'I think we should do him now. It's too dangerous keeping him alive. Everyone thinks he's dead, anyway.'

'Kill him?'

'You know it's the right decision.'

'Murder a policeman?'

'Does it bother you?'

'Of course it bothers me! I don't kill people. I rob, I thieve, I extort, I exploit – but I don't murder.'

'Keep your scruples. I'll call daddy. He'll sort it out. Her too.'

Dermot gripped her arms. 'If he touches her I'll feckin' kill him!'

Stacy pulled herself free. 'That's all I needed to know.' There were tears in her eyes.

'I'm sorry. I can't help it. She means a lot to me.'

Stacy curled her lip. 'Well enjoy her while you can.'

Audrey heard the front door open and smiled. It was joyous to have Tina live with them. She missed her married sons in the south of England and, not having a daughter to dote on, Tina was a very special addition.

'Would you like a cup of cocoa?' Audrey called from the kitchen.

'Hot chocolate?'

'Of course.'

Tina appeared in the doorway. 'Where's Malcolm? I didn't see his car.'

'He's up at the Rorty Crankle. It's the board of trustees' annual general meeting. He couldn't wait to give them the good news.'

'What news?'

'That the same person who managed to sell the old boarding house is now on the case selling the main school.'

Tina's mouth dropped open. 'I think I feel a bit of a panic attack coming on. I may need something stronger than a hot chocolate.'

Audrey laughed. 'There's a lovely white in the fridge.' She opened the door and retrieved the bottle, unscrewed the cap and gave Tina a generous glass.

'Thank you. I hope the weather's better tomorrow.'

'I heard it's going to be sunny but with a biting easterly.'

'Good. I need decent light for the photographs. In the rain, the school looks really depressing, and not a little frightening.' She took a sip of wine. 'I want to get drunk, but I know it won't help.' She put her glass down on the worktop.

'What is it, Tina?'

'I can't get balanced. I can't think straight. I'm all over the place. Sometimes, I forget that my parents are even dead. I feel dislocated from reality.'

Audrey put her arms around her. 'That's how I felt when my husband died. I think I was still dislocated from reality when I first came up here.' She gently stroked Tina's hair. 'It takes time. Your emotions are going to be up and down for a while, not helped by the carbon monoxide poisoning. You must be kind to yourself. Just go with the flow unless, as my mother said, you're in the Niagara River.'

Tina pulled back and smiled. 'Or the River Hawk.'

'Too true.' Audrey poured herself a glass of wine and put the bottle back in the fridge. 'How's your brother?'

'He's holding it together – just. In truth, we're a bit of a pathetic pair.'

Audrey picked up her wine. 'You're there for each other. That's all that matters.'

'I've met someone I like.'

Audrey stared; the wine glass frozen, mid air.

'He's an Irish traveller in charge of the migrants up at the old school. Until I know what happened to Gary how could I even think about starting a new relationship? I feel guilty as hell. What sort of wife am I?'

'Until death do us part.'

'You think he's dead?'

'I didn't say that, but we marry to share our lives. When that is no longer possible it behoves us to move on. We have to.'

'Do you really believe that?'

'What I do believe is that love comes in many guises and from many directions. How could I fall for someone who was indirectly responsible for the death of my brother? I wasted eight precious months agonising and if it hadn't been for you inviting me to your wedding, I would never have met the real Malcolm. I would not have experienced three years – and counting, I hope – of love, of companionship, of joyous marriage. He's brought me a happiness I thought was gone for good.' She put down her glass and took Tina's hands in hers. 'Sweetheart, the past is the past. The real sin is to deprive our hearts of love out of a sense of pointless guilt, or duty.' She released Tina's hands and took a gulp of wine. 'Mmm, it *is* good.'

'What about my parents? What would they think?'

'All parents ever want, is for their child to be happy.'

'Despite everything, you think I should see him?'

'What's the alternative? Netflix?'

'You know what, I'm going to focus on selling that old school, and then see where my heart takes me.'

A voice spoke from the hallway. 'Now that's the kind of fighting talk I like to hear.'

Tina grinned as Malcolm hung up his coat.

# 25

Gary shuffled down the corridor to the headmaster's study. He was wearing his regular ankle and handcuffs. Since being discovered in his hideaway, he'd been escorted everywhere he went by at least two burly travellers, one he'd come to like.

'What happened to your face?' Gary asked Martin who had a fresh cut on his left cheek and jaw.

'I was in a pub and all I did was state a fact.'

'Very dangerous, especially for a man with your accent.'

'What is it with you people? Why are you so antagonistic to folks like us?'

'You don't pay tax. You fly tip. You break into homes. You do house renovations and extort additional payments. You park your caravans in beauty spots and when you're forced out, you leave all your crap.'

Martin slowly nodded his head. 'I take your point.'

'What was the fact you imparted?'

'I was sittin', havin' me pint, when some blokes were makin' thick Irish jokes. You know the sort of thing. *Which is the quickest way to Hawksmead?* Are you going by foot or car? *Car.* Then that's the quickest way.'

Gary smiled. 'I know a few more.'

'I bet you do.'

'What was your response?'

'I asked them a question. *What d'yer call the few good-looking girls in Undermere? The ones that aren't obese?*'

'What do you call them?'

*'Polish.'*

Gary laughed. 'I bet that went down well.'

'Can yer believe it? Some bloke with a fat bint of a girlfriend took exception to my observation. I won't be partin' with cash in that pub again.' Martin knocked on the headmaster's door and pushed it open. Gary sauntered in, as best he could. Sunlight brought the shabbiness of the decor into sharp focus.

Dermot lounged on the old sofa. 'Thank you, Martin. You can go.'

Martin nodded to his boss and closed the door behind him.

Dermot looked up at Gary. 'Why did you do it?'

'I'm a police officer. It's my duty to uphold the law.'

'Is it also your duty to put your wife in danger?'

'She was already in danger. At least now I know she's got you to protect her.'

'But for how long? If Tina finds a buyer and we get notice to quit, who knows what will happen?'

'You could give evidence in court against the Cottee family. That would earn you a reduced sentence. I'd speak on your behalf.'

Dermot gave a dry laugh. 'You really don't understand us at all, do you?'

# 26

The heavy rain lasted longer than usual for the time of year. Tina found it incredibly frustrating waiting for the clouds to break, but the rain did finally stop and the weather looked fine for at least a day or two. She parked her Golf away from the school's main entrance, and away from a clutch of vans, lorries and old German cars. The Porsche Spyder had either gone or was hidden from her view. She lifted a tripod and camera out of her car boot and, without announcing her arrival, moved around the grounds seeking out good angles from which to shoot. The photo she liked best was when she placed the old abbey ruins in the foreground with the autumnal sun giving the low stone walls long, dramatic shadows. In the background was the red-brick Victorian edifice, its sharp angles in stark contrast to the ancient moorland's gentle shapes and hues.

Pleased with her work, she carried the camera and tripod into the school via the main entrance and, from the hallway with its worn stone floor and panelled walls, she entered the refectory, the largest room in the building. At one end, was a stage with a classic proscenium arch, framed with sun-bleached, raggedy curtains. She considered the sunlight probing the exterior ivy and grubby windows and tried to find an angle that truly reflected the scale of the room. On the camera's LCD screen she saw a figure standing on the stage. Her heart thumped as she watched him jump down with an easy grace and manoeuvre his way towards her, around numerous oak dining tables and benches.

'What do you think of this room?' she asked.

Dermot stopped and smiled as he looked about him. 'I can almost smell the school dinners, can't you?'

'I smell chlorine.'

He sniffed. 'No, it's definitely boiled cabbage.'

She laughed. 'Now you come to mention it, I can smell it too.'

'Where did you get chlorine from?'

'I was imagining a swimming pool and spa. It's easily big enough and wouldn't need much digging as the basement is below.'

Dermot nodded then his face turned serious.

'What's up?' she asked, as the muscles in her gut clenched.

'When we first met, and in the Falcon, and the next day up at the Rorty Whatsit, you plucked a chord in my heart. I mean it. You can have no idea how much you mean to me.'

Her mouth went dry.

'And it's because of my feelings for you I have to snuff out what I had hoped would be something pretty special – pretty special, to me, anyway.'

She couldn't respond. All joy from the sunny day had evaporated.

He continued. 'I have this t'ing with another woman and, right now, I cannot afford to break off the relationship. I'm sorry. I genuinely am.'

It was a punch to the gut that forced her to find a resting place at the end of one of the long benches. She looked at him, all gossamer joy of a new romance gone. 'Are you married? Is that what you're telling me?'

'To Stacy?' He grinned and sat down on the bench a few feet from her. He reached for her hand but she pulled it away. 'If only it were that easy.'

Tina was surprised by how hurt she felt after such a brief acquaintance. She summoned all her resolve and stood. 'I must get on.'

He nodded. 'Of course.' He got to his feet and for a moment they looked into each other's eyes. As she watched him leave the room, a new sadness enveloped her.

Later, satisfied with her work but feeling totally deflated, she carried the camera and tripod back to her car and put it in the boot. Her mind kept wandering as she tried to run through the shots she had taken and whether she had enough to spark the imaginations of potential buyers. She slammed the lid and was shocked to see Dermot standing just a few feet away.

'Don't go yet. Please. I have a jar of instant coffee in my office and Barmbrack fresh from Ireland.'

'Barmbrack? What's that when it's at home?'

'It's a cake we eat in the month of Halloween, rich in fruit and spice, and with a dash of whiskey. Let me cut you a slice.'

It was enough to breach her resistance. They walked with unseemly haste to the main entrance, across the echoing hallway and down the long corridor to the headmaster's study. The door was barely closed before he cupped her face in his hands. Their lips came together and his tongue entered her mouth. He pressed his body against hers, pushing her up against the door. She wanted this man and pulled apart the popper at the top of her jeans, wishing she'd worn a skirt. But there were so many hazards in and around the old school it had made sense to protect her legs.

Dermot helped her peel off her jeans and she kicked them aside. His fingers stroked her hair, her breast and the thin fabric at the top of her thighs. In the small of her back she felt the door handle turn and it opened an inch.

'Private business,' he yelled, and slammed it shut with his hand. 'Come back later.'

'Let me in.' Tina recognised the woman's accent as typical Essex.

'I'll join you in a minute,' Dermot said. 'I'll see you in the staff kitchen.'

'Who've you got in there?'

Tina unravelled her jeans and pulled them on as fast as she could.

'It's the estate agent. She's a little upset. You know, what with what's happened to her parents.'

Tina took the cue and poked both her eyes. She sat down on the sofa and put her face in her hands. The door opened.

'I lost my mother when I was a child,' the woman said. 'She'll get over it.'

'I wasn't expecting you, today, Stacy me darlin'.'

'Daddy sent me. He's not 'appy about the current situation.'

Tina had poked her eyes a bit too hard and they were both watering profusely. She looked up at the blurred woman.

'Grief comes back to me in waves. Mr O'Hanlon was being very kind giving me some privacy.' She got up from the sofa and wiped away her tears. 'You're very beautiful.'

Stacy ignored the compliment and opened the door.

'Leave us,' she said.

Tina nodded and left the room. The door slammed behind her. For the second time that day she felt totally deflated. Somehow, she had to protect herself more. Her emotions were all over the place.

# 27

Tap. Tap.

The knock on the guest bedroom door told Tina who it was and she looked up from the screen of her borrowed laptop. For the last couple of days she'd been sitting at an escritoire trying to find the right words that would spark the interest in a certain type of investor.

'Come in.'

The door opened and Malcolm entered carrying a tray with a small cafetière, milk jug, cup and saucer, and a plate with a slice of Victoria sponge, cake fork and napkin. 'I thought you may be ready for elevenses.'

'Elevenses?'

'An old expression.' He placed the tray on a rosewood bureau. 'How are you getting on?'

'Struggling a bit. I'm trying to get into the brains of billionaires; trip their levers, but it's not easy.'

'They are a unique breed. Perhaps I can help.'

Tina was a bit slow responding. 'That's very kind of you.'

Malcolm smiled. 'I know what you're thinking. You're wondering whether an octogenarian can have any ideas that are relevant today.'

'Not at all, Malcolm. I just didn't want to take up your time with my problem.'

'Ah, but it's my problem too. The trustees are relying

on you and me to get the school sold. Don't forget, after I gave up teaching I used to make my living writing advertising and marketing copy.'

'Of course! It had slipped my mind. I'd love to have your help.'

'Let me pour your coffee. Caffeine got me through many a tough brief. The worst jobs were producing brochures for the big insurance companies. They paid well but boy were they happy to peddle half-truths.'

He carried the cup and saucer over to her. She noticed a slight shake as he placed it next to the laptop. 'You are brilliant at selling, Tina, and my recommendation is that you should trust your first instincts. In my opinion, one's initial ideas are invariably the best.'

She laughed. 'I wish that were true.'

'Let's look at the market.'

'You sit down at the desk.' She got up from her chair. 'And I'll prop myself up on the bed.'

'Deal.'

Malcolm took over the upright chair and Tina plumped the pillows on one of the two single beds she'd been sleeping in.

'I'll create a new file,' Malcolm said, 'where I can type a few notes.' He clicked and tapped like an old pro, surprising her by how adept he was using the computer. Two-hands typing, not the usual single digit. He looked at her over his shoulder. 'Who are we targeting?'

'The big property developers – all the ones who have *"Homes"* in their company name.'

'Do we really want to replace the old school with an identikit housing estate?'

'No. But do we have a choice?'

'You tell me.'

Tina got off the bed and took a sip of coffee. 'Mmm, this is good.'

'Coffee connects the dots like nothing else.'

'You're right. I hate those big housing developers. They could build with style if they wanted to, with good materials, decent insulation, quality green spaces, but all they do is try to get around the regulations. They couldn't give a stuff about the natural environment, and nor do most councils. If developers had had their way, Audrey's old school boarding house would be a block of flats instead of a beautiful, tranquil memorial garden.'

'Unfortunately, the trustees cannot afford to donate the land, as Audrey did, and also follow through with their plans to build a youth centre with year-round sports facilities.'

'So, we have to approach the right kind of buyers. Problem is, I'm struggling to find an angle.'

'Have another sip of coffee.'

Tina did as instructed. 'The person we need to attract must be an entrepreneur who has courage in his DNA...'

'Or her DNA,' Malcolm interjected.

'Nice thought, but unlikely.'

'Forgive me. Go on my dear.'

'It has to be someone with the financial resources to capitalise on opportunities the typical, unimaginative, business majority simply cannot see.'

'Who do you have in mind?'

'Someone I once saw kissing a former friend.'

# 28

Abel Cornfield looked out of the side window of the helicopter as his pilot circled above Hawksmead College. He could see the ruins of the monastery overshadowed by the former Victorian workhouse. There were a few remote barns that may have to go, and assorted caravans parked on the rugby pitch – they would belong to the travellers.

'Drone,' said the pilot's voice through his headphones.

Abel looked at him. The pilot pointed to a small object tracking the helicopter.

'Interesting,' Abel said. 'It looks a bit bigger than a toy.'

'I think it's the Matrice – the go-to drone for aerial photography in Hollywood. Six rotors for a perfectly steady shot.'

'The estate agent's really on her game.'

'Where shall I put you down, sir?'

Abel looked at the gravelled area in front of the school. He saw a number of parked vehicles and a white car coming to a halt.

'As near to the front of the building as possible.'

The pilot swooped away from the drone and came to a gentle touchdown on a patch of level grass. Abel looked at the austere facade, parts exposed and parts almost entirely hidden by ivy, as he waited for the rotor to slow. In his late forties, tall, slim, with good posture, a strong handsome face, crowned with an excellent head of light brown hair, he always dressed well because he only had smart clothes. He turned to the pilot. 'Come with me. I'll see if I can get you a coffee.'

'Thank you, sir, but I have a flask and I don't like to leave the helicopter unattended until I know who's around.'

'I'll be an hour or so.' Abel saw a young woman emerge from the white car. 'That's the agent.'

'She looks well turned-out,' the pilot stated.

Abel laughed. 'She is. We've had many face to face chats online. I'm impressed with her.' He opened the door and carefully stepped down to the ground. Keeping upright, confident that his head was well below the slowly turning rotor blades, he strode across the sodden grass towards the gravelled apron.

'Lord Cornfield. Welcome,' Tina said, offering her hand.

'Abel, please.' He felt her fine bones as they briefly shook hands. 'It's good to meet you in person, Christina.'

'Everyone calls me Tina.'

'I like Christina.'

She smiled. 'Let me show you around.'

An hour later, after showing the prospective purchaser the Victorian interior, but only the places where Dermot had told her it was safe to go, they were standing almost midway between the dilapidated barns and milking parlour, and the caravans belonging to the travellers.

'Let me get this straight,' Abel said. 'The school building is Grade II but the ruins are Grade I.'

'That's right,' Tina nodded. 'But I think you'll have plenty of latitude when it comes to planning, short of tearing the whole lot down, of course. The school was good for the town and the loss of its business is sorely missed. Any plan that will help to regenerate Hawksmead will be looked upon favourably, I'm sure. Are you thinking of an hotel?'

'More ambitious than that. I want to reinstate the farm, build tennis courts, squash courts, and a couple of golf courses, one to be PGA standard. We could have clay-pigeon shooting and guided tours on the moor. One of the barns could be converted into a luxury cinema showing the latest films. As for the school building itself, I've examined the floor plan and it will have to be completely gutted. Part will be set aside for recovering addicts, rich ones of course, and the remainder will be a five-star hotel with indoor and outdoor swimming pools, his and her gyms and spas, and two or three fabulous restaurants, one open to locals.' He turned to Tina. 'What do you think? Can you see it?'

'Yes Abel. I think it's an excellent plan.'

He smiled. 'Christina, would you mind if I took you somewhere special to celebrate our deal? Purely business.'

The man's hazel eyes were fixed on her as heat spread to her extremities. She curled her toes, hoping that the concentration would stop her cheeks pulsing red. She was a far cry from the confident young woman who had married Gary. And her start-stop relationship with Dermot had driven all balance from her mind.

'Of course, Lord Cornfield. Where would you like to go? There's a lovely gastro-pub a few miles from here called The Rorty Crankle Inn.'

'I was thinking of a few days in the Eternal City. I take

it, you do have a passport?'

'Should I accept?' Tina was enjoying a late lunch in the little cottage. 'We've only met once, although we've talked a lot via Zoom and on the phone.'

'How old did you say he was?' Malcolm asked, standing, as he poured her a glass of sparkling elderflower.

'According to Wiki he's forty-eight.'

'Nearly double your age,' Audrey observed. 'I cannot imagine why he wants to take you to Rome?'

'He wants to thank her, my dear,' Malcolm said. 'The way billionaires like to do.'

Audrey laughed and looked at Tina. 'Do you want to be thanked by him?'

'I haven't been thanked since Gary.' She looked at her half-eaten salmon. 'Anyway, he said it's purely business. He wants me to look at properties. I should probably say no.'

Audrey took Tina's hand in hers. 'You have many challenges ahead. Take this time out. Enjoy Rome... the paintings, the statues, the Coliseum.'

Malcolm interjected. 'The Basilica will feed your soul like no other place on earth.'

'He's right,' Audrey said. She squeezed her hand. 'Relish the opportunity.'

'But,' Malcolm stared down at her, glass jug slightly shaking. 'Remember, this a business trip to thank you for services already given.'

Audrey squeezed her hand again. 'You don't owe him anything.'

'You're not bait to be gobbled up.'

Tina looked from one concerned face to the other.

Audrey squeezed her hand, yet again. 'Trust your instincts but also listen to what your heart is telling you. If you like him, let him know. Don't waste time.

Life really is too short.'

# 29

The AgustaWestland AW109 lifted off from in front of the old school. Tina watched her white VW Golf getting smaller and smaller as the spinning rotor above her head swept her away. She was seated to the left of the pilot wearing headphones that matched his.

'Would you mind circling over the school?' she said into the microphone.

'It'll run us a bit light on fuel,' the pilot replied. 'But, if I feather the rotor, we should just about make it.'

'No, no... that's fine. Don't waste fuel.'

He ignored her and swept low over the main school building. 'Don't worry, Mrs Burton. Fuel's not a problem.'

Tina kicked herself for being taken in by the handsome pilot with his perfect vowels and consonants. This was her first flight in a helicopter and she loved the view out of the window. From the air the school and surrounding land looked amazing.

The small figure of a man ran out of a side entrance. He waved at the helicopter with both hands, tripped and fell on the grass. She watched him scramble to his feet and wave frantically. Tina gave him a little wave back although she knew he wouldn't see it. She watched the man jumping around and was about to ask the pilot to go lower when he swept her high up into the sky, leaving her stomach somewhere below her seat.

Gary fell to the ground and wept. He had seen Tina's VW Golf and had kept out of sight. If she had seen him, Dermot would have taken her captive and made some excuse to the pilot. But once the helicopter was safely in the air, he hoped she would recognise his frantic waving and let him know that she was getting help.

A large, long, slobbering tongue washed his face, which cheered him up, just a bit. Hector, the scarred and brutalised bullmastiff, would always tug on his chain to be petted whenever he saw Gary, often receiving a kick from Eamonn for *going soft*.

Hands grabbed Gary and he was dragged along the ground, back into the school, accompanied by Hector's barking.

'Leave us.' Dermot ordered his brother and another who had helped him. He squatted down and looked at Gary, constrained by both hand and ankle cuffs. 'Did she see you?'

'The police will be on their way very soon.'

'What would you do in my position?'

'Go back to Ireland… disappear.'

Dermot smiled and shook his head. 'She didn't see you. I know Tina well enough to know she would never leave you. That girl's got courage. She would've got the pilot to land.' He stood up. 'Gary, you're forcing my hand.' He gripped the chain linking Gary's handcuffs and hauled him to his feet. 'I think you'd better make peace with your maker.'

'I didn't take you for a killer.'

Dermot shook his head. 'I'm not… unfortunately, I know someone who is.'

Tina loved the views out of the window but was keen not to distract the pilot who seemed to be focusing hard. She saw the meandering swathe of the River Thames and felt her stomach flip as the pilot swooped the helicopter above the grey river. They followed it downstream giving her an excellent view of the Houses of Parliament, Nelson's Column, St Paul's Cathedral, and the Tower of London. The pilot performed a u-turn and they flew back upstream past the glacial Shard towering above; and past the great wheel of the London Eye before setting down on a circle with an H at the heliport near Battersea Bridge.

'Stunning views. Thank you, Graham.'

'Lord Cornfield wanted me to give you a little tour of London.'

The pilot guided the aircraft along the ramp towards the heliport's futuristic reception building and parked it within a marked circle. She wanted to thank God for a safe landing but she and God had been distant since Gary's disappearance.

'I'll bring your bag,' Graham said.

The wind ruffled her hair as she carefully stepped down in her trainers to the deck. She was both incredibly excited and incredibly nervous. Graham carried her small, grey suitcase, borrowed from Audrey, and walked with her to a smart reception and waiting area.

Abel, wearing a lightweight suit and tie, and immaculate, soft-leather shoes, opened his arms. 'Welcome to London, Christina. Your car awaits.'

She sank back into the impossibly soft leather seat of a Bentley Mulsanne. The last time she'd been in the rear of a chauffeured car was on her wedding day. She pushed the memory to the back of her mind and determined to relish the luxury experience as much as possible. The exterior of the car had almost taken her breath away. She loved its nose with its wide, vertical grille below the sweeping Bentley marque. The car looked so solid, so sleek, so James Bond. The first thing she noticed about the interior was the phenomenal aroma of fine leather. She should have worn heels. The unbelievably soft mat in the foot well was too good even for her almost new trainers. In front of her was a touch-screen tablet for her personal use. The cream-leather interior and seats, monogrammed with the striking Bentley logo, were beyond any luxury she had ever experienced. She peeked between the front seats and saw a futuristic dashboard set in traditional, highly-polished wood.

The driver glanced over his shoulder. 'All good, sir?'

Abel turned to Tina. She smiled and clicked her seatbelt.

'Thank you, Gary,' Abel replied. 'All good.'

*Damn. Why did the chauffeur have to be called Gary?*

'It's Sebastian, sir. Gary's not well, today.'

*Phew.*

'I must pay more attention. Thank you Sebastian.'

'Heathrow Terminal Three, sir?'

'Yes.'

She felt the beating thud of her heart. What was it telling her? She'd only known this handsome, powerful man for such a short while. She turned to him and put on her brightest smile. 'Thank you for meeting me.'

'I would've come in the helicopter but I was arranging funds for the purchase of the school.'

'You don't have it sitting in your current account?'

'I don't have it sitting in the UK.'

# 30

'That's a Ford Galaxy,' Malcolm said from the kitchen.

Audrey was sitting at the rosewood dining table with her tablet propped up by *The Mill on the Floss* by George Eliot and held from slipping by an embossed, leather-bound edition of *Romola*. On the tablet's screen was a YouTube video demonstrating how to use a Singer sewing machine for beginners.

'My mother used to run-up little tops and skirts for me all the time,' Audrey responded. 'I'm not sure I'm going to master this. To think I've gone through the majority of my life not really knowing what a bobbin actually is. I thought it was called a cotton reel. How wrong was I?'

'It's probably a taxi, one of the older ones,' Malcolm pressed on. 'My hands are covered in flour. Could you do me the honour and open the door, my darling?'

'The bell's not gone, yet.'

'It won't be Tina, so it's bound to ring.'

'Ours isn't the only cottage.'

'The taxi's going. Could you see who it is?'

Audrey paused the video on her tablet. 'Perhaps I'll just keep my mother's sewing machine in the front room as a curiosity, a talking point, and let another generation learn how to use it.'

'I don't understand why they've not rung the doorbell yet.'

Audrey got up from her chair. 'I'll see who it is.' She walked through the sitting room into the hall and pulled open the front door. Kneeling on the flagstone path was a young man Audrey immediately recognised but had never met. She hurried to him and took her time to squat down. Tentatively, she rested a hand on his shoulder.

'Sam?'

He roughly wiped away his tears. 'Yes, I'm sorry. Please forgive me. I get overwhelmed.'

'Come inside.'

'I don't want to bother you.'

'I live near an old mill town once renowned for its textiles and am struggling to sew in a straight line. I can assure you you're not bothering me, as long as you help me up.'

Sam got to his feet and she took his hand.

'I've been trying to get in touch with Tina,' he said, 'but her phone's off.'

'She's gone to Rome.'

'Alone?'

'Not exactly.'

'With the Irish traveller? I know she liked him.'

'Come inside and I'll tell you all about it.'

'I don't understand why she didn't let me know she was going.'

'It was all a bit rushed. Last minute. She said you were away in London.' Audrey guided Sam into the hallway and through to a seat on the sofa.

'I was seeing old mates. I grew up in Hawksmead but I only truly felt accepted in London. I needed a break.' He paused. 'Audrey, my mother told me about my Uncle Mark and how he and your little brother had a special relationship. It meant a lot to me to know that.'

Malcolm closed the front door and stood in the entrance to the hallway. 'Would you care for some Dundee?'

Audrey and Sam looked up at the slim, elegant man with white flour decorating his blue-striped apron.

'Malcolm?' asked Sam.

'At your service.'

'Tina has told me so much about you.' He turned to Audrey. 'Thank you both for taking care of her.'

'You're more than welcome to stay with us,' Malcolm said. 'There are twin beds in your sister's room.'

Sam chuckled. 'Thank you. I don't think Tina and I have ever shared a bedroom. It's so kind of you to offer, but the Falcon is a friendly place and it's near my parents' home.' He searched his rain jacket and found a handy-sized pack of tissues. 'The police have confirmed it was an accident. The boiler was old and the battery in the carbon monoxide alarm had run out.' He blew his nose.

'An easy oversight,' Malcolm said. 'I must test our smoke alarms.'

Sam looked at Audrey. 'I heard about your fire.'

Malcolm untied his apron. 'Tina drove like the clappers to get Audrey to hospital. Gary was the policeman in hot pursuit.'

Sam smiled. 'She told me more than once how she fought the law but the law won!'

'It was a beautiful wedding,' Audrey said.

'I am so sorry I missed it. I've seen photos, of course, but I never met Gary, except online.' He looked up at Malcolm. 'You created a wonderful memorial garden. I'll go there to pay my respects before I return to New Zealand.'

'Next door is the Methodist church,' Audrey said. 'It has a charming graveyard.'

Sam looked at her. 'You think my parents could be buried there?'

'Reverend Longden married your sister.'

'Believe you me,' interjected Malcolm. 'William Longden admired your parents so much he would pick up a shovel himself.'

Audrey looked at her husband. 'I'm not sure about that, Malcolm. Not everyone is as sprightly as you. And he is eighty-nine.'

# 31

Tina watched the chauffeur remove Audrey's loaned suitcase from the boot of the Bentley and place it next to Abel's. He extended the handle.

'Would you like me to wheel the bags in for you, sir?'

'Thank you, Sebastian,' Abel replied, 'but we can manage from here.'

'Have a lovely trip, sir.'

'I'm sure we will.'

Sebastian nodded to Tina and got back in the car. She watched it glide away.

Abel smiled at her. 'Are you all right pulling your bag?'

She gripped the handle. 'Nobody drives it but me.'

He laughed, the automatic doors opened and she followed him into the most futuristic airport terminal she'd ever experienced. She tried to take in the dramatic ceiling, the space-age lighting, the shops and restaurants while also keeping up with Abel.

'Good morning Lord Cornfield.'

He stopped by a perfectly coiffed woman in uniform holding a tablet.

'Good morning, Annabel. I hope you are well?'

'I am, sir. Rome should be lovely at this time of year. Not too hot.' She gave Tina a welcoming smile. 'Have a good trip, Mrs Burton.'

'Thank you.' Tina blushed and followed Abel to a check-in desk, seemingly opened especially for them. He produced his phone and offered the screen for scanning together with his passport. The smartly uniformed man looked at Tina and she handed him her passport, which he held under a scanner and then passed back to her.

Abel placed her bag on the conveyor belt. The man fixed a tag and she watched it disappear.

'I thought you'd want our bags in the cabin with us?' Tina said with a smile.

'Don't worry. The airline will ensure there's no delay waiting for them at the other end.'

She followed Abel through security and down a private corridor to a First Class lounge where wealthy-looking people were sitting at tables staring into their phones, accompanied by flutes of Champagne and tiny espresso cups. To one side was a long, luxury bar leading to sound-proofed picture windows that brought the vast expanse of runways, taxiways and Boeing airliners into the room.

They settled at a table and were immediately offered Champagne, which they both declined. 'May we have coffee and orange juice, and...' Abel looked at Tina with an enquiring expression.

She smiled up at the waiter. 'Do you have almond croissants?'

'Yes madam.' He turned to Abel.

'Make it two.'

'Thank you, sir.'

The waiter headed for the bar and Abel looked at his watch, which Tina recognised as a Piaget.

'It's so nice in here,' she said. 'We could forget time and see our plane take off through the window.'

Abel laughed. 'Very true, except they know where we are and when the time is right, will invite us to board the aircraft.'

She looked away and took a breath. The experience was already overwhelming. What was to come? She felt Abel's hand on hers.

'I want you to relax. It's special for me, too. Arrogant men talk about creating their own luck – but, did they create their parents, the era they were born into, their country, their trust fund that provides a safety net, enabling them to take extraordinary risks? There's a cliché which holds true today – the first million is far and away the hardest. The man, or woman, who risks the family home to pursue a dream, is the one with true courage.'

Tina liked the way the conversation had turned. Until she had met and married her policeman, she had been very ambitious, but the move to London swiftly followed by Gary's disappearance had snuffed out much of her lust for success. But meeting this smart, sensitive and supremely successful older man had re-ignited her ambitious flame.

'I have something for you,' Abel said. 'It's a gift, not an inducement. I've also had it engraved, so I can't take it back. Please accept it as a simple thank you, with no strings.'

Tina looked at Abel and wondered what the gift was. 'May I see it?'

He reached into his jacket pocket. 'Before I show it to you, I want you to understand how important it is, for perfect running, to have it serviced every five years.'

She kept still, held her breath, her excitement building.

Abel placed a red leather box on the table and she

immediately spotted the brand name: Patek Philippe, Genève. She glanced at her wrist and at the watch her parents had given her on her eighteenth birthday.

He smiled. 'I know what you're thinking. *I already have a watch.*'

Almost involuntarily, Tina placed her right hand over her left wrist.

'Today, you're travelling in trainers,' Abel continued. 'But, for dinner, you'll probably select another pair of shoes. That's how you should think about this watch.' He pushed the clasp and opened the box.

She gasped. She couldn't help it.

'This is a travel timepiece, a Calatrava Pilot by Swiss watchmaker Patek Philippe, to record your first flight in a helicopter. As you can see, the styling is aeronautical and incorporates a second time zone little hand, set to Rome time.'

She tried to control her breathing.

Abel took the watch out of its box. 'But, most importantly, it is self-winding. No battery to run out. It is also water resistant down to thirty metres. That's about a hundred feet – pretty deep. The case...' He rubbed the watch between his thumb and forefinger. '...is made of rose gold, and the strap is calfskin.'

Tina's mouth was dry.

He held out his hand. 'Please try it on.'

'What's the engraving?' She heard her voice crack.

'Take a look.'

Gary shivered. This was the end game, of that he was sure. His one consolation was that Tina was ignorant of his existence and so not in immediate danger. A tear crept out of the corner of an eye and he swiped it away. He would not beg. He had no belief in a God or an afterlife. When his time came, he would embrace oblivion. At the moment, all he could embrace was a hard floor and a long chain coiled around old water pipes in the basement room. A little daylight came through fixed, thick glass high windows that were a little above ground level.

The bolts slid back and the door opened. Eamonn recoiled. 'A bit of a stink, eh?' Gary said, sprawled on the stone floor.

Eamonn edged his way in and grabbed an old metal bucket containing body waste.

'What about food, or am I to be starved to death?'

'You'll get it when it suits me, you feckin' bastard!'

'I could've killed you, Eamonn, but I didn't.' Sprawled on the floor, Gary looked up at the big man and hoped he wouldn't empty the bucket's contents over him. 'Help me and I'll make sure you're in the clear. No jail time.'

'Me. Help an Englishman? A policeman? Save your breath.' He reached for the door.

'Leave it open, Eamonn. Please. I'm chained. I can't move. Please.'

Eamonn stared down at him. 'Now you know how we feel. Ireland has been chained to Britain for centuries. What mercy did you show us? We starved but did you send food? No. When we fought back, you hanged us.'

Gary looked at the man's angry face and chose his words carefully. 'I apologise for all the hurt we've caused.'

'Still. Mustn't dwell on the past.' Eamonn's mouth curled up. 'At least your wife is safe in the arms of the rich bastard who's buying this place.'

Gary tried not to betray any emotion.

Eamonn's expression softened. 'Tina's a nice person.

Beautiful. Me and the dog scared the shit out of her but she's got courage, I'll give her that.' He walked away, swinging the stinking bucket, but leaving the door open.

Tina sat back in her seat and watched the world rush by. She felt a surge in her back as the nose lifted and the jet soared into the sky. She turned to Abel who was looking at her. 'I like travelling First Class.'

'And you will. This is Business Class… they don't have First Class on this flight. But, when we go to New York for Christmas, we will fly First Class, although the seats are a bit too far apart for my taste.' He smiled and rested his hand on hers.

She enjoyed his touch and wondered what sex with this handsome, wealthy man would be like. She'd really fancied Dermot who had an enigmatic charm, laced with massive sex appeal. Abel was different. He was completely deferential, was scrubbed, manicured and polished, but behind his smile and perfect white teeth he clearly had a spine of steel.

She looked out of the window at the wisps of cloud scudding by and wondered about her own judgement. The death of her parents had driven out the last vestiges of balance. She knew she was out of control and that she was vulnerable. But, she wasn't scared. There was nothing bad about Abel on the internet, just his business successes, estimates of his vast wealth, and the small matter of his marriage.

She turned back to him. 'I Googled you.'

Abel smiled. 'So that's what it was. I thought I felt something.'

'I didn't realise you're a widower. I thought you were divorced.' She waited for his response, but it was slow coming.

He took his hand away. 'We met in a restaurant. Claudia was studying English at university and was out with friends. I was also a student celebrating my first business deal. We were nineteen and, I'm embarrassed to say, it was love at first sight.'

She looked into his eyes and knew she liked this man. 'What happened?'

'Claudia was about your age. Felt terrible, went to bed early. At midnight, I called an ambulance. By morning she was on life-support. Her parents and her sister came to say goodbye. She died.'

'Why? How?'

'Sepsis.'

Tina had heard of it but wasn't exactly sure what it was.

'They didn't know what caused it. It could've been something as minor as a scratch having her nails done. She went into septic shock. Her organs failed one by one. They fought the virus as best they could but she was overwhelmed. I have never felt so helpless.' He took a deep breath and smiled. 'It taught me to live in the moment. Have an eye on the future, but not live there.'

Tina felt her new watch with her fingertips. 'Thank you for my present. And thank you for taking me out of myself.'

Lunch arrived in white ceramic dishes. Tina wanted to tuck in but there was a bit of turbulence and she was anxious about spilling food on her top.

'Timing is everything in life,' Abel laughed. 'May I help you?'

She allowed him to cover her top with a cloth napkin. 'Thank you kind sir... sorry, my lord.'

He chuckled. 'I'm still not used to it.'

'Is your father an earl? Or a duke?'

'He was a tailor. Originally from Lithuania. His parents were shot by collaborators but a non-Jewish family managed to hide him. After the war, a surviving uncle took him to the new State of Israel and then in the 1950s he came to England, ostensibly on holiday. Thanks to help from the Jewish community in Finchley, he was able to evade deportation and learn the rag trade. He met my mother in the mid 1960s. She was a fashion model. They married. My sister arrived, and then me.'

'Is your mother alive?'

'Lung cancer took her. She smoked as a model to help keep thin and it killed her aged thirty-nine. My dad has never really got over it. He's had three wives since but they didn't stand a chance. He's in his late eighties and has decided it's time to hang up his gun.'

Tina smiled. 'My dad always used cowboy analogies. If a business meeting went wrong he'd sometimes describe it as Custer's last stand. For years, I thought he said *custard's* last stand. As in, he had a bit of a wobble.'

'I've had meetings like that.' He touched her hand. 'I am so sorry about your parents. At the very least, I hope Rome will give your mind a break, a chance to rest.'

The journey from Fiumicino Airport took longer than Tina expected. Sitting in the back of the taxi with Abel she felt a bit awkward. They really knew so little about each other and lived in very different worlds. But, as Audrey had reminded her, opportunities like a luxury trip to Rome come but once and she was determined to treasure every minute. And judging by the increasingly beautiful buildings they were passing, there was an awful lot to attract her estate agent's eye.

The taxi entered a large cobbled piazza. Encompassing the entire square was a low wall adorned with countless marble statues. Within the pedestrian centre were two highly intricate fountains where gargoyles spouted water, boys blew horns, and giant naked men with bulging muscles and strange animal heads prepared for battle. Most striking of all was a commemorative column, exquisitely carved, rising out of a mass of writhing serpents. Tina couldn't quite see who or what was standing at the top.

'Almost there,' Abel commented.

'It's stunning. Everywhere I look it is unbelievable.'

He turned to her. 'I hope you will come to love Rome as much as I do, and that this is the first of many trips we make.'

She didn't know how to respond, so took his hand.

The driver turned into a narrow street, turned into another, turned again, and halted the taxi. He got out and opened Abel's door.

Tina pushed open her door and looked at the classic Italianate facade. *Massive kerb appeal*, said her estate-agent brain.

'Buona giornata, signore e signora,' welcomed the liveried doorman. 'Spero tu stia bene, Lord Cornfield.'

'Very well, Luciano. I hope life is good for you, too.'

'I live in Rome and I have a wonderful job. Seriously, sir, my life could not be better.'

Tina spotted Abel slipping a couple of hundred-Euro notes into Luciano's hand.

'Signore, we are honoured that you have chosen the best hotel in Rome for a vacation with la tua bellissima moglie.' He gave Tina his most winning smile.

Abel turned to look at her. 'Luciano, I would like to introduce you to un'amica molto buona, Christina

Burton.'

The doorman bowed his head. 'Welcome to Hotel di Santa Benita, signorina. I hope your stay will be very happy.'

Tina smiled. 'Thank you.' She looked through glass doors into the extravagant reception and imagined the wealth of beauty within. She was confident about how she looked, albeit a bit on the thin side, but her clothes were chain-store stylish rather than high-end designer.

The driver removed the bags from the car's boot and wheeled them to a uniformed porter.

Abel gently put his arm around her shoulder. 'Let's get settled in.' The glass doors opened and he guided her to a large reception desk and to a beautifully groomed, smiling receptionist.

'Lord Cornfield. How lovely to see you. My name's Gabriella.'

'Thank you Gabriella. Have we met before?'

'I don't believe so. This is my first week.'

'Congratulations.'

'Thank you signore.' She placed two glossy folders on the counter. 'Is this your daughter's first visit to Rome?' She smiled at Tina.

'Mrs Burton is a friend, not my daughter,' Abel said. 'È anche una vedova.' He handed her his passport.

'Many apologies, signore.' Clearly embarrassed, Gabriella placed his passport on a scanner and returned it to him avoiding eye contact. Tina handed over hers with what she hoped was a reassuring smile.

Gabriella scanned her passport and gave it back. She turned to Abel. 'I think Signora will enjoy the Augusta suite.'

'I agree,' Abel said.

'Mario will take you to your rooms and your luggage will be with you, shortly.'

A young, liveried valet guided Tina and Abel towards the only lift in the ancient building. The doors slid open and Tina entered, followed by Abel and Mario. They stood in stiff silence until the lift came to a halt. The doors slid open and they followed Mario down a short corridor. He removed a white entry card from one of the folders and put it in a door slot. A light turned from red to green and he pushed the door open. He looked at Tina and she and Abel entered.

'Signorina, it is necessary to put entry card in slot for lights to work.' She watched Mario place the card in a wall-mounted slot. 'When you leave, take card. All lights go out. Simple. Save planet.'

Abel peeled off a fifty-Euro note and gave it to Mario. 'I can take it from here, thank you.'

Although Mario looked pleased to see the large tip, he could not hide his disappointment. He turned to Tina. 'I can show you how to work everything.'

'That's all right,' Abel said. 'I've stayed here many times.' He relieved Mario of the folders and ushered out the flirtatious young man.

Tina looked around her room with its luxuriously embossed wallpaper and extravagantly gilt-framed oil paintings. There was a button-back, silk-covered sofa and matching armchair; there were low-level tables bedecked with cut flowers in decorative vases, or with exotic lamps; and a large wall-mounted TV. On the screen appeared a message: *Welcome Signora Christina Burton to the Hotel di Santa Benita.* She smiled. 'But where's the bed?'

'Next door. It's a suite.'

He guided her through to an even larger room with

an enormous double bed, side tables with drawers, fitted wardrobe units and another widescreen TV. A silk rug depicting classic Roman carvings covered much of the carpet. She spotted her borrowed suitcase sitting on a raised stand and thought it looked distinctly shabby in comparison.

Abel picked up the TV remote control. 'There's a simple menu for ordering room service et cetera and we can also message each other via the TV. Of course you can also dial my room from the phone by the bed.'

'Or I can use my own phone.'

'Exactly.' He smiled. 'My suite is just next door. Relax, have a drink, there's Champagne and chocolates; unpack if you want and I'll come back in, say, thirty minutes? We could then go for a stroll, look at some world-renowned shops and stop off for a little light refreshment. Tonight, I suggest we dine in the hotel, get a good night's sleep, and explore the cobbled streets of the old city in the morning.'

'Fabulous.' *When were they going to make love for the first time?*

'I'll freshen up and see you in about half an hour.'

'Great.' She watched Abel leave the room and a moment or two later she heard him close the door to the suite. She took a few seconds to take in the five-star surroundings. The furnishings were high-end and everywhere she looked was another little touch of luxury. No need was left unrequited. She unzipped Audrey's suitcase and quickly hung up her clothes in the large wardrobe. She had been unsure as to what to bring and was still not certain she'd made the right choices. However, she was confident about her underwear, which was almost unworn. Gary had loved seeing her dressed all in white, but he had disappeared so soon after their marriage that much of her smooth satin lingerie had remained in her bottom drawer, untouched.

She took her toiletries and make-up to the en-suite bathroom, beautifully appointed in Italian marble and with concealed lighting. Snow-white towels, perfectly rolled, were displayed on recessed shelves with matching monogrammed bathrobes and slippers.

Her new watch, displaying the hour in Rome, told her she had time. She removed it, read the inscription, then kicked off her trainers, peeled down her jeans and removed all her clothes. She looked at her naked form in the tinted mirror. She had forgotten about her complete wax... and smiled at the memory.

She stepped into the large shower and stood back before turning on the tap. Within a few seconds she was cascaded by lovely warm water from a giant-sized showerhead as she lathered her whole slim frame in luxurious, complimentary Nuxe body wash.

Wrapped in the softest towel she'd ever felt against her skin, she stepped onto an equally soft bath mat, warmed by underfloor heating. Once dry, she used Borghese body cream, another high-end courtesy product, to moisturise her arms, legs and torso. She dug in her toilet bag for a toothbrush and gave her even, white teeth a good going over. Happy, she ran a comb through her damp hair and carefully touched up her make-up, to preserve her natural look. Finally, she used the hotel's powerful hairdryer and added volume to her thick, blonde locks. She picked her clothes up from the floor and hung them in the fitted wardrobe. Her briefs she balled up and placed in a pocket within her suitcase. She selected a pair of white satin knickers and slipped them on. They felt good. She put on a long

T-shirt and looked at herself in a full-height mirror. Too thin *but still pretty hot!*

A sudden thought. She hurried back to the bathroom and retrieved from her toilet bag a small plastic bottle of lubricating gel and a top of the range packet of condoms. She hated using them but she had given up the pill following Gary's disappearance. She placed both items in a bedside drawer.

She was ready. She glanced at the TV to check the time, then heard a soft knock. She took a deep breath and tried to keep her cool as she walked through the suite and opened the door.

Abel, wearing a lightweight suit and tie, stood tall and very handsome. For a moment, he seemed lost for words. She reached for his hand and took it in hers. 'I thought you might like a little rest before we go out.' She smiled. 'Work up an appetite.'

'If we go out now, I can show you the famous Spanish Steps and the Pantheon. Or, we can do a bit of shopping. Stretch our legs.'

Had she got the whole situation wrong? The first clue was Abel booking two suites. Putting aside the cost, most men would not be so considerate. 'Come in. I'll pop on some clothes.' She hurried through to the bedroom. What to wear? Her jeans? No. She put on a bra, changed her satin knickers for comfortable cotton and rolled on a pair of tights. She lifted a pleated tartan skirt that Gary had loved off the rail in the wardrobe and chose a top that was not too clingy, in case they went into a shop and she had to try something on.

Shoes.

Trainers were ideal for cobbles but were definitely not the look. High heels were also out. Luckily, she'd had the sense to pack a pair of leather ankle boots. She pulled on a jacket and reached for her bag, which had a long shoulder strap.

A full-height mirror confirmed she looked good. Abel clearly wanted to treat her before getting his wicked way.

She smiled.

Patience, girl!

Patience.

# 32

The doorman bowed his head as Tina and Abel stepped out of the high class hotel. She slipped her hand through Abel's arm and they strolled down the narrow cobbled street. The sun was on its way to setting but it was still full daylight and pleasantly warm. She marvelled at the beauty of the historic buildings, with their stunning facades, sculpted stonework, and pastel shades.

'Wow... what a lovely street.'

'Historic Rome is as big as it is beautiful. We could walk for days and only see a tiny part of it. It's my favourite city. Stunning. Every visit I'm amazed. On each corner is a church with magnificent carvings, statues and paintings, often by renowned masters.'

'Have you seen the Basilica?'

'Yes. If you think it looks big on TV, wait till you get inside. It's beyond description. We will have to queue in St Peter's Square but it doesn't take long to get in.'

'Fast track?'

Abel laughed. 'No. It's not like Disneyland.'

'I can't imagine you in a queue.'

'Tina, I'm a man of the people. I suppose I could donate to a Vatican charity and buy my way to kissing the papal ring, but who knows where that chunk of precious metal's been?'

'God knows, I presume.'

He chuckled.

Her arm through his, they strolled along cobbled streets lined with fabulous little restaurants, ice cream parlours, boutique hotels, and guest houses with large oak doors set in pale pink stone facades. Almost on every piazza corner was a church named in memory of a saint. They went in one; dimly lit, the peace in the vast enclosed space was awe inspiring. Everywhere she looked were unbelievable examples of intricate artistry.

'I have no words,' she whispered.

Abel smiled. 'We are not even scratching the surface of what this incredible city has to offer. Tomorrow, we have tickets for the Vatican museum. I have only been there once and could take in just a fraction of the Renaissance art on display. It is almost beyond belief. I also found it hard to get my head around that I could walk right up to giant-sized statues, in perfect condition, that were carved before Jesus even walked this earth. As for the Sistine Chapel... forget swimming with dolphins. Michelangelo should be on everyone's bucket list.' They stopped strolling and looked up at a vast painting of the Mother and Child.

'I'd like to swim with dolphins,' Tina said.

'Then you shall.'

She turned to him. 'Have you?'

'Tame ones in Florida.'

'Is there anything left on your bucket list?'

'Yes.'

She waited for him to expand. 'May I know?'

'It's what we all want.'

They strolled into Piazza di Spagna and Tina stood for a moment to take in the enormous square with its tall palm trees, boat-shaped fountain, exquisite shop fronts, horse-drawn carriages, and seething mass of tourists. Her arm through Abel's, they meandered past colourfully dressed people towards the north end of the piazza where they paused and looked at a white-stone facade. Above each of the small windows was a little white awning, and above the modest entrance was a bronze plate, stamped with the name, *Versace*.

They entered a world that Tina, or Christina as Abel liked to call her, really appreciated. The decor was style perfection, from the beautiful, tiled flooring to the soft-white curved shelving, subtly lit, displaying the finest leather accessories.

An hour later, after trying on the most expensive clothes Tina had ever worn, all her sadness had evaporated. Every time she came out to model another outfit for Abel, the shop seemed to have swelled in numbers. Tina was catwalk thin, and her good posture and innate style carried the designer clothes off to perfection.

When she finally put her own clothes back on, they felt cheap, almost shabby, but the applause she had received every time she came out of the changing room wearing another beautiful outfit had pumped her full of confidence.

It was dusk when they left the shop. Tina gripped Abel's arm and gave him a very long peck on the cheek. 'That was fun,' she whispered.

'You looked gorgeous in everything.'

'Thank you.'

'Let's go via the Spanish Steps then swing by the Trevi fountain. Photos cannot convey its scale and beauty. You have to see it. The Spanish Steps, on the other hand, are slightly underwhelming but they're en route.'

'I feel so spoiled.'

Abel placed his hands on her upper arms. 'Nothing and nobody can spoil you, Christina. You are the most remarkable young woman I have ever met. You appreciate the finer things in life but they don't turn your head. You have integrity. Grace. Charm... I admire everything about you.'

Tina's heart was pounding as she tried to control her breathing. She didn't know how to respond. Abel offered his arm and she took the cue.

They walked in silence.

She was the first to speak. 'Computers. What attracted you? It seems at odds with your appreciation of culture and art.'

'There's a part of me I cannot control. It's a gift for recognising talent in others. Believe you me, it's the only skill I possess. I was eighteen, at university studying maths, and I met a guy who told me that one day we would all have our own phone, our own individual phone number. At that time, phones were so big and heavy it seemed a preposterous idea, but I knew the guy was clever. I asked him if he could design a computer program that could anticipate currency movements. He did. I bought it. I made my first thousand pounds playing the market... in one hour. I sold the program to a commercial bank for a million. I asked my friend to design an accounting program. I gave him all the parameters but what he produced was so much cleverer. In fact, it was a financial modelling tool the basis of which is still used by leading software packages today. I didn't sell that. I sold licences and by the time I was twenty-five I had about fifty million. So did my friend. I used some of the money to buy property and land. But I was over-confident and invested in start-up businesses during the first dot com bubble. I lost a few million but learned a lot. I kept on investing, backing ideas, and gradually built a portfolio. I've been lucky. I have good instincts. I have no talent but I recognise talent, and I back it.' Abel stopped walking and turned to face her. 'As soon as I met you, I knew you were special. You have a gift. You attract others to you. Look at Versace today. People waited, paused their shopping, to see you model the next dress.'

Tina had always believed in herself but she was embarrassed by the level of his praise. In most circumstances, she would write off compliments as solely a ploy to get her into bed but Abel had already passed-up the first opportunity.

'Are we nearly there, yet?'

He laughed and did a grand gesture to a wide, high, flight of steps. In the twilight, people took selfies with the steps behind.

'Shall we run up?' she asked.

'Let's…' He grasped her hand and they ran to the base of the steps.

She took a deep breath and looked at her would-be lover. 'Thank you Abel.' She let go of his hand and started running up the steps. Her feet pounded the old stone as she rejoiced in the exuberant exercise. For the first time in oh so long, she felt happy.

The cold really bit into Gary's bones. He was already thin but now he knew he was seriously malnourished. His skin lacked thickness and was scarred and bleeding from where the cuffs rubbed his wrists and ankles. He felt beaten. They couldn't let him live if they were to escape justice. He was a loose end Stacy would ensure was squared away. How could somebody who looked so angelic be so ruthless? If she wasn't a psychopath she certainly bore most of the traits.

He looked up at the high window and saw a little dwindling daylight poking through into the basement room. There was no escape. He was not dealing with amateurs. He was a slave waiting for the end. And it would come soon, very soon.

'I love these narrow streets,' Tina said. 'I love the little alfresco restaurants, and the food market we just passed. And I love the enormous piazzas with their amazing dramatic fountains and bizarre, erotic statues.'

Abel laughed. 'Rome does boast a lot of naked men.' Arm in arm they ambled-on as the sun set. Long shadows were cast by tall stone buildings with dark alleyways lit by ancient street lamps. They entered another historic square and joined a horde of tourists from almost every nation on the planet.

'Fontana di Trevi,' Abel said, 'is without question the most beautiful fountain in the world.' He took her hand and weaved her through the craning visitors to the edge of the fountain. She looked up and saw a vision of such magnificence it almost stilled her heart.

Abel continued in tourist guide mode. 'The fountain is fed by fresh water brought here by an aqueduct constructed by the Romans, nineteen years BC. These days, I think the water's recycled so it's not wasted.'

Tina pressed herself closer to the man she was falling for, big time. She relished his body heat and knew that the feeling in her heart was real.

'Every time I come here,' he continued, 'I am astounded by the artistry. The scale is mind-blowing. The facade behind the fountain with those columns and statues is mightily impressive in itself, but those winged horses galloping through the water touches something deep inside me.' She felt him fishing in his pocket. 'Throw these in.' He handed her a few coins. 'They say it will bring us luck, and the money goes to a good cause.'

She looked at the Euros in her hand and threw them into the frothy, white water. His arm slid around her shoulders and she snuggled into him.

'I think we can squeeze in one more item,' he whispered into her hair.

She took his arm and he led her down Via delle Muratte, another cobbled street with stylish shops and pizzerias. The route they were taking seemed complicated and, at times, Abel was forced to consult the map on his phone. And then they arrived at Piazza della Rotonda. Tina looked up in awe at the majestic stone colonnades that line the entrance to Rome's famous, former pagan temple.

'Wow.'

Abel smiled at her. 'Wow indeed. It was commissioned in the second century by Hadrian, the Emperor who built the wall in the north of England. The reason it looks so good today is that Emperor Phocas gave the temple to the Vatican early in the seventh century. Of course, it would look even better if Pope Urban the eighth hadn't robbed the temple of most of its bronze. Let's take a look inside.'

'Can we go in?'

'Yes. It's the perfect time of day.'

He took her hand and guided her past the towering Corinthian columns and through the giant-sized doorway and vestibule into a rotunda that was beyond imagination. She looked up in awe at the domed roof. 'Oh my God.'

Abel pointed to a hole at the top. 'The oculus is lined with Roman bronze and is the largest of its kind in the world. Its size allows the sun to light the Pantheon by day and for us to view the stars at night.'

She tried to soak up the magnificent artistry and geometry of the Pantheon's coffered dome. 'Is the oculus covered over with glass?'

'No, it's open to the elements. When it rains, it falls onto the floor. If you look carefully, you'll see it's concave with numerous holes for draining the water into original Roman waste pipes. When it snows, I understand it looks incredible.'

She turned her attention to the square and circular-patterned marble floor then lifted her eyes to take in the granite columns, elaborate tombs, and many ecclesiastical statues.

'Shall we sit?' He guided her to several rows of wooden pews in front of the altar. She sat down and he slid in beside her.

'It's so peaceful,' she said.

'There's something about the perfect symmetry of the spherical interior that relaxes the mind.'

In the still, cool, evening air she closed her eyes and tried to shut out the conflicting emotions that tore at her heart. Was she betraying Gary? His voice echoed inside her head and his face was so clear, so alive, she had to snap her eyes open to erase his image. She stole a glance at Abel and immediately felt a deep longing to be in his arms, to be protected by him, to be loved. But was it him or his wealth she found so intoxicating, so alluring? Could she ever love him with the same intensity she had loved Gary? She took a breath and leaned against him.

# 33

Dermot O'Hanlon lay back in the king-sized bed and luxuriated in the fine-cotton sheets. The White Hart Hotel in Undermere had good ratings online. He hated splashing the cash but giving a convincing performance was essential if he was to protect the woman he truly wanted. There was nothing he could do to save her husband and he pushed the thought of what was to happen to him out of his mind. In truth, he should never have got involved with one of the most violent and crooked criminal gangs in England, let alone Essex. But, lust and greed had got the better of him. Now, all he wanted was to wriggle out of the situation without jeopardising Tina's life.

The door to the bathroom opened and he felt a stirring. Backlit by the bathroom light, Stacy looked exquisite in her sheer nightdress. How could somebody have the face and figure of an angel, yet be so cruel, so lacking in empathy? He could understand why Gary had let his guard down in the presence of such a woman. He felt no love for her but his desire to consume her bountiful body was as great as ever.

'Hello, my sweet,' he said. 'You are beyond delicious.' He saw Stacy fight a smile. 'I swear, in all the places I have travelled, never have I seen, let alone met, anyone who can hold a candle to your beauty.'

'Do you love me?' Her voice was husky.

His response had to be convincing. 'Enough to make you my lover, my betrothed, my wife, until death do us part.'

Stacy laughed and Dermot felt a chill that wilted his erection. She hurried across the plush carpet and hurled herself at him. Her arms wrapped around his neck and he felt her gym-trained sinews.

'What a team we make, my lover,' she said. 'We'll rule the world.'

'Rule the world? Not getting banged-up is enough for me.'

She pulled away and looked into his eyes. 'What's the problem? Tell me and daddy will deal with it.'

That was the problem. Gary's dick had ruled his head and Dermot had fallen into the same trap. He looked into her sparkling eyes. 'I may have to disappear for a while.' He saw her sparkle turn to flint, but pushed on. 'I thought we'd have longer but Cornfield looks set to buy the old school.'

Stacy lay down on the bed. 'Daddy has dealt with bigger problems than Cornfield.'

'What can he do?'

She turned her face to him. 'Please. Don't pretend you're not part of the game.'

All sexual desire evaporated. The Cottees had a fearsome reputation for a very good reason and the apple of her father's eye had not fallen far from his violent tree. Getting out from under her high heel without incurring daddy's wrath, or attracting the attention of the authorities, was going to require some very fancy footwork.

He felt the tips of Stacy's long, manicured nails on his chin. 'Kiss me.' Her fingers traced a line down his neck and bare chest.

He took her hand and kissed her palm.

'Wait,' she said.

'I'm not sure that I can.'

She went to her suitcase and from a pocket removed a blister pack. He watched as she popped a pill into her mouth and swallowed. She smiled down at him. 'I want an all-nighter.' She threw the pack onto the bed and opened a glass bottle of sparkling mineral water, standing on the bedside unit. She took a sip and held out the bottle for Dermot. He took it and watched as she peeled off her nightdress.

'Holy Mother of God, I don't need any blue pill.' He put the open bottle and blister pack on the bedside unit. He moved across the bed and she lay down beside him. He pushed her onto her back and kissed the firm mounds of her perfectly created breasts. He caressed and kissed her golden, toned skin, working his way down to her sheer thong. He pulled a tie string and pushed the fabric to one side.

'Go for it, lover. Go for it.'

A sweet smile framed by blonde locks floated into his mind's eye.

'Come on, sweetheart. Don't keep a girl waiting.'

Tina felt Abel's arm in the small of her back as they followed the liveried waiter to a square table with a white cloth, laid with highly polished silver cutlery and sparkling crystal wine glasses. The head waiter pulled out a padded chair and she sat down as he pushed the seat under her. As quick as a magician he placed a pristine white linen monogrammed napkin on her lap. Meanwhile, Abel helped himself to the chair opposite.

Two waiters, each holding a glass bottle, came up to the table. 'Frizzante o naturale, signora?' asked the more senior of the two.

'Naturale per favore,' she said, smiling encouragingly.

He picked up her glass with a white-gloved hand and poured the still mineral water.

'Lo stesso per me, grazie,' Abel said.

The waiter glided around the table and filled a second glass with the same careful attention.

'Champagne?'

She looked into Abel's hazel eyes and Gary smiled back. His no nonsense, defined features were immediately dismissed only to be replaced with Dermot's phenomenally attractive mishmash. Abel was different. He had clean, even features that were sculpted to perfection. Perhaps they had been, but it was not a question she was about to ask.

'Christina? Champagne?'

'Thank you. A glass would be lovely.'

He turned to the waiter. 'Please ask your sommelier for a bottle of Louis Roederer Cristal.' He grinned at Tina. 'A glass is never enough.'

She smiled. 'I feel intoxicated by Rome, already.'

'Christina, you look stunning.'

Following their excursion, Tina had taken her time to freshen up and moisturise her body. After selecting her very best lingerie, she had opened her wardrobe door to decide what to wear and discovered, hanging on the rail, three of the dresses she had tried on in the Versace store and had loved the most. How had they got to her room, her suite? She tried on all three and found it almost impossible to choose. Finally, she settled on an almost-sheer dress that hugged her contours. When Abel knocked on her door to escort her to dinner, she had glanced into a full-length mirror and knew she was at her peak; she would never look better than she looked tonight.

'It's thanks to Donatella,' she smiled, and sipped some water to deflect the compliment. Her parents' union had created two children whose looks had always attracted attention, even when they were very young. From his late teens, men had been drawn to her brother. He was cool, calm, collected and deeply sensual in a wholly masculine way that had broken many hearts until he had found the man for him. In her late teens, Tina had put her career, her ambition ahead of love until she dated a good-looking inventory clerk she'd met whilst measuring up a property. There was a lot about him that had appealed to her but his love of football outbalanced any desire he may have had to build a career or business. A brief dalliance with a Russian property developer ended that relationship.

'A penny for them.'

It took a moment for Tina to drag her mind back to the present and to understand what Abel was saying. 'A penny? I can assure you they're priceless.'

He laughed. 'I bet they are.'

She smiled and contemplated the man seated across the table. Baron Cornfield of St Mawes plied the aphrodisiac of power in a body that told its own story. He was tall but not too tall with the kind of lean, athletic torso and limbs that were toned by gym machines and masseurs. Everything about him was polished, complemented by a ready quip and self-deprecating humour. Despite his enormous wealth and power to influence, he shrugged off his status as purely his ability to capitalise on lucky throws of the dice. Well, tonight, he was going to have a very lucky throw of the dice.

'The menu is yours for the eating,' Abel continued.

'Don't hold back.'

'There are no prices.'

'I should hope not.'

She laughed and chose the lightest food as she did not want to make love with her handsome suitor for the first time on a full stomach. 'For starter may I have the asparagus and parmesan salad?'

'Good choice. And for your main course?'

'I think I'll be fine with just a starter.'

'You may think that now, but when you smell the aroma of my veal ossobuco, I'll hear your tummy rumbling across the table.'

She grinned. 'You're probably right.' She picked up the menu and ran her eyes over the choices of fish. 'Turbot with morels and escarole sounds good.'

'It does.'

'The only problem is, I don't know what morels and escarole actually are.'

'I was once asked that question and pretended I had to take a call so I could Google the answer. Morels are wild mushrooms, I believe, and escarole is a type of bitter lettuce, like chicory.'

'Were you on a date?'

For a moment, he looked puzzled. 'No. It was a business lunch with a Japanese client. To this day I have no idea why I didn't just ask the waiter.' He reached across the table and took her hand in his. 'Christina, thank you for coming with me to Rome.'

She felt a warm glow glide through her body.

'I have a proposal,' he continued.

What was coming next? The air sucked out of her and her head began to spin. She wasn't quite ready for marriage yet, but it would only be a matter of time.

He squeezed her hand. 'Thanks to your initiative, I

am starting a great new venture in a part of the world that I had never visited. You have an instinct for what people want, even if they don't know it yet, and I cannot think of anyone who will do a better job.'

*What was he talking about?*

'I want you to mastermind the development of my new hotel and leisure complex at the old school. It won't be easy, and it will take several years of your life, but if you accept, I know it will make a massive difference to the success of the project… and to your own financial wellbeing.'

She breathed out, slowly. Shouldn't she be thrilled by the offer? Why wasn't she? She looked into his eyes and knew what she really desired. 'Thank you, that's such an honour. I'm deeply touched.'

'Don't give me your answer now.'

She smiled to hide the disappointment that washed through her. 'Lord Cornfield…'

'Please, don't call me that. To be frank I am ashamed of it. I contributed an eye-watering amount of cash to a certain political party that needed the money and was rewarded with a peerage for…' he did quotation marks in the air. '…services to computing.' He laughed at his own joke.

'You bought your title?'

'Like a car, all shiny and bright. I'm a cross-bencher. In other words, I don't, officially, support any political party. But it proves that wealth can buy almost anything.'

She pulled her hand out from under his and placed it on her lap, out of his reach.

He looked at her intently. 'I am forty-eight, twice your age, Christina. I am active, but with each passing year, I will get older as you climb to your prime.'

What had brought this on? She was completely puzzled. 'Why did you bring me here?' she asked, her mouth, dry.

'When we arrived at the hotel, the receptionist mistook me for your father. Rich man with woman half his age is not news, but I care for you too much to exploit you that way.'

'Nobody exploits me unless I want them to.' She felt tears spring to her eyes as the sommelier showed Abel the bottle of Champagne. He nodded.

She stood up and spoke directly to the wine waiter. 'Signore, please don't open it.' A tear escaped much to her annoyance. 'Goodnight Abel.' She hurried out of the hotel's restaurant, feeling several pairs of eyes on her.

# 34

Abel nodded to the waiter who took the Champagne and ice bucket away. He looked at Christina's recently vacated chair. Could he have handled it any worse? Simply put, he had fallen for the beautiful, charming, smart, grieving young widow and wanted nothing more than to wrap his arms around her. If she were any other beautiful young woman, he would have already bedded her several times. Usually, at the end of a long weekend, he'd had enough and was keen to part-company. But Christina was different. Of course, she was expecting to have sex and he would have enjoyed it, but he would also have been ashamed. If he were his usual self, he would show her off to his chums in London by escorting her to his favourite clubs and restaurants. As much as people would smile and as good-looking for his age as he was, everyone would know that Christina was on his arm and in his bed solely because of his wealth. He could delude himself that he could have pulled her even if he were... what? An accountant? After all, Christina's late husband had been a police officer, so her head wasn't turned by money. But, an accountant? No, he wasn't that good looking, or witty.

He placed his napkin on the table and stood. Several diners looked in his direction. He took out his wallet and dropped a hundred Euros on the white table cloth and strode out of the restaurant.

Standing in the lift, as it took him to the fifth floor, he tried to form a plan. He was falling in love with Christina, of that he was sure. The doors opened and he strode down the corridor towards her suite. What could he say or do to repair his clumsiness? He tapped on her door and waited. He tapped again. He knocked. He knocked harder. He banged. He pulled out his phone and swiped the screen. He waited for her to answer her mobile phone but all too quickly it went to voice mail. He dialled again. Voice mail. He tried calling her room phone via the hotel operator. He could hear the phone ringing. He held on.

Tina tilted her tear-stained face up to the large shower head and the hot water cascaded over her.

She'd been a fool.

How could she have ever imagined that someone so famous and important as Abel Cornfield would be interested in her, romantically? He wasn't even interested in sleeping with her! Had he brought her to Rome simply to seduce her into accepting his job offer? She wanted to talk to her mum, as she always had, but her mum was dead. Her daddy, who was her anchor in all things, was dead, too. She sank to her knees as the tsunami of grief overtook her. She tried to imagine Gary taking her in his arms, looking so handsome in his uniform, but she couldn't summon the image. Her life that had started off so well had peaked when she married aged twenty-two, then shattered into a million pieces. She was sliding backwards to a place where all light was gone.

Abel ate, sitting at the dining table in his suite. The

food in the hotel was second to none, but his mind was far away from haute cuisine. He had been so crass. Christina was expecting to sleep with him and all the job offer had done was act as a rejection. He'd only felt this way once before in his life and sepsis had stolen her from him. He loved Christina but more than that, he admired her and wanted to protect her from the advances of a man twice her age; a man who had used his wealth to woo her at a tragic time in her life when she was at her most vulnerable. All it had taken to prick his conscience was the receptionist referring to Christina as his daughter.

What a mess. He had allowed his conscience to overrule his heart and destroy his second chance, perhaps his only chance, of finding happiness.

He called down to reception and asked for the food to be removed. He tried Christina's numbers again but she wasn't picking up. He got ready for bed and switched on the TV. He flicked from Italian show to Italian show then checked out the movies. None of the new ones appealed to him. He was about to turn it off when Roman Holiday came on the screen starring Audrey Hepburn and Gregory Peck – they had a big age gap, didn't they? He turned out the lights and let Christina's sweet and beautiful face fill the screen in his mind. In the morning he would take her hand and tell her how much she meant to him. How much he loved her.

A valet opened the door to Tina's suite. It was still early but, after a sleepless night, Abel was desperate to be with her.

'Christina. It's Abel. I was worried about you.' He listened for a response. Hesitantly, he entered the sitting room and looked at the half-open door to the bedroom. 'Christina? Are you there?'

No response.

He pushed open the bedroom door. The first thing he noticed was that the bed was fully made and had not been slept in. Now he was worried. His eyes flicked around the room looking for her suitcase. It was gone. He slid back the door to the closet and saw the three dresses he'd bought for her. He checked the bathroom. No toiletries.

She must've snuck out without anyone noticing.

He tipped and dismissed the valet then sat down on the edge of the bed and put his face in his hands.

# 35

Malcolm didn't much enjoy driving into Undermere. In the last few years the traffic seemed to have doubled and there were now cameras everywhere, ready to ensnare the unwary driver. He swung into the station car park and saw Tina standing near the taxi rank. He pulled on the handbrake and leapt out as fast as his ageing muscles would allow.

'Thank you, Malcolm.' There was a note in her voice that spoke volumes. He opened the boot and Tina slid in her bag. She looked up at him. 'I'm in trouble.' He saw tears gush into her eyes and he wrapped his arms around her.

'You will get through this, darling. It won't be easy, but you will.' He felt the young woman shake in his embrace.

Audrey heard the bell, hurried down the hallway and pulled the door open. Standing on the step was Samuel.

'The coroner has released their bodies.' She guided him into the cottage and sat on the sofa next to him. 'I should've been home,' he whispered. 'I left this country for selfish reasons. I should never have gone.'

She squeezed his shoulders. 'We all feel guilt when someone dies. My mother never got over the guilt of sending my brother to a boarding school from which he never returned. Malcolm feels guilt. I feel guilt. But remember this... your parents would not exchange their lives for yours. They would not want you to feel any guilt. It was an accident.' She looked up at Malcolm standing in the doorway to the hall.

'She's asleep,' he said. 'Absolutely exhausted.'

Audrey nodded.

'I'll make a pot.' A few seconds later, she heard the clatter of crockery coming from the kitchen.

'Sam.'

The young man looked at her.

'Malcolm and I are here for you. We can help arrange the funeral. Please let us.'

The Reverend William Longden entered the Methodist Church from the vestry, wearing a long, plain black robe. He had already checked that there were enough order of service pamphlets in each of the pews. Aged eighty-nine, once over six feet three inches tall but now stooped, with a bald pate and a hooked nose, he put his sharp mind down to his love of language.

'Reverend Longden.'

He recognised the voice immediately. 'Mr Cadwallader, you're here early.'

Malcolm approached with his hand outstretched. 'You know me, William. Just in time is late.' They shook hands. 'Difficult day ahead.'

'It is. I will do my best to provide a crumb of comfort but only time can ease the tremendous sense of loss. Of course, what is truly tragic is the terrible fate of young Gary.'

'What a glorious wedding that was.'

'I've married many young couples but that late summer's day in your beautiful memorial garden I mark as my finest.'

Malcolm laid a hand on the older man's arm. 'If we're not careful, we'll both be weeping.'

William offered a tight smile. 'Without doubt.'

'How is the church?'

William looked around the interior. He saw plain walls, plain Victorian windows with plain Victorian panes, contrasted by surprisingly decorative cast-iron pillars supporting galleries for additional worshippers, rarely required, on each side of the church. 'Thanks to Audrey's largesse the decor is much improved but we've had to invest in a new bucket as the constant rain has found a way of entering the ladies' facilities.'

'What about the gents? I hope there are no unintended leaks there?'

William chuckled.

'Here's another thought,' Malcolm continued. 'Have you considered crowd funding to improve the heating? I don't know about you, but these days I can detect the merest wisp of a cold draught.'

William glanced down at a metal vent in the plain flagstone floor. 'Are you suggesting that the warmed air pumped under the floor is inadequate?'

'It may have been good enough for Victorian worshippers used to hardship but oldies like you and me need more wraparound comfort.'

'Well, I'm astounded. I'll have to take your complaint to a higher authority.'

'I hope you do, Reverend, as a schooner of sherry prior to the service simply doesn't cut it anymore.'

Audrey was seated in a funeral car between Tina and Sam, holding each of their hands as they followed the two hearses to the front of the Methodist church. She was not surprised to see so many people standing outside. Malcolm hurried up to the car and opened a rear door. He took Tina's hand and helped her out. Meanwhile, the driver opened the other passenger door for Sam and Audrey.

Tina exchanged Malcolm for her brother and Audrey took her husband's arm. They followed Tina and Sam through the arched entrance into the Victorian church. Most of the pews were full but four spaces had been reserved at the front.

They sat down on crushed felt cushions that provided scant protection from the cold, solid-wood pew. Elgar's solemn masterpiece, *Nimrod,* was being played by Eleanor, usually seen wearing an apron in the Olde Tea Shoppe, now all in black, hands and feet working the traditional piped organ.

Audrey picked up the order of service. On the front was a photograph of Tina and Sam's parents on their wedding day; below were their full names and against each the date of birth and the date of death. She opened her bag and removed a pressed, linen handkerchief, one of Malcolm's she'd sneaked from his drawer. She stemmed the tears that spilled out and then snuck a sideways glance at Tina, who was sitting bolt upright and wringing the lace hankie Audrey had given her.

The organ music swelled and there was a ripple from behind as the congregation stood.

Audrey turned and saw the first of the coffins brought in, carried on the shoulders of four men in dark, formal suits. The coffin, of light wood veneer, was placed on one of two biers at the front of the simple church. Once both coffins were in place the pallbearers retreated and the congregation watched the Reverend William Longden, dressed in a full-length cassock and white surplice, climb the few steps that led up to the wooden pulpit.

His church was packed. People were pressed together in pews, several stood by the entrance and a few had ventured upstairs to sit in the galleries. William surveyed the expectant congregation but took little pleasure from their numbers. As the organ music came to an early conclusion, he looked down into Tina and Sam's tear-stained, upturned faces, each gripping the other's hand; and at the two boxes containing the remains of two people William had grown to like. On each coffin was a beautiful bouquet of fresh flowers, rich in vibrant colours, their heady scent imbuing his soul with renewed energy.

In front of him on the lectern were a few notes, but he didn't need them. He knew precisely what he wanted to say. The eulogy had taken longer than usual to write but he hoped his words would bring some comfort. He opened his mouth to speak but before he could make his first utterance, the air was filled with the pulsing chop-chop of rotor blades.

Abel Cornfield peered out of the helicopter's side window as it circled above the Methodist church. A dozen people were crowding around the entrance, shielding their eyes as they stared up. In the church's graveyard were two freshly dug plots, with duckboards on each side and straps coiled ready to lower the coffins into the ground.

Christina's parents.

He should be with her, supporting her, but despite all his efforts, they had not spoken since Rome. He signalled to Graham, his regular pilot, to fly off and within a few seconds they were approaching the old school standing in solitude on the moor. Abel caught a glimpse of a handful of men carrying pot plants to a curtain-sided truck. The pilot circled the helicopter above a number of caravans and assorted vehicles. A man with a large dog on a leash emerged from the side of the building.

'What the...??' The pilot forced his stick over and the helicopter lurched to the left hurling Abel into the side panel. The pilot regained full control and guided the helicopter down to the flat patch of grass in front of the gravelled apron. 'Sorry about that, sir. Bloody drone.'

Abel waited for the rotors to come to a rest. The man with the dog stood some way off but everything in his demeanour seemed threatening. Abel was now the legal owner of the old school and grounds and his law-yers had given Dermot O'Hanlon notice to vacate. They had a month. If the travellers didn't comply, Abel could take them to court but his preferred Plan B was to pay them to go.

'It's safe now, sir,' the pilot said through the head-phones.

'Thank you, Graham.' Abel removed his headset, reached for the door handle and pushed it open. The strength of the wind caught him by surprise. He looked back at the pilot. 'I don't know how long I'll be.'

'Take your time, sir. I have coffee and a whole moor to piss on.'

Abel laughed and stepped down from the helicop-ter. He carefully closed and secured the door. The rotor above was turning slowly. He stood upright and walked over to the man with the dog. 'Mr Dermot O'Hanlon is expecting me.'

'He's said nothin'.' The man snarled the words, al-most like his dog.

'That's your beef,' Abel replied. He stepped off the

grass onto the gravel and strode towards the front door. As he approached, it opened and he was met by Dermot's scowling face.

'I thought you were coming tomorrow?'

'It's not a problem is it? I'm not expecting you to have tidied up!' Abel laughed at his own joke.

Dermot didn't smile.

Abel felt his blood pressure begin to rise. 'I own this place. I've been generous with your notice to quit.'

'Come back tomorrow.'

He looked into the Irishman's eyes and knew the man had something to hide. 'As you've been here for a considerable amount of time I, politely, ask if you would act as my guide.'

'Didn't Tina show you around?'

'I was a bit more focused on her than the building. With you I won't be.'

Dermot stepped aside and gestured for him to enter the grand hallway.

The first thing Abel noticed was the smell. It was a mix of aromas; that of an old institution and something else he couldn't readily identify.

The pallbearers lowered the second of the two coffins into its final resting place and pulled up the straps. The area around the two open graves was carpeted in green to protect the assembled shoes. At the head end of each grave was a large mound of earth and, a short distance away, was a small mechanical digger. The bouquets of flowers that had been placed on the coffins were now at the foot of the open graves.

Tina gripped her brother's hand. This was it. This was real. This was when she had to grow up. This was the goodbye, the farewell that Gary's disappearance had denied her. The pallbearers bowed their heads to the deceased, and slipped away.

The Reverend Longden stood slightly to one side. In his hands he held the Methodist Prayer Book but, when he spoke, he didn't refer to the text open in front of him. 'God of all grace, we pray for one another, especially for Helen and John who we commit to your immortal care. In our loss and sorrow be our refuge and strength, and enfold us in your everlasting arms.'

# 36

Stacy looked up from the mass of green plants to the ceiling as she listened to the receding chop-chop of the helicopter. Good. Dermot had got rid of Lord Cornfield. His sudden arrival had interfered with the removal of the marijuana, which was to be processed in a drying facility in Essex before the weed, pot, grass, ganja, skunk, bobo bush, whatever... was to be distributed via a network of dealers.

Unfortunately, the workers could not be distributed quite so easily. They were all men from Vietnam, illegal migrants who knew that if they went to the police their families would suffer back home.

But what to do with them now?

Not speaking English was a positive. Perhaps they could be transported to Scotland and let loose in the Highlands? Stacy hated involving her father especially when she knew he disapproved of her associations. Sleeping with the enemy had been embarrassing for both her and her father, who had genuinely liked Gary. Although Dermot was on the right side of the law, as far as her father was concerned, the involvement of so many Irish travellers in the Cottee family business could end up being a costly mistake.

She didn't want to undermine Dermot's authority; she fancied him like hell and wanted to be Mrs O'Hanlon, but she had a job to do and that was to clear the old school of all the incriminating evidence, including the rat chained to a water pipe in the basement pantry.

'Jesus said, *do not let your hearts be troubled.*'

Tina listened to the wonderful Reverend Longden and wished her heart was not troubled.

'*Believe in God,*' he continued, his voice strong, almost theatrical. '*Believe also in me for I am the way, and the truth, and the life.*'

'Amen.' The word came out louder than Tina had intended. It was immediately repeated by those closest to the graves.

A pallbearer approached her with a copper bowl and matching trowel. Her vision blurred by tears, she scooped up a little earth and took a careful step forward. She looked down at her mother's coffin, appreciably smaller than her father's. Audrey's hand rested gently on her shoulder. More than any words, it gave her the maternal comfort she needed as she tossed the earth onto the box below.

The chop-chop of rotor blades lifted all their eyes to the sky and she watched as Abel's helicopter disappeared from view into low cloud. A few spots of rain splashed her cheeks.

'I cannot believe how many people have come, despite the rain.' Sam had not responded positively when Audrey first suggested the Methodist Church Hall as a possible venue for the funeral wake.

'I told you.' Tina gripped her brother's arm at the head of a mass of local people queuing to pay their respects. Inside the entrance was the tall, imposing figure of the Reverend Longden who had spoken so movingly, so powerfully, about their parents.

213

Huddled under umbrellas, old friends and acquaintances had the good grace to introduce themselves to Sam, to speak words of consolation, briefly, and to move on. But, Tina took her time with each guest and very quickly she and Sam had to seek shelter inside the hall so that people were not kept standing out in the rain.

Hair slicked by the deluge, Tina was delighted to see one of Hawksmead's greatest champions. 'My sincere condolences, Sam,' said Andy Blake. 'My wife and I got to know your parents well over the last few years. We are profoundly saddened by your terrible loss. If there's anything I or my paper, the Hawksmead Chronicle, can do, please let me know. My office is just down the High Street.'

'Thank you. I'm so grateful for all the support Tina and I have received, today.'

'I meant what I said.' The tall man looked intently at both Sam and his sister. 'Wherever you go, however long you are away, Hawksmead is your home and will always welcome you.'

Tina leaned across and gave Andy a kiss on the cheek.

'Last point,' Andy said, 'then I'll leave you two alone. I know you have the inquest to get through but if you need any help sorting out wills and probate, I have experience in that area and would be more than happy to help.'

'Thank you,' Sam said. He held out his hand then changed his mind and gave Andy a surprise hug.

Cloud encased the AgustaWestland helicopter in an impenetrable blanket of white, compounded by torrential rain. It had been particularly bad over Elstree Aerodrome where Graham had tried to land. He had sought permission from Air Traffic Control to head south to

Redhill Aerodrome, where the helicopter was based. He hoped the rising heat from London's buildings would at least lift the cloud base. Through the murk he made out the meandering River Thames and followed it downstream, which was the specific flight path for private helicopters.

*Keep cool.*

All he had to do was follow the river, between low and high water marks. The problem was, he could barely see the grey ribbon. If he flew too low, he risked flying into offices and apartments, built near the river's edge. Then there were the cranes. At night, their warning lights were easy to see but in thick cloud during the day, by the time he saw a warning light it would probably be too late to change course. He was tempted to go higher, away from lethal obstacles, but the risk of getting lost over south London, outside of official helicopter lanes, was too great.

*Keep cool.*

Magdalena wrapped her arms around Tina and squeezed. 'I love you, my sweet. I would give anything to take pain from you.' She held Tina's face in her artisan hands and kissed her on each cheek. 'May God bless you and protect you. And if he's too busy, I am here.'

Tony Blake accompanied by his wife, Eden, interrupted Magda's flow and Tina felt quite relieved.

'We are so sorry about your parents. Your father calmed my nerves on your wedding day. I was terrified of giving the Best Man speech.' He took both her hands in his. 'I was very fond of Gary and was honoured to be at his side on such a special day. He adored you, as we all do. When you left Hawksmead for the bright lights, Eden and I talked about uprooting our family and following you south. Then Gary... disappeared. I should've come to see you. But I didn't want to impose. It's my biggest regret. I'm so sorry, Tina.'

She saw tears in his eyes and released her hands. She blinked hard and looked at his voluptuous wife.

'Please come and visit, as soon as you can,' Eden said. 'Georgiana remembers being your bridesmaid as though it were yesterday. She loves the dress she wore even though she's way too big for it now. That summer preparing for your wedding was so very special.' Eden's eyes brimmed over.

'We can't turn back the clock. I wish we could.'

'No. But we can go forward, together. We want to be here for you, to help you build a new, happy future. So many people have come today because they care. We all really care.'

He was sweating. His shirt clung to him. The cloud base was zero and it wasn't even truly winter yet. He couldn't see a damn thing. The radio was tuned to Air Traffic Control. He pressed the transmit button. 'Cornfield requesting permission to divert to Battersea Heli-Port.'

'Request pending. Maintain holding.'

Graham held position but decided to go lower to try and get a bearing. It was a great risk as the helicopter may have drifted away from the river and the rotor blades could easily clip a tower block or crane.

The radio burst into life. 'Cornfield. Diversion approved. Contact Battersea on 122.9.' At that moment, through a break in the cloud, Battersea Heliport appeared, stretching out into the river. He couldn't believe it. Relief flooded through him. He tuned into the new frequency and was about to open his mouth to speak when the helicopter jerked and jolted and spun in circles like a winged sycamore seed.

The party was in full swing. There was no other word that could accurately describe the wake. Tea had turned into wine, and black ties were loosened as people relaxed and laughed, albeit suppressed. The last time Tina had seen this many friends and acquaintances was at her wedding in the neighbouring memorial garden. Three years later, her parents' funeral had brought the same wonderful folk together again and, for a brief while, she could park her grief. Deep down, she had hoped Abel would come to the wake but when she heard his helicopter fly back south, she was disappointed but not surprised. The man had done all he could to reach out to her, but she had given him nothing in return. Was it too late?

'I expected to see your young Irishman here.'

Tina looked into Harry's florid face. The last time she'd seen him was when she and Dermot had dined at the Rorty Crankle. That seemed such a long time ago.

'Thank you for coming, Harry. Is Cathy with you?'

'Yes. We shut the pub and jumped the condolence queue as we were both in need of a drink. She's chatting to Audrey and Malcolm. We are both so sorry for your terrible loss.'

'Thank you.' She kissed him on the cheek.

'And the Irishman?'

'He had a previous engagement... with another woman.'

'Ah, I see.'

'There is somebody I like, but I cocked it up.'

'I think, my dear, you are permitted multiple cock-ups.'

She nodded slowly. 'Would you excuse me? I need to give that someone a call.'

Tina moved away from Harry and smiled at guests

as she sought a private place. She would have gone outside but it was bucketing with rain. She opened a door and felt for a light switch. It was a storage room with old items of furniture. Feeble daylight probed the grimy window pane. She took her phone out of her small handbag and scrolled through her contacts.

Graham refused to accept that all was lost. He used his training and innate skill to regain control of the helicopter, which was no longer plummeting but still spinning like a Frisbee. Thank God he was alone.

*'You get on back before the weather closes in. I'll catch the train.'*

He was so pleased his best client wasn't with him now. Not only was he about to sink several million pounds in the grimy brine below, he'd be lucky to escape with his own life, let alone also that of a trusting passenger.

'Christina!'

The moment she heard his voice her heart flipped. There was something in his tone that enveloped her soul. She opened her mouth to speak but couldn't find any words.

He continued, 'I owe you an apology. I acted like a fool.'

'No. There was only one fool, and that was me.'

'Where are you?'

'The Methodist Church Hall. The funeral wake is still in full swing.'

'May I see you?'

'I would like that.'

'Tonight?'

'Aren't you in London?'

The tail rotor which Graham had given up on slowed

the spinning helicopter and he managed to regain some control. Almost crab-like, he edged the cumbersome machine towards the helipad and it spun slowly as it descended. As soon as the tyres touched the deck he altered the pitch of the blades spinning above and cut all power.

It took a few minutes for the rotors to come to a stop. By that time, a fire tender was standing by, and a tow truck. He opened his door and stepped onto terra firma – at least it felt like that to his rubbery legs – and walked down to the tail. The damaged rotor blades were stained with blood.

'Geese,' he confirmed to himself.

Sofie leant back against the storage room door and placed a Viceroy between her lips. She fired up a Dunhill lighter and sucked in the smoke. 'I hope you don't mind. I can't get on with e-cigarettes.' In the two years since Tina had last seen Sofie in London, she had bulked-up.

'What are you doing here?'

'I wanted to make sure you're all right.'

'I can assure you I am far from all right, no thanks to you.' She gave her old neighbour a long hard stare.

'It was Gary's decision. He wasn't forced. He knew the risks.'

'Did he? Did he really know the risks?' She took a breath. 'Why are you here, Sofie?'

'I'm sorry about your parents.' She stepped closer to Tina. 'I am really sorry.'

'I can't blame you for what happened to them, so thank you. How's Miroslav?'

'He's well.' She took another long drag.

'You weren't really a couple, were you?'

'No.' The admission came out with the smoke.

'And your name's not really Sofie, is it?'

'No.'

Tina reached for the doorknob. 'I have to go.'

'I am happy for you, Tina. Abel is one of the good guys.'

'So you were in a relationship?'

'There was a terrorist attack on London Bridge. I happened to be passing and was cornered by an attacker with a knife. Abel fought him off.' She looked around for somewhere to stub out her cigarette and selected an old inkwell. 'He's a special man. Very special. A knight in shining armour, but we didn't have an affair.'

'I saw you kissing that day in St James's.'

'What you saw was a goodbye kiss. He had much too high a profile for me to get involved. But I had hoped when I left the service we could reignite the spark. Unfortunately for me, his interest lies elsewhere.' There were tears in her eyes as she rested her hand on Tina's arm. 'Be happy.'

'Can you deputise for me?'

The ageing former photographic model and ballerina turned her kind face towards Tina who whispered, 'I have to go.'

A frown wrinkled Audrey's brow. 'Go where?'

'The old school. Abel's waiting for me. I'm going to pick him up.'

Audrey gripped her hand. 'I'm so pleased.'

'I'm sorry to leave you in the lurch.'

'Go. Malcolm and I will take care of everything here. You get your man.'

Tina felt herself bubbling over with nervous excitement. 'I may not be home tonight.'

'I'd be disappointed if you were. Take every happy,

blessed moment.'

'I will. I promise.' She looked at the Patek Philippe watch on her wrist.

'I'll find Malcolm,' Audrey said. 'He'll drive you. His motor is parked by the entrance to the memorial garden.'

'Thank you, but I rang Station Cars. There's a taxi on the way. We're going to be staying the night at the White Hart in Undermere.'

Audrey smiled. 'I know it well.'

'Have you seen Sam?'

Near the rear of the deserted Methodist church Sam was seated in a pew. He wanted to stand by his parents' graves but the torrential downpour had driven him to seek shelter. Now he was alone. Truly alone. God was not with him.

Many times he'd been told by Christians and those of other faiths that being homosexual was a lifestyle choice. That God had given him free will and that he had chosen to disregard Leviticus, chapter eighteen, verse twenty-two: *Thou shalt not lie with mankind, as with womankind: it is an abomination.* For the avoidance of doubt, he had checked other versions of the Holy Bible. They were all full of Don'ts: *Don't have sex with your mother* – no problem there. *Don't have sex with your sister* – no problem there, either. *Don't have sex with another man's wife* – he never had the desire. *Don't have sex with an animal* – never in his wildest dreams. *Don't have sex with a man* – why not? He looked across the empty wooden pews to the plain cross sitting on a simple wooden table.

'Why not!' he shouted. His voice bounced around the walls. 'Why not, God? Jehovah? Allah? Whatever you care to call yourself.' He stood and gripped the back of the pew in front. 'Why can't I have sex with the man I love? Why? What harm does it do? You don't have to look, you all-seeing being. Turn away. Focus on something else, like all the misery dished-out to honour your name.'

'Brutal.'

Sam turned and saw a tall man standing near the entrance. 'I'm sorry. I was having a bit of a moment.'

The man walked down the side aisle towards him. 'No apology required on my account.'

'Do I know you?'

'I knew your parents. I was at school with your Uncle Mark. He was a couple of years below me.' The man came up to Sam and held out his hand. 'My name's Vincent. I guess I've missed the funeral.'

Sam shook his hand. 'Yes. But the wake is still going on.'

'I just wanted to pay my respects. I'm sorry for your loss, Sam.'

'Thank you.'

'I've seen you in the Falcon.'

'Ah, yes, I remember.'

'Drink does get the better of me. I er... I agree with your sentiments. I've not said this out loud, before, ever.' He swallowed. 'I was married... to a woman. Divorced. I should've owned up a long time ago.' He paused. 'I'm gay. Homosexual.'

'Vincent, coming-out is not owning-up. '

'I've not been honest. I loved a boy, once. He was thirteen, I was fifteen. We were in a school play, together. I was Cyrano de Bergerac and he was Roxane. He was so beautiful, so tender.'

'You were in love with a girl, not a boy.'

Vincent shook his head. 'No. I was in love with Robert, not Roxane. He will always live in my heart.' He sat down and wept. 'He didn't have a life and I've wasted mine denying who I am.'

Sam put his arm around the elderly man. 'It's not too late, Vincent. It really isn't.' For the first time since coming home to Hawksmead, Sam felt strong.

Tina hurried out to the waiting taxi and climbed in the rear seat of the Toyota Prius. 'Sorry to keep you.'

The driver did not respond but pulled away from the kerb before she had a chance to click her belt, and headed out of the small town.

'Dreadful weather,' Tina said, trying to make small talk.

'Perfect for a funeral,' replied the driver.

She recognised his voice immediately. 'Sean?'

The driver glanced over his shoulder. 'Hello Tina. My condolences. Terrible.'

'Bridge!'

Sean turned back to look at the road as the wipers frantically swept the downpour from the screen. They were approaching the humpback bridge over the River Hawk and going too fast. He slammed on the brakes and the car snaked. He managed to straighten it up and Tina's stomach flipped as they bumped down on the far side.

'Sorry about that.'

'Take it easy, Sean. No rush. How come you're a taxi driver?'

'I got bored with inventory work; bored with freezing my nuts off in cold houses; bored with photographing chips and mould. It was driving me crazy, and when Gemma got pregnant, I decided to chuck it in.'

'Gemma?'

'Someone who appreciates me for who I am.'

'I always appreciated you. Don't forget to turn right.'

'You're the passenger not the driver.' He swerved right and entered the mile-long drive that led up to the former school. The rain came down even harder.

'I'm sorry if I hurt you, Sean.'

'Hurt me? You stuck in a knife and cut out my heart.'

'Slight exaggeration.'

'First you left me for a Russian property developer, then you ran off with a cop. The fact you preferred a lousy traffic cop to me said it all.'

'Well, you've got Gemma, now, and a baby.'

'Chelsea.'

'As in King's Road, London?'

'I dunno. We heard the name on TV and liked it.'

They approached the old school. Several vehicles were parked close to the back entrance near the abbey ruins including a curtain-sided lorry. Sean swung around the large gravelled apron and brought the taxi to a halt near the main entrance, where several cars were parked including the Porsche Spyder.

'What's going on here, then?' he asked.

'I found a buyer so the travellers are leaving.'

He pulled on the handbrake and looked at her. 'You sold this?'

'Yes. Would you wait here while I get the buyer? We're going on to Undermere.'

'Undermere? Is that where he lives?'

'He's staying at the White Hart.'

'I get it. No need to explain further.'

'Please, Sean.'

'So who is the rich bastard?'

Tina sighed. 'His name's Abel Cornfield and he's a decent man. He'll give you a good tip, I promise.' She gripped her handbag and opened the door. Heavy rain pounded the front of her black dress. 'I'll be back in a few minutes.' She wrapped her raincoat around her and ran as best she could in her heels to the front entrance.

# 37

Gary stank. He was amazed at how quickly a human could sink to a putrid mess. Something was going on, of that he was sure. They would have to get rid of him soon, one way or the other. As far as Tina was concerned, she was widowed a long time ago. He didn't want her to go through it all again on top of her parents' death. What about his family? He had a brother and a sister. He was the bonus, his mother always said. A lovely pre-menopause surprise. He wondered how his elderly mother was coping. His brother and sister both had their own families, one living in Exeter and the other in Bristol. He hoped they were all well and happy. Occasionally, a tear would sneak out but Gary wasn't going to feel sorry for himself. There was nobody else to blame. Calling Frank Cottee's beloved daughter Tina instead of Stacy, in the age of the all-will-be-revealed era of the internet was suicide, as it had proved to be.

The door opened and it was the woman herself. 'Jesus!' she gasped.

'No, Stacy. It's Gary. I've just not had a shave for a while.'

Abel followed Dermot up the wide wooden stairs to the top floor. Every instinct told him that something was fishy. He'd started his wanderings of the Grade II building in the basement rooms but some woman called Stacy had gripped his arm with steel talons in her determination to steer him away from certain parts. As soon as she opened her mouth, he recognised her for what she was but decided to keep his own counsel. The victor in almost every fight is the one who gets to choose the battleground. Occasionally in his business career he'd come across dodgy individuals who'd tried to launder their ill-gotten gains through one of his businesses. There had been times when veiled threats were made but he'd always stayed firm and, fortunately, his own security team had kept him safe. He had considered bringing a personal protection officer with him to the school the first time he visited, but he'd communicated with Christina on Zoom and had been attracted to her, immediately – a minder would have cramped his romantic overtures.

Dermot opened a door to a large dormitory and flicked a bank of switches; neon strips hummed into life revealing a long room with innumerable beds and old school blankets, and three large chests of drawers down the centre.

'This is where the migrant workers sleep. They are moving on tomorrow,' Dermot said.

Abel walked into the room and the boards creaked. 'The floor feels warm, even through my shoes.'

'We keep the heating on. These men have suffered enough, already. Plus, most come from a tropical country. There are two dormitories on this floor, shower and toilet facilities, and various smaller rooms. I presume you'll want to gut the whole place?'

Abel looked intently at Dermot. 'Let's go down.'

They went back the way they'd come, down the

flight of stairs to the landing. Abel gestured to a pair of double doors. 'What's in here?' The wired glass was blocked-in by black material.

'A few classrooms. Nothing of interest.'

'Everything's of interest.' He tried the doors.

'They're bolted,' Dermot said. 'The floor's not safe to walk on. We can go via the back stairs and enter at the far end, if yer like.'

Abel took a couple of paces back and ran at the doors, slamming the sole of a handmade shoe against the metal fingerplates. The doors flew open. Immediately ahead was a wooden frame encased in black plastic sheeting. He looked at Dermot, questioningly. Coming up the stairs, behind, was the oaf with the big dog. At that moment, his phone rang. 'Christina. Where are you?'

'Looking for you,' came her reply.

'Listen to me. Get back in your car and I'll meet you a bit later at the hotel.'

'I have a taxi waiting.'

'Good. Go now.'

'I'm happy to wait.'

Dermot snatched the phone out of Abel's hand. 'Tina, it's Dermot. Lord Cornfield is going to be tied up for quite a while. You go. Bye.' He terminated the connection, dropped the phone on the floor and stamped on it. He looked at Abel. 'Shall we go?'

Abel was pushed through an overlap in the plastic sheeting and was met by a forest of green, almost luminescent under the abundant overhead lighting. As they walked, the cloying odour was overwhelming. At the far end, men were carrying away plants.

He was pushed through more plastic sheeting and entered a smallish area with windows on each side.

Rain was still lashing down. The door ahead was opened and he was shoved through plastic sheeting into an almost identical room where only a few plants remained. A steady stream of silent young Asian men and teenage boys, dripping from the rain, passed them as they walked, each carrying a plant rich in foliage. By the time the trio had reached the far end, Abel felt sick. The pungent smell was nothing like the whiff of grass he'd occasionally caught on the breeze when at university.

Where was Sean and the taxi? Getting soaked, Tina ran in her high heels across the gravelled apron searching beyond the parked trucks for the Toyota Prius. The sun was setting, although it had barely made an appearance at all during the miserable day.

'Bastard!'

Drenched, she made her way back to the entrance, stopping, momentarily, to admire the Porsche Spyder. She entered the hallway, took her phone out of her handbag and tried Abel's number. It went straight to voicemail.

Abel was pushed through into another open area at the far end of the building, and towards a stone staircase, narrower than the one in the main entrance hall, and made narrower still by the air-conditioning pipes trailed along the side. He followed Dermot down with Eamonn and the dog panting behind. When they reached the ground floor, he expected to follow the air-conditioning pipes out into the rain but a shovel of a hand told him he was to go on down to the basement. Here, the stairs were even narrower, and the way ahead dark. At the bottom, Dermot flicked a switch and old neon strips flashed and hummed into life, revealing a large bare room, lined with shelves which must, at one time, have stored the farm's produce. They walked on through another door into a boiler room.

'Impressive,' Abel said, pausing to look at a large, barrel-shaped boiler.

'It's a Paxman,' stated Dermot. 'A classic. It should be in a museum. I hope you won't sell it for scrap. But, if you do, give me a shout and I'll take it off your hands.'

Their conversation was interrupted by the dog barking and scratching at the door ahead. Dermot gripped Abel's arm and guided him through into a room with old wiring, a stench of diesel fuel and an incredibly noisy engine.

Dermot shouted into Abel's ear as though explaining something interesting to a friend. 'Yer see, we needed extra electricity to keep the marijuana plants happy. Can you imagine my surprise when I found this little monster? It's a diesel powered, water-cooled old Lister generator from the 1970s. It means we didn't have to draw extra electricity from the national grid and attract the attention of the authorities.'

'Move on.' Eamonn's command was followed by a shove in Abel's back. More rooms came and went. Below ground level, in almost darkness, he wondered whether he had arrived at his final resting place.

A vast ancient kitchen opened up and to one side he spotted a dumb waiter, a lift on a pulley system for taking food up to the refectory above. His old boarding school had had a similar system.

Ahead was an arch and a long passage, with doors to the left and right. At the far end, barely discernible in the gloom, stood a figure he recognised from earlier.

Two bolts, top and bottom of a solid oak door were thrown back and Dermot pulled it open. Despite all the smells Abel had experienced in the last ten minutes, he was completely unprepared for the stench that assaulted his senses.

The dog barked, making him jump, and pushed its way past Abel with such force even Eamonn couldn't maintain his grip on the leather lead. The dog bounded in and smothered the stinking occupant's face with licks.

'Hello Hector. How are you, old boy?'

The man was English and Abel was touched by the reunion.

Eamonn picked up the lead and pulled hard. With the help of his brother, they hauled the yelping hound out of the room.

Abel had considered trying to fight his way out of the building but had been confident that he would be freed once all the evidence of illegal activity had been removed. Christina was his main concern, but as crooked as the travellers may be, he did not believe they would harm her, although he began to have his doubts when the door was slammed shut, the bolts rammed home and he was locked in with a stinking, bony, bedraggled man. Luckily, the light worked.

'My name is Abel Cornfield.' He looked at the long chain and cuffs binding the man's thin, bleeding ankle to an old iron pipe. 'I will get us out of here.'

The response was a chuckle that was profoundly disturbing. 'I am Detective Constable, Gary Burton.'

*The Gary Burton?*

'The Irish are fine,' he continued. 'They will sweep this place clean and move on, as they always do.'

'That's good to hear.'

'But not Stacy and Frank Cottee. They can't afford to let me live, or you.'

Tina was soaked through following her fruitless search for her wretched ex-boyfriend taxi driver. She was also puzzled by the way the phone call with Abel had ended. What was going on? She decided to wait in the main hallway for him to finish his tour of the school before ordering another taxi.

'Hello.'

She swung round and looked at a figure standing by the open door to the basement stairs.

'Stacy?' She was wearing a black, double-breasted trench coat, high-heeled ankle boots, and a Gucci shoulder bag with a long chain looped over her head.

'I'm here to help Dermot with the move,' Stacy said. 'By the way, he's with Lord Cornfield.'

'Could you take me to them?'

'They're busy.'

'Doing what?'

'Looking around.' She came up to Tina and gripped her arm. 'I'll walk you to your car.'

Tina recognised the threat in Stacy's pressing fingers and shook her arm free. 'I can walk myself, thank you. I wouldn't want you to get wet.'

'You're very considerate.'

Tina looked beyond Stacy across the hallway to the main stairs. 'Please ask Lord Cornfield to call me when he's finished here.'

'No problem.'

'Thank you.' She walked back through the porch and out of the main entrance into the torrential rain.

*Dermot and Stacy were still an item.*

She felt a surprising pang of jealousy as she hurried around the end of the building and found shelter with a few rusting bicycles. She tried Abel's number again – voicemail. She tried Dermot's and a recorded voice stated, '*The mobile phone you have called is not available*'.

She called Station Cars. '*All our drivers are out at the moment. We'll get one to you as soon as possible but it could be as long as an hour.*'

She shivered. She was getting cold, very cold. Her thumb hovered over Malcolm's name.

# 38

Audrey and Malcolm had taken over the roles of host and were standing near the entrance within the Methodist Church Hall, thanking people for their good wishes on behalf of Tina and an absent Sam. Gradually, as the hall emptied, they spotted their friend who had played the organ earlier.

Malcolm leaned close to Audrey and spoke quietly in her ear. 'I'm relieved that Tina and Sam resisted asking Eleanor to play the modern classics.'

'Yes, there was no *Wind Beneath My Wings,*' came her whispered response.

'No *Flying Without Wings* either.'

'No *You Raise Me Up.*'

'No *Angels* from Robbie.'

'*Morning Has Broken*, usually hits the spot.'

'Not this afternoon.'

'*Time to Say Goodbye* always makes me sob.'

'Me too,' Malcolm agreed. 'As soon as I hear the strings followed by Sarah Brightman, I'm doomed.'

'I can usually hold it in until Andrea Bocelli goes from singing Italian to English. And then I'm awash.' She reached for Malcolm's handkerchief in her bag.

'On such a sad day as today,' Malcolm added, 'I fear the church would've been flooded.'

Audrey dabbed her eyes and then called to her friend

across the room. 'I hope the Olde Tea Shoppe hasn't lost too much business, today.'

Eleanor came over and joined them. 'My loss is inconsequential and I did manage to hand over a few "two-cakes-for-the-price-of-one" cards.'

'Any spare?' asked Malcolm.

'Agnes does not approve of my promotions,' Eleanor said. 'She also thinks I allow customers to hang around for far too long chatting over a cup of tea. I've had to ask her more than once not to slam the bill down on the table in front of them.'

Audrey laughed. 'Agnes? Is that what you call her?'

'She thinks it sounds more English than Agnieszka. I tell her that more English is allowing people to change their minds after placing an order. She's really tough on the customers but they still seem to like her.'

'And what about you?' Malcolm enquired 'How are you getting on?'

'Still manless. Apart from that, I'm hunky-dory.'

'Have you tried any of the apps?' A smile hovered at the corners of his mouth.

'I'm tempted. Agnes meets loads of boys that way.'

'Perhaps you should consider dating men!' interjected Audrey.

Eleanor burst out laughing. 'Ah, it's so good to see you both. I've really enjoyed today, catching up with everyone. Is that terrible to admit?'

'It's why we have a wake,' Audrey said. 'We all need a rest from grieving. None more so than Tina and Sam.'

'Where is he, by the way?' Eleanor asked.

'I'll check on him,' said a familiar voice. 'I saw him enter the church.' They all looked at Reverend Longden. 'The young man has quite a bit to work through.' He turned to Eleanor. 'Thank you for playing, today.'

'My pleasure.'

He looked pointedly at Malcolm. 'Eleanor has become one of our regular organists at Sunday matins.'

Eleanor laughed. 'At the end of each service William very kindly reminds the congregation that the tea shop is open. His sermon is a small price to pay!'

They laughed but it was swiftly suppressed by guilt.

Malcolm offered his hand to William. 'Good job, Reverend. I think you'll pull in a big crowd after today. Your eulogy was spot on.'

'Thank you Malcolm. I find in life that one is never too old to accept praise.'

They all laughed, again.

'The caterers will clean up in the morning,' Audrey said, gesturing to the hall. 'After, they'll call by the church and drop off the keys.' She stepped forward and gave William a kiss on the cheek. 'It was a lovely service.'


Bedraggled, Tina climbed the stairs to the first floor, pushed open the double doors and faced the long corridor with classrooms to one side that she had first seen when escorted by Dermot. She searched for a light switch and neon strips all the way along flickered into life.

'Abel?' She listened for a reply. 'Dermot? Stacy?'

She let go of the door and headed up the stairs to the next floor where she was met by an overwhelming smell coming through the open doors. Beyond was black plastic sheeting, partly ripped. She stepped forward and peeked through the gap. Where partition walls had once stood, there were umpteen waist-high tables bedecked with lush foliage. At the far end, migrants were carrying potted plants out through the doors. The tropical heat was welcome as she was chilled to the bone, but the smell made her feel sick as did the realisation that Dermot dealt in drugs and was not simply a petty criminal bending the rules to survive. What a fool she had been.

Where was Abel? It was clear he was in danger. She had to find him. But first, she had to call the police. She opened her bag and with a shaking hand removed her phone. She had a signal, not great but good enough.

Manicured talons snatched it from her and twisted her arm up behind her back.

'Ow!! You're hurting me.'

'Walk,' snarled Stacy. 'Or I'll break it.' She shoved Tina in the back and forced her to walk past the marijuana plants.

# 39

Gary, in their short marriage, had taught Tina two things: fight hard from the get-go and emit the loudest, most annoying, ear-piercing scream as possible.

At the far end of the second vast room was another set of doors leading to the back stairs. The men removing the pots of marijuana plants kept their eyes averted, but a couple of teenagers were brave enough to steal a glance in her direction.

Tina bided her time until they were mingling with the migrants. As they exited the growing room, she screamed loud enough and sharp enough to almost rupture eardrums, and wrenched her arm free of Stacy's grip. Rage poured through every muscle and with nails manicured by Magdalena, she scored Stacy's left cheek. The shocked woman screamed, adding to the cacophony. Tina kicked off her high heels and barged her way past the plant-carrying men down the back stairs to the floor below. She contemplated going to the ground floor but she'd seen too many travellers near the entrance by the abbey ruins. She decided to run down the two long corridors where the classrooms were located towards the main stairs at the far end. Without shoes, she ran fast but bits of grit and discarded classroom tools scattered on the worn linoleum caused her to yelp as they dug into her soles.

Where was Abel? She had to find him. If she'd been more thorough when she first took on selling the school and less enraptured by Dermot, she would have discovered the marijuana. It was her fault Abel was in danger and she was not going to leave without him.

Just before she pushed open the final set of doors, she stopped. Barking was coming up from the entrance hall below. She was trapped and it wouldn't be long before they would come looking for her.

She had to do something.

But what?

She opened the nearest classroom door. It was the science lab with its old work benches, wooden stools and aged equipment. She grabbed a high stool and rammed it under the door knob. At least it would buy her a few extra seconds while she thought what to do.

Below each workbench, were several gas cylinders, some attached to rubber pipes leading to Bunsen burners. She could try and blow-up the school but that could kill her, kill Abel and all the other poor souls. But, if they smelled gas, everyone would clear the building and in the confusion she could escape outside and hide in the dark until the taxi arrived. She squatted down to a cylinder and tried to undo the tap at the top but it was too stiff. She tried another and it gave. After a few turns she heard the hiss of gas.

Stacy barged her way into the Headmaster's private toilet facility on the ground floor and switched on the light. She hurried to the mirror and stared at her face in horror. Her entire life, people had complimented her on her stunning looks, which she valued almost above everything else. Smoking had etched a few fine lines, but she was still a to-die-for stunner. But now she had three deep scratches that had penetrated the epidermis and would take weeks to fully heal and months for the marks to fade – perhaps they never would entirely disappear.

*Scarred!*

The vile, little bitch had scarred Stacy Cottee, the daughter of Frank Cottee, known as King Cottee for his absolute rule of every strand of his business empire. She searched her bag and removed a tube of hand cream. It would have to do. At first it stung but after a few seconds it soothed the pain and she felt better, though no less bitter.

Her hand shook as she searched her bag for a pack of Newport menthol cigarettes and placed a filter tip between her lips. She flicked back the lid of a Ronson flip-top lighter and put the flame to the tobacco.

'Stacy,' said familiar, warm, enticing Irish tones.

She turned to the handsome face. 'Look what she did to me!' She pointed a talon at her cheek. 'I'm going to destroy her for this.'

'No you're not. You're not going to touch a hair on her head.'

She felt the heat of rage turn into the arrow of pain. 'What? You like her. I knew it!' She spat the words.

'More than that. What you and I have done to her is evil. Sure, Gary was nosy filth but it's no excuse. I see that now. I'm letting the migrants go. I'm letting Cornfield go. I'm letting the policeman go.'

'Daddy will never forgive you for this.'

'Daddy sets foot in Ireland, or any of his oikish thugs, we'll take their kneecaps first.'

She recoiled. Dermot's words, full of bile, spoke to her the way she'd rarely experienced before. She wanted to hurt him. Really hurt him and there was only one way to do that.

She took Tina's phone out of her bag and tossed it into the lavatory bowl. There was a satisfying plop. She smiled. 'Well lover... I'll be off.' She expected him to grab her arm or to try and make peace, but all he did was wait for her to go.

# 40

Audrey looked around the Methodist Church Hall and was pleased with the work that Malcolm, Eleanor and she had put in to make it look respectable. The caterers would come in the morning to pick up boxes of dirty plates, glasses and tea cups.

'Shall we go to the pub?' Audrey smiled at her own words.

'That's an invitation I've not heard for quite a while,' Eleanor said. 'Actually, for a hell of a long time.'

'We'll find you a man, yet.'

'I'm in my sixtieth year. I've more chance of winning the EuroMillions. Any man my age wants a woman half his.'

'More fool them,' responded Audrey, emphatically.

'She has a point,' Malcolm said as he stacked a final chair. 'I went for a younger woman.'

'Not half your age,' Eleanor laughed.

Malcolm approached the two women. 'Yes she is. At least, that's what she told me.' He cocked his head to Audrey. 'It's the big four oh coming up isn't it?'

'More like the big seven oh!' Audrey kissed her husband.

'You two love birds are just making it worse.'

Audrey turned to her friend. 'Once Tina is back on an even keel we're going to scour the planet for the perfect man for you.'

'One thing's for sure,' Eleanor said. 'You ain't gonna find him in Hawksmead!'

'Audrey found me in Hawksmead.'

Eleanor and Audrey both looked at the tall man pulling a mock-offended comical face, and laughed.

Abel rattled the door to the basement pantry.

'It's bolted on the other side,' said the bedraggled younger man. 'There's no way out.'

'You think they're going to dispose of us?'

'I know it.'

'Two years on, you're still alive.'

'That's Stacy Cottee for you – keeping me alive is the greater punishment. I'm the mouse to her cat. She likes playing with me.'

'At least Christina's in the clear.'

'She's in danger until Stacy and Frank Cottee are behind bars.'

'Then I have to get you out of here. You're the one person who can give evidence in court.'

'Good luck with that.' He rattled his chained ankle.

Working as fast as she could, Tina dragged five heavy cylinders towards the door. She undid the valve to each one and soon the gas made her feel heady. Taking great care, she opened the door and looked both ways. No person or dog was about. She dragged the first cylinder into the corridor.

It was almost dark when Stacy stepped out of the school's main entrance. 'Eamonn,' she called. A deep throated growl from the bullmastiff startled her.

'Going already?'

In the fading light she looked at Eamonn's bulky figure sucking on a cigarette and holding his snarling

243

hound in check.

'I was looking for you.'

'And why would that be?'

'We've lost Tina. Do you think your dog could help me find her? She's hiding somewhere in the school. Probably in one of the classrooms on the first floor.'

'Have you anything of hers he could sniff?'

'Will a shoe do?' She held out one of Tina's discarded shoes.

'Okay, we'll give it a go.' He took the shoe. 'Come with me.'

She followed the man and dog back into the school hallway and watched as he squatted down and placed the shoe under the drooling jaws.

'Now listen here, Hector. We've got a pretty girl to find. You know, the one with the blonde hair and those fabulous long legs.'

'Not that fabulous.'

Eamonn looked up at Stacy. 'Don't interrupt.' He turned back to the dog. 'Listen to me, Hector. Here's her shoe. That's right, have a good long sniff. Find the pretty girl and I'll give yer a big, juicy, meaty, bone.'

The dog barked, making Stacy jump, but Eamonn didn't seem bothered at all.

'She's probably hiding in a storage cupboard wetting her knickers,' Stacy smirked.

'Hector'll find her.' He stood up and Stacy followed the man and dog as they ran up the wooden stairs to the first floor.

Tina barged her way past the men carrying marijuana plants and hurried down the back stairs to the ground floor. She opened the internal double doors and looked down the long corridor. She knew that one of the rooms towards the far end was the headmaster's study where she'd nearly given all to Dermot. Perhaps she should thank Stacy for interrupting? Could Abel be locked-in down there? She had no choice but to check every room.

'Come on, Hector!' growled Eamonn.

Stacy stood back from the double doors to the first floor corridor as Eamonn tried to coax his whining dog. Far from being a ferocious hound, the beast looked scared.

'What have you got there? A bloody poodle?'

Eamonn turned to her and she didn't like the expression in his eyes. 'Call Hector a poodle again and I'll set him on yer. Do I make meself clear?'

'Crystal.'

'Something's spooking him.' Eamonn almost did a pirouette as Hector ran in circles wrapping the long lead around him.

Bored with waiting, Stacy pushed open one of the double doors and recoiled. 'Whoa! Gas.'

'That's what he's smellin'.'

'It's not the mains supply, just gas from some old cylinders.'

'Come on Hector. Let's get out of here. This whole place could go up.' He led the dog back down the main stairs.

Stacy called after him. 'Where are you going?'

'To find me brother.'

Tina banged open each room door on the ground floor and called out for Abel. She waited five seconds for him to reply, and then moved on. Her torn, stockinged-feet were sore and bleeding.

She came to the headmaster's study and opened the door. The light was on but the sparsely furnished room was deserted. She hurried across the worn carpet to the toilet facility and looked in.

Empty.

'Daddy, I can't do that.'

'Listen girl,' Frank said to Stacy all too clearly out of her iPhone. 'This is your mess to clear up. I said I would deal with it when we found out what your lover-boy was really all about. But you wanted your plaything. You wanted to make him suffer. I told you it was a massive risk. You assured me the gippos were tough enough to handle him. It's clearly gone tits-up. Deal with your mess and get the hell out of there.'

'It's not just Gary,' Stacy said, putting on the little-girl's voice she saved for her daddy when she needed his help. 'There's someone else we have to top as well.'

'Spit it out, girl.'

'His name's Lord Cornfield. He's locked up with Gary.'

'Geezuschrist!'

'Daddy, the scrambler app on our phones is making it very hard to hear. Shall I come home?'

'Don't you dare! At the very least get rid of Gary. Anything he's told Lord Cornfield is hearsay in court.'

'How? I've never killed anyone.'

'Dealer's choice, sweetheart. Just do it. And don't come home till it's done.'

Stacy heard her father end the call. She was standing by her Porsche wanting desperately to get away but knowing she had a job to do first. She never batted an eyelash when her father spoke of clean-up operations but actually doing it herself, and to a policeman she had slept with and had sort of loved, was a very tough gig.

What about Tina? Where was she?

And what about Dermot? It was his fault she was in this mess. One way or another he and the blonde bitch were going to suffer.

Gary heard approaching footsteps before Abel and braced himself for what he felt sure was the inevitable. The bolts were pulled back and the door opened to reveal Dermot. Gary watched him recoil at the smell before regaining his composure. He kept his distance as he threw a key ring at Gary. It bounced on the floor. He turned to Abel. 'Lord Cornfield. I apologise for any inconvenience we've caused you. You're free to go.'

Abel rose to his full height. 'I think you owe Mr Burton a great deal more than an apology.'

'I do,' Dermot said. 'It's a debt that can never be repaid. All I can do now is ensure Gary is reunited with his wife.'

'Where is she?' Gary asked.

'She's here. Somewhere. She's looking for Lord Cornfield. I think she has a soft spot for him.'

Abel met Gary's gaze. 'I assure you, nothing happened between us.'

'Unlike between you and Stacy Cottee, eh Gary?' smirked Dermot.

Shamed, Gary looked at the stone floor.

Dermot continued his punishment. 'Both me and the good Lord here, we did all we could to make Tina our own, but she held her ground. There's a tiny part in her soul that always believed you'd come back to her.'

Gary picked up the key and struggled to release the handcuff. 'There's something wrong with the lock. The key's not working.'

Abel slipped on his jacket and squatted down beside him. 'Once this is off, I think your first port of call should be the shower.' He tried to turn the key in the lock. 'There must be a technique to getting this open.'

'Well gentlemen, I'll leave you be.' Both Abel and Gary

looked up at Dermot standing in the doorway.

'Dermot, please don't leave me like this,' Gary implored. 'Can we at least part as gentlemen? I was sent to help bring down King Cottee. We're not interested in you or your family of travellers. As far as I am aware, you don't have blood on your hands.' He hoped his words would have some impact.

'Lord Cornfield, please step away and not by the door,' Dermot requested.

Abel moved to the back wall below the high window.

Dermot entered the room and squatted down. He turned the key and the cuff snapped open. Gary whipped the linking chain around his neck. 'Help me!' he yelled.

Abel rushed forward and threw his weight on Dermot who fought with sinews toughened from generations surviving on the road. He clawed at the chain blocking the air to his lungs as Gary pulled with all his diminished strength.

'Are you going to kill him?' Abel gasped.

Gary gritted his teeth and continued to pull on the chain.

*BANG!!*

Both men looked at the door which had been slammed shut. Abel leapt to his feet but before he could cross the room they heard the first bolt slide home. Within moments, the second was also slammed into its keep.

# 41

Tina couldn't find Abel anywhere. She'd tried calling the police from the landline in the headmaster's office, but it was dead. The work emptying the forest of marijuana plants was still going on and from the sound of engines starting-up outside, some of the travellers were already making a move. Perhaps Abel was trapped in one of their caravans or trucks?

Dermot.

She had to find Dermot. He liked her and she was confident he would protect her from anything that Stacy was planning, and would draw the line at hurting Abel.

She had put off searching the basement level as it was dimly lit with many, dark, windowless rooms, sealed by heavy oak doors with solid iron bolts. In her torn and bleeding stockinged-feet she walked into the main entrance hall – no one was about – and hurried across the stone floor to a battered door, twisted its iron ring and pulled it open. Stretching down into the darkness were stone steps and an old, worn handrail. She ran her fingertips over the dirty wall and found a switch. A bulb struggled into life.

'Tina.'

Stacy's voice cut like an ice pick. Standing in the middle of the hallway, she was still very beautiful despite Tina's best attempts to scar her face.

'What are you doing?' demanded the voice from Essex.

'Where is Abel? What have you done to him?'

'He's fine. He's with his mates, Dermot… and Gary.'

It was a sucker blow.

'Did Dermot tell you about Gary?' Stacy moved a couple of steps closer. 'I introduced them. Me and Gaz screwed our way to heaven but then I found out he was filth spying on me dad, and had to be punished.'

Tina's mouth was dry. She couldn't speak.

Stacy laughed. 'Cat got your tongue?'

'Is he… alive?'

'Who? Which luvver-boy are you talkin' about? Posh Abel? Gypsy Dermot? Or Gary the cop?'

Tina couldn't catch her breath. 'You're evil.'

'No Tina. I'm not evil. I'm an angel. Daddy says so.'

Tina looked at her feet. Without shoes, she could not outrun Stacy. 'Where is Abel? Please tell me.'

Stacy opened her mouth but her words were cut short by an explosion from above.

'Oh my God!' Tina turned and looked towards the main stairs.

'That'll be one of the gas cylinders,' Stacy said. 'If Abel's dead, it's your fault.'

Tina whirled round. 'What are you saying?'

'He's upstairs in a top floor dormitory, tied to a bed.'

'Show me. Please.'

Stacy smiled. 'Goodbye Tina.'

'Where are you going?'

'Home.'

Tina rushed up to her and gripped her arms. 'Please Stacy. Help me find him.' She looked into her eyes and saw only victory.

Stacy peeled off Tina's fingers. There was another explosion followed by pops and cracking. 'Oh dear. Poor Abel. The Cornfield is on fire.'

Malcolm opened the passenger door to his Honda and Audrey climbed in. Once he was sure that her coat was fully clear, he closed it and walked to the driver's door. As he clicked in his belt he looked at Audrey. 'Well done. Congratulations.'

'I don't feel I can accept congratulations for a funeral.'

'You should. It went off very well. Everyone enjoyed catching up with old friends.'

He saw Audrey reach for her bag and remove his borrowed handkerchief. She dabbed her eyes.

'Are you okay, my sweet?'

'I love that girl,' Audrey said. 'My tears are for her, for all the pain she has suffered these last couple of years.'

Malcolm slid the key into the ignition. 'I'd better get driving before you set me off too.' He started the engine.

'I hope she's having the most wonderful evening with Lord Cornfield.'

'In my dealings with him re the sale, he came across as a fair and honourable man.'

'Well I trust he's going to be very dishonourable tonight.'

Malcolm laughed. 'I don't know what you mean!' And he pushed the lever into drive.

Stacy pressed her car's fob and her beloved Porsche Spyder sparked into life. Daddy had wanted her to have a more solid vehicle, one higher off the ground with decent fenders at the front and rear, but as soon as she'd seen the beautiful soft-top car, she'd fallen in love. Daddy hated the idea that she was driving around with a *"rag top"* instead of toughened steel, but in the summer, cruising down London's fashionable streets, for all the envious women to see and all the men to admire, gave her the kind of buzz she craved. The car was fast, too, and incredibly responsive. She'd taken it to Brands Hatch race circuit and burned so much rubber, all four tyres had to be replaced. Daddy had not been pleased when he'd seen her credit card bill but it had been worth a few minutes of his ire.

She fired up her throaty beast, switched the lights on full beam and thrust the gear lever into reverse. The wheels spun on the wet loose gravel as she backed up. She stamped the sole of her Christian Louboutin boot to the brake pedal and the tyres skidded as the discs locked. She depressed the clutch, found first, and stamped the accelerator so hard the rear wheels spat grit.

Ahead, one of the travellers' trucks had the audacity to block her path. She blasted her horn and turned onto the marshy grass, sliding sideways before her spinning wheels secured enough grip for the Spyder to leap ahead of the truck. She glanced in her rear-view mirror and hoped the fiery glow would turn into a mighty blaze that would consume the whole building and solve the problem of the three men locked in the basement room.

She tugged at her seatbelt but the strap was caught in the door. She'd sort it out when she stopped at traffic lights. All she wanted to do now was get home. She accelerated and the Spyder tore down the mile-long drive to the Old Military Road.

Tina pushed through the plastic curtain at the entrance to the first long growing room and was shocked by the intensity of the fire. On the floor above were the dormitories and judging by the ferocity of the flames eating up the old timbers it wouldn't be long before the whole top floor and roof would be ablaze. Was Stacy lying when she said Abel was trapped up there? Tina had firsthand experience of what smoke and heat can do when Audrey was trapped by fire in the old school boarding house.

Stacy liked driving at night in the countryside; she could see whether vehicles were oncoming and there were fewer speed cameras to spoil her day. She had lost her licence more than once and despite being forced to attend two speed awareness courses, driving fast gave her an exceptional thrill.

Her xenon headlights lit the hedgerows on each side of the mile-long drive. She took a risk and averted her eyes to set the satellite navigation system for home. By the time she was back with daddy, all her problems should've gone up in smoke.

She came to the T-junction at the end of the school drive and the sat nav instructed her to turn left. She swapped gears with great precision and the alloy wheels spun the car to more than sixty miles per hour in just a few seconds. The speed of the Spyder ensured Stacy had plenty of work to do holding the car on the wet, meandering road, lined with dark-shadowed ditches and solid-looking hawthorn hedges. A road sign warned her she was approaching the humpback bridge spanning the River Hawk at the north end of the little town. She'd seen no other vehicles so kept her smooth leather sole pressed against the accelerator pedal.

The Honda headed up Hawksmead High Street, turned

the corner at the top end, and drove towards the humpback bridge.

'Look at that.' Audrey pointed at the windscreen.

Malcolm glanced at her. 'What?'

'There's an orange glow in the sky.'

He kept driving as he peered through the windscreen. 'It could be the travellers burning their rubbish. Let's go up there and double-check.' He turned onto the humpback bridge and was blinded by xenon headlights.

Tina ran up the wooden stairs to the top floor where the dormitories were located. She shoved open the double doors and searched for the light switch. Neon strips flickered on, lighting the long room, divided into sections by wooden partitions. She ran down the dorm looking at each of the narrow iron beds with their thin, stained mattresses. Some were made up with sheets and old school monogrammed blankets. The floorboards beneath her almost bare feet were getting hot, and she saw the first trails of smoke.

She pushed open the doors at the far end, looked left and right, and slammed back the double doors ahead. It was another dormitory. She found the light switch and neon strips revealed an even longer room, with more partitions and many more beds. She ran down the long room, dancing from foot to foot, as she desperately sought Abel. Thickening smoke made her slow and caused her to cough. A flame licked her toes.

Stacy stamped her foot down on the brake pedal and her discs responded immediately, but the recent heavy rain prevented the rubber on her low-profile tyres from gripping evenly. The car skidded sideways causing the rear to bounce off the stone wall lining the bridge. The nose shot forward with such force into the opposite wall, the rear end of the car lifted and the inertia flipped the vehicle over.

*'Daddy!'*

The soft top crushed as it hit the water and the air was driven out of her lungs.

Malcolm brought the Honda to a halt on the north side of the bridge.

'What happened?' Audrey looked over her shoulder into the darkness.

'I think we've had a miraculous escape.' He reached into the glove compartment and removed a torch. 'I'll have a look. Wait here.'

'Take care. There may be other cars.'

'I will.' He opened his door, switched on the torch, and walked carefully in the dark towards the bridge. Sections of wall on each side were dislodged and badly scraped but had held. He leaned over the side and his beam picked out the underside of a car, held by one of the arch supports, but almost entirely submerged in the fast-flowing river.

'Good grief!'

Tina felt sick and light-headed as she worked her way to the far end of the dormitory. Flames, no longer tentative, were voraciously eating up the dry floorboards and decades of debris. The heat became too intense for her feet and she was forced to jump onto one of the narrow beds. To protect her soles, she wrapped each foot in an old school sheet. The dorm was now properly on fire with flames licking to the ceiling. Abel was not up here. He was either trapped in the basement, taken prisoner by the travellers, or already dead. She had to put the last thought out of her mind.

What about Gary? She didn't believe a word Stacy had said. But she was from Essex and she knew that was where Gary had been working undercover. Could he still be alive?

And what of Dermot? Where was he? Or had he driven away with the other travellers, together with their illicit organic hoard?

She heard a crack and watched in horror as part of the wooden floor fell into the former growing room below, followed by several iron beds and burning mattresses.

'The school is definitely on fire,' Audrey said as Malcolm got back into the Honda.

He closed the door. 'There's a car lying upside down in the river.'

'Did you see anyone get out?'

He returned the torch to the glove compartment. 'No. I don't hold much hope for them. The police are on their way. I said I'd wait.'

'I'm worried about Tina.'

'Have you tried calling her?'

'Straight to voicemail. I think we should get up to the school, just to make sure she's not there.'

'I said I'd wait.'

Audrey opened the glove compartment and handed him the torch. 'You wait here for the police and I'll drive up to the school.'

Malcolm took a breath. 'I don't like the sound of that.'

'You didn't jump in the river and I'm not about to run into a burning building.'

'You promise?'

'I give you my word.' Audrey eased herself out and hurried around the nose of the car. Malcolm held the driver's door open for her. She put her arms around his neck and gave him a kiss. 'Be careful.'

'*You* be careful.' They both looked towards the orange glow across the moor.

'Your phone has battery?' she asked.

'Yes. I only turned it on to call the police.'

'Good. Keep in touch.' She slipped into the driver's seat and reached for the handle to adjust the position. She turned to her husband. 'You'd better call the fire brigade, just in case nobody else has.'

Tina dragged a couple of school blankets into the washroom. She entered the communal shower area and was so relieved to feel the cool water. She soaked the blankets and soaked her feet, each wrapped in a sheet. She kept thinking about Audrey and what she had had to do to escape a burning building. But Tina was not ready to escape. Before she got out, she had to find Abel.

The soaked blankets felt heavy as she draped them over her wet hair and around her body and face. Gripping them from within, she looked through a narrow gap.

Shuffling in her sheet-wrapped feet, she opened the door and was shocked by the amount of smoke. She gripped the blankets tighter and through eyes, barely open, shuffled to the stairs. The sheets around her bare feet almost caused her to trip and so she decided to kick them off. Luckily, the flames weren't licking through the stair treads yet although the wood felt warm to her tender soles.

As she approached the floor below, the smoke was more dense, more acrid, more damaging to breathe. Everyone appeared to have left the building. The only company she had was the roar from flames voraciously eating up the old wood. The heat was intense and even though she filtered the smoke through the blanket, each breath hurt her lungs.

She carried on down to the first floor where she had released the gas from the cylinders. The air was now unbreathable, even through the blanket. She could argue that her hasty plan had worked as she was sure help was on its way, but at what cost?

Abel's life?

Her life?

The heat in the storage room was getting intense. It glowed down from the ceiling. Surprisingly, the light bulb still worked. Abel had tried to smash the high window and only succeeded in bruising his elbow to such a degree he was sure it was fractured. Dermot lay on the floor, his ankle chain-linked to Gary's.

'Let's all look on the bright side.' Dermot's voice was hoarse following his near strangulation. 'At least the woman we all love is not in here with us.'

At that moment the power went, plunging the room into darkness.

Dermot chuckled. 'There is one thing I'm sad about.'

Abel waited for him to continue, then got impatient. 'You can't leave us hanging, Mr O'Hanlon. What is the one thing? I can think of plenty.'

'Dear Lord, I'm sad that Gary's is the last face I'll ever see. Of course, it's different for him and for you, 'cause I'm so bloody handsome.'

Abel decided he had to take control. 'It's clear we're about to be roasted. We're locked in a room with a solid door, bolted from the outside. Even if we could break the window, the gap is probably too narrow for us to squeeze through.

'I'm thin enough.'

Abel was pleased that Gary had an edge of hope to his voice.

A burning ember fell from the ceiling.
Too late. They were out of time.

# 42

Audrey indicated she wanted to turn right off the Old Military Road onto the mile-long drive up to the school, but the stream of vans, four-by-fours towing caravans, trucks and lorries prevented her, whilst the red glow in the sky got more and more intense.

She hooted her horn to no effect.

'Enough is enough.' She flicked her lights to full beam and swerved around the nose of a curtain-sided truck, almost ending up in the water-logged ditch beside the mile-long drive. With two wheels on the verge, spinning on wet grass and mud, she forced her way back onto the tarmac, making the on-coming stream give her room. After passing a few more vehicles the way ahead became clear and she pressed the accelerator. The last time she had seen the old school was when Malcolm and she walked out together on their first date, over four years ago. It was not a place she enjoyed visiting. Within forty seconds, she was confronted by a blaze that dwarfed what she had experienced a few years previously. The size and power of the conflagration was truly shocking.

She parked the Honda on the furthest reaches of the deserted gravelled apron and got out of the car. The blast of hot air and the appalling smell of burning triggered terrible memories she had tried hard to forget.

The skin on her scarred legs tightened, and her breathing became raspy and short. She fought to quell her growing panic but the more she tried the more memories of acrid smoke tearing at the fabric of her lungs, and ferocious flames stripping her calves and thighs, brought the whole terror back into sharp focus.

Tears poured down her cheeks as she stood and watched the Victorian building crackle and roar. Small explosions on an upper floor added to the cacophony of sounds. Soon the school would be little more than a burned-out shell, unlamented by the many generations who had had the misfortune to reside within its walls.

Tina knew she should get out. She couldn't see, she couldn't breathe, she couldn't hear. Something large rubbed against her and she would have screamed but the fear of the acrid smoke and burning heat was far greater. She reached out a hand and felt sharp teeth.

'Oh my God!'

The dog barked. Whimpered. What should she do? Unable to see, she tripped over the air-conditioning pipes and fell on the hard floor. The dog licked her face and she grabbed his collar. She tried to get up but lost her balance and was dragged down the stone steps, landing in a bruised heap in the basement. The air felt cooler, at least not as hot as it had been, and less smoky, although it was almost pitch black. The dog rubbed against her and she felt for his collar, more scared of being alone than of his fangs. Almost blind, she allowed herself to be led through the bowels of the building, banging into all manner of hazards, pulling open doors and lurching into blackened rooms.

Suddenly, she could see. She was in a kitchen, lit by the light of flames coming through high windows.

Burning embers were falling all around her and one fell on the dog. Without a second's thought, she swiped it away. The dog ran ahead through an archway and barked and clawed at a closed door.

Staccato cracking made her turn her head as part of the kitchen ceiling fell followed by a crashing dining table from the room above. Flames, where there had been none before, suddenly appeared and within seconds the whole kitchen was a raging furnace as more wooden tables and benches crashed down.

Malcolm could not see the face of the young police officer without shining his torch into her eyes, and he was sure that would not go down well.

'What speed were you travelling?'

'About ten miles an hour. Needless to say the other car was going considerably faster.'

'How long ago did the accident happen?'

'Ten minutes, possibly twelve.'

The police officer leaned over the stone parapet and shone her torch down. She spoke into her radio but the sound of rushing water from the river below drowned out her words. Malcolm assumed she was asking for help – a tow truck with a winch, maybe, and divers to retrieve any bodies.

Finished with her radio call, she approached Malcolm. 'Right, Mr…' She shone her torch on her notebook and the reflected light gave Malcolm a chance to see her face, which looked as young as she sounded. 'Mr Cadwallader. I'd like to examine your vehicle.'

'Ah, yes… my wife has it.'

'She drove away from the scene of an accident?'

'The car was unscathed.'

'The car is evidence.'

'Exactly my thought, but my wife is worried about a

friend.'

'Worried. In what way?'

He turned his head and gestured to the bright orange glow clearly visible across the black expanse of moorland.

Abel was the first to hear the bolt. Or was it the sound of cracking embers as they fell to the floor?

*Clunk!*

He was sure it was definitely a bolt. He pushed open the door with his good arm and was shocked by the intensity of the heat. The giant dog almost leapt past him and felled Gary in a canine embrace. The room immediately filled with burning, acrid smoke and his eyes were seared by the heat. A figure shrouded like an Egyptian mummy staggered into the room and collapsed in a heap of blankets amongst the burning embers.

'Christina!' Abel bent down and tried to pick her up but the pain in his elbow was too great. 'Gary. Help me,' he shouted above the crackling wood and roar of the flames.

Gary pushed away the amorous hound as burning embers from the ceiling continued to float down, and scrambled to his feet.

'I'll carry her.' Dermot shouted to Gary. 'Unchain me.'

'You're joking,' Gary said. 'She's my wife, I'm carrying her out.'

'For the love of God, Gary, release me.' Dermot shouted and then coughed. 'The chances of us getting out are almost nil, but I'm far and away the fittest person here. The good Lord has a broken elbow and you're not up to the job. Release me and I'll carry her to safety.'

Abel hugged Tina's wrapped body to him. 'Do as he

asks, Gary. I promised Christina, she would one day swim with dolphins, and I'm keeping that promise.'

In the blazing light from the flames, Gary removed Dermot's ankle cuff. 'Don't try to escape,' he shouted into his face.

'I thought escape was the plan,' Dermot retorted. 'Although cremation is far more likely.'

Both Abel and Gary helped lift the unconscious Tina into Dermot's arms, making sure that the blankets protected her body as much as possible.

'Gentlemen, it's been a pleasure,' Dermot said and coughed.

Abel looked at Gary. 'You lead us out. You know this place much better than me. I'll follow Dermot.'

Abel waited for Gary to push back the door and as he did the heat and brightness of the flames terrified him. The dog, their saviour, stuck close to them as Dermot staggered through the thick fog of toxic smoke. Gary led the way down the corridor, constantly looking back to check that Dermot and Christina were close behind. Abel admired the young man's determination and bravery. There was almost no chance they were going to make it out.

# 43

Audrey watched the firefighters working in twos as they manned the large hoses. There were three tenders and countless men in protective gear carrying breathing apparatuses on their backs. Some could have been women but she couldn't tell. Despite the power of pumped water aimed at the ground floor, and at the end of ladders fitted to turntables, it was clear to her that the fire was going to win and destroy the entire building. Thick black smoke was billowing out of the main entrance, with the rest of the former school burning with a ferocity that Audrey had not witnessed before.

She retrieved her phone from the Honda and tried Tina's number again.

Gary had been down to the basement many times and was quite familiar with its umpteen rooms sealed by heavy doors. Fortunately, the main entrance hallway had a stone floor and stone steps leading down to the basement. Other rooms on the ground floor had wooden floorboards which were clearly already alight and dripping embers. The great hound had an instinct for survival but also a love for Gary, so kept hanging back. Burning embers had scorched the dog's coat and Gary had burnt his hands dealing with them. Soon the fire raining down would turn into a storm.

Sharp, blue flashing lights penetrated high, ground-level windows on the far side of a former changing room, and cut through the thick, acrid smoke that was so searing and toxic. After all that time hoping, help had finally arrived, albeit just too late. The room swam and swayed and Gary fell backwards as black sheets enveloped him.

A drop of water splashed on Audrey's cheek. She looked up and several more drops landed on her face. The weather had been atrocious for weeks thanks to a stream of Atlantic storms, but she welcomed the rain. Within seconds it was coming down in torrents. Would the pelting rain preserve some of the building? She hoped not.

Out of the school's main entrance bounded a large dog, its fur singed and smouldering. The now lashing rain was a mercy for the whimpering beast as it coughed and vomited onto the gravel. She wanted to encourage the dog to get further away from the ferocious flames. As a child she grew up with Lhasa Apsos, and would normally avoid getting close to big dogs, but the poor animal was in such distress she felt compelled to comfort it. She hurried over and gripped its collar, and felt something attached to it. In the blazing light she saw a Patek Philippe watch.

This was it. For all his wealth and considerable achievements in school, university and in business, Lord Abel Cornfield lay down to die. In one hand he gripped Gary's and in the other he held onto Tina's. His last act had been to remove her watch and strap it to the dog's collar. At least there was a chance the firefighters would realise someone was trapped in the building. He couldn't breathe, he couldn't see, he couldn't move. He vomited.

'The police want you back here.' Audrey listened to Malcolm's words and wondered how she was going to break the news. 'They've got lights on the car but the river is too fierce for divers to fix a tow hook. The rain's not helping, but it has to be good your end.'

'Tina's in the building!' Audrey heard Malcolm's intake of breath. 'The firefighters have gone in with thermal imaging equipment to try and locate her. Malcolm, I think we've lost our little girl.' Her words came out in a massive sob. 'The school is all but destroyed.' She looked at the entrance. Surely, nobody could survive such an inferno? And then, out of the dense smoke appeared a firefighter in full breathing apparatus, dragging a body by the shoulders. 'They've brought someone out!'

'Is it Tina?' Malcolm's voice shouted out of her phone.

'I can't see. The firefighters are fitting an oxygen mask. The Chief Fire Officer has ordered me to keep away.'

'What about medics?'

'They've not arrived, yet.' The heat was beyond intense as she hurried to the person lying on the gravel, whose face was covered by an oxygen mask. She shuddered with disappointment. 'It's a man,' she shouted into her phone. 'I don't recognise him.'

'Is he alive?'

'I think so.' She looked towards the entrance where the firefighters were pointing their hoses. 'There's someone else being dragged out!'

'Who?'

'I can't see.' She watched as two firefighters dragged

a second person away from the entrance.

'Is it Tina? Audrey!! Is it Tina?'

'I think it's another man.'

'Can you talk to the fire officer? See if they've located her.'

'I will, but they're busy saving the two they've brought out.'

Two more firefighters appeared, one dragging a man and the other carrying an inert body, wrapped in blankets, as if it weighed nothing.

'There are two more.'

'Tina?'

She watched the firefighter carry the person to a safe distance followed by another with an oxygen tank who fitted the mask.

'I can see her blonde hair. It's Tina!'

'Is she alive?'

Audrey rushed over, her wet clothes steaming from the blazing heat.

'Madam. Keep back!' shouted the Chief Fire Officer.

The rain continued to pound down. 'Where are the ambulances?' she shouted, trying to make her voice heard above the incredible roar.

'We have to wait,' said the breathless man. 'A massive pile up on the motorway has sucked in every paramedic in the region, not helped by the weather. There should've been more tenders here.'

'I'll take them to A&E in Undermere. Put them in my car. You can radio ahead.'

'I can't allow that. It's outside my remit.'

'This young woman saved my life when I was injured in the fire at the old school boarding house. I am not leaving her here to wait in the pouring rain.' She pointed to the youngest-looking and most raggedy of the three injured men. 'And he looks like Gary Burton, the policeman who's been missing for over two years.'

The Chief turned to his men and touched their shoulders to get their attention. 'Right, lads. Get them in the lady's car, with oxygen.'

'I want Tina in the front with me.' She spoke into her phone. 'Malcolm, are you still there?'

'Right here.'

'Tell the police officer that I have PC Gary Burton, and three others, all seriously injured by fire, and I need to be escorted as fast as possible to Undermere A&E.'

'You mean, our Gary is alive?'

'Yes, but only just.'

She heard Malcolm cough several times. When he was able to speak, his voice sounded strained. 'Audrey, take the Old Military Road across the moor. A tow truck's arrived and the bridge is entirely blocked.'

# 44

Heather brought over a glass of brandy and placed it in front of Sam before sliding into the booth seat, opposite.

'Thank you.'

'Have you heard from Tina?'

'She's in good company. Certainly, better than mine.'

'We all need a rest from grieving, including you.'

He nodded and took a sip of his drink. 'Wow, that is good.'

'Finest cognac we have. You deserve nothing less after the day you've been through.'

'Tina's had it rougher than me.'

Heather reached across the table and took his hand. 'It's good you're home.'

Tears filled his eyes. 'Everybody's been so nice to me. I don't deserve it.'

'People care about you. About Tina and what your family has suffered. Please allow us to support you through these troubled times. What about your husband?'

'I asked him to stay away. I didn't want to embarrass anyone.'

'Hawksmead has open arms, especially since the arrival of a certain special lady. She sat in this very booth the first night she arrived in Hawksmead and, frankly, changed all our lives for the better.'

'Audrey and Malcolm are beyond words.'

She smiled. 'They don't see themselves that way. Audrey came to lay to rest a family tragedy and in so doing found a new home, new friends, and a new husband, in many ways all thanks to your sister.' She squeezed his hand. 'Hawksmead is a special place, not because of the bow-fronted shops, or the humpback bridge, or the moor, or this wonderful pub...'

Sam grinned.

She pressed on. '...but because of people like you, and Tina.'

The rain was exceptional. Low pressure had scooped up water from the Atlantic and was dumping it on a little Japanese car trying to negotiate an unlit, twisting strip of slicked tarmac across a sodden moor. The road had hidden brows and steep drops into small lakes that the Honda aquaplaned across. Bends came with little warning, causing the car to slide more than once before the tyres gripped.

Four lives depended on Audrey's driving skills. The smell of smoke, and singed skin, was almost overwhelming but if she opened a window she knew the heavy rain and cold air could bring on pneumonia to smoke-damaged lungs.

They rounded another water-filled bend and dived into a flooded dip. Blinding lights filled Audrey's vision and she had no choice but to jam on the brakes and hope the anti-locking system would prevent her from skidding off the road. Headlights on full beam, she focused on the narrow strip of wet tarmac, all the time trying to slow the car until it came to a slithering halt.

A man shone a torch through her side window, which she lowered an inch.

'A bit of an accident.'

'Eamonn, is that you?' Dermot's voice from the back of the Honda sounded pained and raspy.

'Dermot, where the feck were you? We're in a ditch. The Asians have scarpered and the marijuana plants are all over the place. If the deer eat it they'll be higher than a kite. I think we should abandon the haul and take this car.'

'Good plan.'

Eamonn pulled open the driver's door as Audrey slammed her foot down on the accelerator. The front wheels spun as his giant paw reached in and tried to turn off the ignition.

Once the car had gathered sufficient speed and left Eamonn sprawled in the pouring rain, Dermot spoke again from the rear. 'Thank you.' His voice was little better than a croak. 'I hoped you'd do that, but I couldn't ask you in front of me brother.'

'How is Tina?' Abel asked, his voice even more pained than Dermot's.

Audrey didn't reply. What was the point? She had to keep focused. Through her swiping wiper blades she saw the faint orange glow of streetlights in the far distance.

Malcolm had done his best to explain to the young police officer what was happening up at the old school and that Audrey was in no position to come back and give a statement.

'It's about saving lives. Whoever was in that vehicle, now upside down in the river, is without doubt dead but inside my car are four people in urgent need of medical attention. I know you have your job to do but surely you can see why my wife had to take the Honda?'

'You were involved in a fatal car accident and then

your wife removed a vital piece of evidence from the scene. It does not look good.'

The grinding of the tow truck's chain interrupted their terse conversation. In the bright spotlights aimed at the dripping vehicle it was clear that whoever was driving had long since been swept away.

'Look at that,' Malcolm said.

'What?'

'The driver's seat belt is caught in the door.'

The police officer noted the car's index number and put a call in via her radio to have the driver identified.

The rain continued to pelt down. Malcolm ventured to ask a question. 'Would you mind if I ordered a taxi to take me home? I'm rather chilled. You have all my contact details.'

'Fair enough. But, crime scene investigators will be examining your car so don't put it in for repair.'

What a relief to be back in civilisation. As Audrey followed the main road that led to Undermere General's Accident & Emergency, three ambulances with sirens wailing and lights flashing whizzed past her.

'Follow them,' came Gary's croaked command from the rear seat. The sign ahead made it clear that only ambulances and other emergency vehicles could turn right and go up the tree-lined drive to A&E.

Audrey didn't care about her driver's licence or a fine. Her sole concern was cutting safely across the oncoming traffic, not easy without blue emergency lights and in pelting rain. But flashing her headlights seemed to do the trick and she was soon across the road and heading up the one-way drive. Ahead, she saw paramedics wheeling broken people from the multiple car crash into A&E. Would there be anyone available to help her passengers?

And then she saw him as if it were preordained and slammed on the brakes. 'Wait here,' she called over her shoulder. She pushed open her door and splashed through the rain towards a tall man in a stylish raincoat sheltering under a large golfing umbrella. 'Mr Bisterzo! Mr Bisterzo.'

The man walked away fast. Perhaps the pounding rain on his umbrella had obliterated her voice. In desperation, she launched herself forward and grabbed his arm. He turned and scowled down at her.

'Doctor, please can you help me?' She knew that she either looked like a drowned rat or a woman released too early from an asylum.

'Mrs Willat?' He remembered her! Willat had been her surname when she first came to Hawksmead.

'Yes. You helped me recover after I fell in the river.'

'Have you fallen in again?'

Malcolm was drenched and exhausted. It had been a long day, not helped by the appalling weather and a near head-on collision with a sports car. He sat back in the rear of the taxi and allowed his eyes to close. His thoughts immediately turned to Audrey and Tina, and her Gary, seemingly back from the dead. He hoped he hadn't misheard.

'Would you mind putting the heat on?' Malcolm asked the driver as a chill rippled through his body. Standing exposed in the rain had been crazy at his age and he feared there could be health repercussions.

'You heard about the fire?' The driver asked over his shoulder.

Malcolm could do with some of that heat now. 'Yes. The old school is no more.'

'I wonder what will happen?'

'It's probably good news for the man who bought it.'

'How's that?'

'He can apply for planning permission for his new enterprise with a clean slate.'

The driver nodded. 'Perhaps it was him that started the fire.'

# 45

Hector cowed in the darkness as he watched the fire-fighters tackle the blaze. His back hurt but he couldn't reach it to lick and rolled over on wet moss to get relief. He was cold and tired and hungry, but he lacked the strength to chase after a rabbit. Keeping to the shadows, he skirted the blazing building and walked amongst the ruins of the old abbey. He'd hidden here in the past, when he'd managed to escape the man who often kicked him. Only hunger had forced him back into his clutches. This time, when the man took off the lead, he wrenched himself free from his grip and went to find his friend. But, now his friend was gone and he was in pain and all alone.

She shivered. She'd tried drying herself by standing close to the hand dryer in the ladies but the airflow had been so pathetic she'd had to give up. Feeling damp and cold, Audrey emerged from the washroom and walked down the long corridor towards where the beds were curtained-off. A&E Consultant, Mr Bisterzo, caught her eye and approached. She'd liked this man when he'd treated her years ago and, for some reason, he'd remembered her.

'Mrs Willat.' She decided not to update him on her latest married name, Cadwallader. Her birth name was

Oakes, but it was almost fifty years since she'd been Audrey Oakes.

'Mr Bisterzo.' She smiled at the handsome Italian doctor.

'I think you should get home,' he said. 'Have a hot bath and a hot drink, and get warm. At a certain time of life, it's all too easy to let pneumonia take hold.'

'I would normally object to the phrase "at a certain time of life" but, on this occasion, I am more than happy to take your professional advice.'

'That's not my professional advice. My professional advice would be to confine you to a secure ward. The last time we met you had endured near drowning and hypothermia in the freezing River Hawk. You then suffered smoke and flame injuries from a fire and, today, you show up with no fewer than four seriously ill people.'

'In mitigation, there's been a gap of nearly four years.'

'Four years? Unbelievable. Well it's very nice to see you again.'

'How are they? Tina in particular.'

'She's stable, but the damage the hot smoke and chemical asphyxiates have done is considerable, and worrying.'

'How worrying?'

'Short term, there is risk of a heart attack but longer term the prognosis is not especially good. We're looking at the possibility of pulmonary disease, recurring bronchitis, asthma, even emphysema. Her system was already compromised from prolonged exposure to carbon monoxide.'

Audrey dabbed her eyes. 'What about the three men?'

Mr Bisterzo blew out his cheeks. 'The smoke was clearly incredibly hot and definitely toxic. I'm not even factoring in burns from falling embers. Lord Cornfield has a scorched oesophagus and a fractured ulna. I understand he used his elbow to try and break a toughened glass window. It must've bloody hurt. Mr O'Hanlon, part of the travelling community, has similar throat and lung injuries but is responding well to treatment, although his head and face are badly burned. Most serious of all is Mr Burton. He's emaciated, vitamin deficient and has suffered burns both in and out. You made the right decision bringing them in.'

Audrey felt her tears flow.

The consultant lifted his arm and it hovered over her shoulders. 'May I?'

'I think I need it.'

He placed his arm around her. 'I'm driving you home.'

'Oh, I have my car.'

'Long gone I'm afraid. Hoisted and carried to a secret pound we call Fort Knox.'

'Fort Knox?'

'It costs more than its weight in gold to get your car back. All proceeds go to the consultants' benevolent fund.'

Audrey laughed and dabbed her cheeks with a hankie from her bag. She liked the Italian doctor, whose skill and courage had saved her life. He was giving her a comforting arm as he would to an elderly aunt.

Dermot luxuriated in the clean sheets. He was the first out of the four to be wheeled from Accident & Emergency to an acute ward on one of the upper floors. He thought about what possessions he had – his wallet and his phone, but no charger, and clothes that were unfit to wear again. There would come a moment when he would need to slip away. He'd managed to elicit from Enya, a sweet nurse from his homeland, that Gary was in a bad way and may not make it. That could be good news, albeit unfortunate for Gary. But when he enquired after Tina, Enya's graphic description of her physical state left him deflated. She was the first woman he'd ever had such strong feelings for. Somehow, he had to protect her from Stacy, in particular her father's henchmen, without endangering himself. He was convinced it was Stacy who had bolted the three of them in the basement room, and then set the building on fire.

On the other hand he could pray that Gary got well and, if Dermot gave evidence in court against the Cottee family, he said he would speak up for him. Sure, it was not the way travellers did business, but the Cottees had to be stopped to protect Tina from the avenging angel. The downside was the risk of him spending his prime years in prison.

Audrey looked at the doctor in the driver's seat of the Mercedes SUV Coupé and could understand why so many patients would fall for the man. He had the heady mix of a classic Roman profile topped with neat, wavy hair; good posture, lightly tanned Mediterranean skin, and long legs.

Chilled and shivering, she was a bit embarrassed that she still appreciated a handsome man with such a good bedside manner at her age.

She spotted Tina's Golf parked on the road outside Malcolm's cottage and thought about the awful day the poor young woman had endured. The passenger door was opened from the outside and Audrey looked at the consultant with surprise as she had been so absorbed by the day's events.

'I don't need to pay a single penny for your thoughts.'

She smiled and accepted his hand as she climbed down from the SUV. Fortunately, the rain had stopped. 'Yes, it's been quite a day that began sad and, without your expertise, would have ended in tragedy.'

'We're not out of the woods yet.' He looked at the cottage. 'The lights are on. Have a hot drink and a warm bath and keep wrapped up.'

'Yes doctor.' She smiled and gave him a kiss on the cheek.

Audrey closed the front door and kicked off her shoes.

'Malcolm?'

She listened for his reply, and then walked up the stairs to the landing. The light was on and their bedroom door ajar. She pushed it open and was about to switch on the light when she saw Malcolm's shape under the covers.

Pulling the door to, she crossed to the bathroom and decided to follow doctor's orders by running a bath. As she cleaned her teeth, she wondered how a single day could deliver so much.

Tina was awake. She knew exactly where she was thanks to her stay following the carbon monoxide poisoning at her parents' house. But how and why was she there? If she lay still, and did nothing, she felt quite comfortable. Covering her mouth and nose was an oxygen mask and almost within seconds of her pulling it away from her face, a nurse appeared and gently told her to keep it on. If she took a deep breath, her lungs tightened and she was forced to take her mask off to cough. It hurt her lungs when she did and frightened her, as mixed in with the blackened phlegm she coughed up was dark blood.

When thirsty, a nurse would help her drink water from a tall cup with a straw. She'd already drunk quite a bit and had wondered why she didn't need the loo, until her fingertips told her she had been catheterised.

She felt for her watch and discovered a plastic hospital band in its place. The nurses must've put it somewhere safe. She hoped so.

Her head ached and her eyeballs felt incredibly sore. What had happened? She tried to think back but all she could grab were flashes. She was at the school. She was looking for someone. Stacy's face, so sculpted, so beautiful, so fearsome, filled her vision, and she shivered.

And then the face most important of all, thin and bearded. She pulled at her oxygen mask and through vocal cords scorched by hot particles she croaked his name.

*'Gary.'*

Warmed-through from her bath and almost overwhelmed with tiredness, Audrey slipped into bed, trying not to disturb Malcolm.

'Goodnight darling.'

All she heard in response was the slight wheeze of his breathing.

# 46

Weak sunrays through a wall of windows in the small ward told Dermot it was morning. He pulled on a hospital dressing gown and shuffled in his hospital slippers into the main reception area. A young woman was sitting behind the raised counter, her eyes fixed on a computer monitor.

'Apologies for the vision before you, me darlin'.' Dermot spoke in his broadest and most charming Irish brogue. 'Any chance you could point me to your facilities?' He saw her look up at him with a smile that immediately froze. She gathered her composure and pointed to a unisex lavatory. 'Thank you. One quick question. The friends I came in with last night – Lord Cornfield and Gary Burton, do you know where they are?'

The receptionist looked at her computer. 'Lord Cornfield is in Acute Ward Two but there is no record of Mr Burton. He may be in intensive care.'

'Intensive care? Is that where they've taken Tina Burton?'

'I'm sorry, I couldn't tell you.'

Dermot nodded and shuffled to the lavatory. Once he was sure the door was locked he looked in the mirror... and recoiled.

To his certain knowledge, Abel had never slept in a National Health Service bed until last night. He was quite impressed. When he decided a little tweak was necessary to his nose as a result of a fist from a prop forward in an opposing school rugby team, the experience within a leading private hospital was much less interesting than the activity in the acute ward. Sleep had eluded him so, at the start of the new day, he was happy to observe all the comings and goings. Most extraordinary of all was the man in the bed opposite who had talked to himself all night and who, suddenly, sat up and yelled, '*This Champagne is bloody awful!*' The exclamation made Abel laugh – and it hurt, it really hurt, but it was worth it.

A handsome nurse came to quell the man's diatribe about the poor standard of service and then he came over to Abel and asked if he was comfortable.

'Thank you. I'm impressed with this establishment,' Abel said, not recognising his own croaky voice. His face felt so tight it was as though his skin had endured a chemical peel. 'A glass of Champagne, even one not to the standard acceptable to the gentleman in the bed opposite, would be most welcome.'

Ari laughed. 'Would you care for it to be accompanied by a selection of our canapés, vol-au-vents, tartes-au-Francais?'

Abel could not resist breaking into a smile and it hurt again. He tried to sit up but could only use his left arm as his right was in a plastic splint, supported by a sling. He knew he looked a mess but was resisting a visit to a mirror. He would let his personal assistant know that for the next few days he was out of commission and that his phone, the finest money could buy, was no longer in his possession. In some ways, it was quite freeing, but it also felt like walking across a tight rope without a net. Nobody went anywhere without their phone.

'Is it possible for me to take a shower or bath?'

Ari examined Abel's chart. 'I think it would be best if you see the doctor first.'

'When will he come?'

'She generally begins her round at about ten.'

Abel looked at his left wrist but his watch was gone. 'What time's it now?'

Ari checked the watch clipped to his tunic pocket. 'Six forty-five.'

'Are you telling me that I have to sit here and simply wait for three and a quarter hours?'

'Probably a bit longer as she'll be starting her round in Acute Ward One.'

'Any chance I can make a phone call?'

'You can use the phone at reception.'

'Thank you.'

'Right, well, I'd better sort out your Champagne.'

Abel sank back onto the NHS pillow. He would've laughed, but it wasn't worth the pain.

# 47

Audrey woke with a start. Something was wrong. She looked at the bedside clock and then looked at the body lying beside her. He was usually up and pottering around for at least two hours before she lifted the corner of her eye mask.

'Tea, my darling. It's time to get brewing,' she said, sotto voce.

No response. She gently rested a hand on his shoulder and his pyjamas were wet.

'Malcolm?' She flung back the covers, leapt out of bed and opened the curtains, filling the bedroom with weak morning light. For a moment she stood, motionless, and then she heard a bubbling croak. She hurried to Malcolm's side of the bed and knelt down to look at his face. His breathing, barely discernible, was short, shallow, raspy. His face was drained of blood and the heat from his brow was like touching the hot plate on a stove.

Breathing deeply herself and trying to quell her rising panic, Audrey reached for the landline phone sitting on a bedside table. Memories flashed through her mind of when her first husband had died following a heart attack. *Please God, not again, not yet.*

'Emergency. Which service?'

'Ambulance please.'

Massimo Bisterzo looked down at the beautiful young woman on a ventilator. Dr Manson, his favourite registrar, handed him the chart and he suppressed the rage against his God that erupted almost every day working to save very sick people. He always talked to himself in Italian, allowing the words to trip off his tongue freely, confident that only a very few would be able to understand his diatribe, hopefully nobody in the medical team accompanying him.

There was nothing he could do for the angelic woman lying before him. At least she was comfortable or, at least, oblivious. Every terminal patient he had treated, despite all their brave words, was a little afraid of death.

He wanted to believe in God, to believe that there was an unimaginably beautiful world that envelops the soul but, in his heart, he believed death was a total wipeout.

He replaced the chart in its slot, checked the vital signs monitor, took a last look at the sleeping beauty and led his team into the neighbouring unit. Here there was a chance for some sort of life, albeit one reduced by malnutrition, smoke inhalation, and burns. The man was receiving oxygen and was breathing on his own.

Bisterzo looked at the vital signs monitor. His heart rate was satisfactory, but his blood pressure was too low for comfort. On initial examination, there were signs of thermal injury of his upper airway and trachea which could lead to obstruction but, at this stage, Bisterzo didn't want to intubate as the very process could exacerbate the damage. He was feeling tired from his late night treating a high number of patients with life-threatening injuries. It wasn't so bad when a patient was getting on in years, but when still young, as the man in the bed before him, he found it disturbing.

Audrey held Malcolm's hand. His skin felt thin and cold, barely covering his long fingers. She'd followed his bed when it had been wheeled out of intensive care to an acute ward. She knew she looked a mess. At least she'd had a bath last night but she'd not had time to brush her hair or teeth before the ambulance came. It had been out on another emergency where a person was treated at the scene and by brilliant good fortune had almost been passing the cottage when they took the call. A swift check of Malcolm's temperature, his sweating and wheezing, pointed to pneumonia and within three minutes he had been helped downstairs and, wrapped in a blanket, wheeled out to the ambulance. Meanwhile, Audrey had grabbed clothes that were robust but not exactly matching and just had time to set the alarm, and grab her handbag and keys. She had sat by her husband in the ambulance and held his hand for the somewhat rocky and bumpy journey to hospital.

At one point, Malcolm had pulled away the plastic oxygen mask and rasped, 'My car. Where's my car?'

'It's all right, Mr Cadwallader.' The paramedic had gently replaced the mask and turned to Audrey. 'Pneumonia can cause some confusion.'

'He's not confused.' She leaned towards Malcolm. 'Darling, your car is at the hospital, safe and sound. We'll pick it up when you're better.' In truth, the car was safe but far from sound. At the very least it would need a deep clean to rid it of the vast array of odours that had accumulated during the helter-skelter drive across the moor.

Sitting beside her husband's bed in the acute ward holding his hand, she looked at the monitor and checked his vital signs. His heart rate was ninety, his respiration twenty-four, albeit a bit wheezy, and his blood pressure was one hundred and thirty-eight over eighty-two. His blood oxygen saturation was ninety-one per cent, thanks to the extra oxygen he was receiving. Malcolm was slim and fit and, although he was less mobile since his accident falling downstairs a few years ago, he took great pride in being active in his eightieth year. She looked at the monitor again; the numbers confirmed that the intravenous antibiotics were already having a positive effect.

She eased her hand away from his but was surprised by the sudden grip of his fingers. 'Darling, I'm not going,' she said, gently. 'I just need to use the facilities. I'll be back in a jiffy.' She got up from her chair and looked about for her handbag. She retrieved it from the floor and stepped through a gap in the curtains drawn along a track. She took a moment to take in the small acute ward which had eight beds, then walked into the communal corridor.

'Audrey.'

She turned on hearing the refined, albeit husky voice, speak her name. Abel had clearly showered since the trauma of the fire and although he was unshaven and his skin a little blotchy, and his arm in a sling, all in all he looked pretty good, if a little odd, in his NHS gown and slippers.

'Lord Cornfield. How are you?'

'Lungs hurt a bit and I have some sort of malevolent vice gripping my head but, apart from those two inconveniences, I've never felt more relieved to be alive, for which I thank you.'

Self-consciously, she ran her fingers through her unkempt hair. 'I look a mess.' He seemed slightly puzzled by her statement and she felt a bit of a flush coming on.

*Good God woman, you're not trying to pull him!*

'My husband was out in all that rain last night following an accident with another vehicle on Hawksmead bridge. He has pneumonia.' She saw immediate concern in his eyes. 'Thankfully, he's responding to antibiotics.'

'Let me get this straight; while you were at the school rescuing us, your husband was getting soaked?'

She nodded.

'Would you care for a cup of coffee? There's a drinks machine down the corridor.'

'I would love a hot chocolate but I have to pay a visit, first.'

# 48

Abel sat at the end of the corridor in the acute unit nursing two rigid paper cups containing hot chocolate, despite one arm being in a sling. He would have liked to be dressed, but his clothes were fit for nothing but the bin. He had no phone, no money and no access to a computer. He was sure Mrs Cadwallader would be happy to help him. It was a long time since he'd been in a position of need. Money bought most people, although Abel had made it a point in his life not to throw his cash around.

He looked up as Audrey came to sit near him. She'd clearly taken a bit of time to sort out her hair and face and it was to good effect. She was a fine looking woman who, in her prime, would have been drop dead gorgeous. She still looked pretty good to his forty-eight-year-old eyes.

'Chocolate.' He handed the cup in his left hand to her and relieved his injured arm of the other.

'Thank you.'

'Dermot, the Irishman, is in your husband's ward. He looks pretty beaten up, but he's tough. He carried Christina so his hands weren't free to swipe away the burning embers that landed on his head. He carried her all the way up the stairs to the entrance hall before collapsing. I know he's a criminal, but Christina owes her life to him. Of course, Dermot's heroic effort would've come to nought without the firefighters and you.'

'We were lucky, Lord Cornfield.'

'Abel, please.'

'If Tina hadn't told me she was meeting you up at the old school, I would not have gone there to check she was all right when I saw the fire. I would not have seen the watch you gave her strapped to the dog's collar. That was a life-saving stroke of genius.'

'It was my last throw of the dice. Thank God the dog made it out.'

'Indeed.'

'Where is the dog, now?'

'I don't know. I have to confess, once I saw Tina's watch I forgot all about the dog.'

'Of course. Have you seen Christina… or Gary?'

'Not since last night.'

'One of us should check on them.'

'I really want to but I don't think I can leave my husband.'

'This is a bit of an imposition but, would you mind if I borrowed your phone for a while?'

He watched as she took her phone out of her bag. She checked the screen. 'There's no pass code to get in and the battery is almost fully charged.' She placed it in his hand, supported by the sling, as his left hand was holding his drink. 'If anyone calls, please tell them where I am and what's happened.'

'Thank you.'

She stood and finished her hot chocolate. 'It's been a pleasure to meet you, Abel.'

'The pleasure is all mine, I can assure you.'

'Tina has very good taste.'

'She is a truly remarkable young woman.' He saw her

eyes fill with tears.

'Shall I take your cup?'

'Thank you.'

He watched her drop the paper cups in a rubbish receptacle and head back to her husband's acute ward. Her phone was at the budget end of the spectrum but it gave him a vital link back to his world of power. Although, using his left hand to tap and swipe the screen felt awkward.

# 49

Time passes incredibly slowly in hospital, so when there is any movement, it's a drama that attracts attention. A vacant bed was removed from Malcolm's acute ward and ten minutes later another bed put in its place, this one with a patient. Audrey noted a bottle collecting urine attached to the side of the bed. There was an oxygen cylinder and pipe to a mask covering the man's face, and a bag of clear liquid was dripping intravenously into his arm.

'Is that…?' Malcolm's voice was croaky but there was more life in it than Audrey had feared. She gripped his hand. 'How are you feeling?'

'Warmer. I did get chilled.'

'I told you not to leap in the river.'

Malcolm chuckled, but it was more of an audible wheeze. 'Any news on the driver?'

'Not that I've heard.'

'That bridge. What can I say? It has form.'

Audrey looked down the ward at where the new arrival was curtained-off.

Malcolm squeezed her hand. 'I hope the Honda is not racking up horrendous parking charges. If you need to go and re-park the car, I'm perfectly fine.'

She looked into his warm, loving face. 'Darling, I think I need to come clean about your motor.'

Gary looked up at the hospital ceiling and admired the modern engineering. Undermere General Hospital was a good place to be ill and, boy, did he feel ill. He had first dated Tina when she was visiting Audrey following her escape from the boarding house fire. Audrey had survived due in part to her own determination, due in part to Tina refusing to stop for Gary's police patrol car, and due in a major part to the skills of the medical staff.

Gary had no idea how he'd escaped the fire in the old school. His last memory was the stink of the smoke, the impenetrable darkness and the scorching heat. He vaguely remembered being in the back seat of a car being tossed about as the driver skidded around bends; and then faces looking down at him, a few weird dreams and waking this morning and speaking to an Italian doctor. He looked at the intravenous drip and felt the oxygen mask. He knew he needed them both but the policeman in him wanted to take action.

'Hello Gary.'

He looked up into the face of the woman who had changed so many lives for the better and pulled away the oxygen mask. 'Hello Audrey.' He was shocked by the sound of his voice. 'It's good to see you.'

She smiled and squeezed his hand. 'It's more than good to see you.'

'Tina. Have you seen her?'

'Not since last night. I will try and find out how she is. Lord Cornfield told me that Mr O'Hanlon's actions saved her from getting badly burned, and worse, at his own cost.'

Gary replaced the oxygen mask and took a deep breath as he digested the information. He pulled it away again. 'Audrey,' he whispered. 'It's important that the press and TV do not get wind of the fact that I am still alive until the criminals I was investigating can be arrested.'

She leaned closer to him. 'What do you want me to do?'

'Can you make sure that O'Hanlon does not tip them off. Could you find him and see if he's fit enough to come and see me. I think it's time he and I made a deal.' He reached for her hand. 'Someone drove us to hospital. Was it you?'

Audrey smiled. 'Across the moor. No cameras, no red lights, no chasing police car – I was able to really pump the gas.'

Gary laughed and it hurt his lungs.

Audrey raised her brows. 'Malcolm doesn't know that his pride and joy was hoisted up onto the back of a flat bed and now resides in a very expensive car park.'

'Priceless.' Gary smiled and that hurt, too.

'Not quite priceless, but a king's ransom to get released.'

'Never mind. You can sell your story. I'm sure the Hawksmead Chronicle will buy it.'

'You rest. I'll see if I can locate Mr O'Hanlon.'

# 50

He ordered his driver to pull up outside the main entrance to the hospital, not caring that the car was in a no waiting zone.

'Keep your phone on. Take a piss. Get something to eat. I'll be at least an hour.' He opened his rear passenger door and slammed it shut behind him. He felt stiff from the long drive and needed to take a piss himself. He pushed the revolving door that was determined to control his pace and entered the main reception area. He looked for male toilets and hurried towards the sign, pressure building with each step. He had always prided himself on keeping fit, and often worked out at his local boxing gym. As a young man he'd been known as Frank the Punch – landing a solid right was always a pleasure.

'Your phone.' Abel looked at Audrey, sitting by an elderly patient.

'Thank you.' She took it off him. 'This is my husband, Malcolm.'

Abel turned his attention to the man who appeared to be enjoying a deep sleep. A half-full bag hung from a stand, dripping into a clear tube that led to his arm. 'How is he?'

'He's on the mend but he'll need a week, or possibly

two.'

'If there's anything I can do please let me know. If he'd be more comfortable in a private facility, no problem.'

'That's very kind of you. We're fine here at the moment. Any news of Tina?'

'All I've been able to glean is that she's still in intensive care. Only a relative can get to see her.'

'What about her brother? Does he know?'

'I presume the hospital has already contacted him. I'll check. I fear she's in a pretty poor state.'

He pushed down the nozzle to the wall-mounted hand sanitiser and cursed as a jet of foamy liquid shot past his hand onto his cashmere jacket.

'Bollocks.'

At the reception desk, a doctor was occupying the focus of two receptionists. He approached the high counter and patted it with his hands as though playing bongo drums.

'Frank Cottee to see Stacy.'

The doctor ceased talking and looked at him. It was what Frank liked best – respect.

'Mr Cottee, my name's Mr Bisterzo. I have been caring for your daughter.'

'No offence, *Mr* Bisterzo, but I demand to see the doctor in charge.'

'That is me.'

'Really?'

'Please take a seat.' He gestured to an alcove with two chairs.

'I've been sitting in a car for three hours plus, I don't need a seat.'

Bisterzo smiled. 'I understand. I'll take you to your daughter.' They walked side-by-side down a wide corridor.

Frank sniffed. 'So, what's the story?'

'I'm afraid Stacy's in a bad way. When she was brought in, the paramedics had fought to revive her, first on the river bank where she had been spotted by a dog walker, and later in the ambulance, pumping her heart all the way. We managed to get her heart beating on its own, but her brain was starved of oxygen during her time in the river. We've conducted several tests to determine -'

'You said her heart's beating,' Frank interrupted. 'So she's alive?'

'Her heart will stop beating once we take her off the ventilator. She can't breathe on her own as there is no brain activity.'

'So, you're saying she can't breathe without a ventilator but her heart's pumping, regardless?'

'The heart in a way has its own brain, its own inbuilt pacemaker. All it needs is oxygen to continue to beat and the ventilator is providing the oxygen.' Bisterzo led the way into a room full of what looked to be up-to-the minute monitoring and technical equipment. A young female nurse was writing on a chart. Bisterzo stopped by the foot of the bed and looked intently at Frank. 'This is the worst situation any parent can face.'

'But she's still alive?'

'Yes, but only with our help.'

Frank walked away from the doctor and went to look at his girl, kicking aside an upright chair. Fixed to her mouth was a tube, pumping air into her lungs. Other wires were connected to her and their numbers displayed on a monitor. Rage rose from deep within. He turned to the Italian doctor and almost spat at him. 'What are those marks on her face?'

Bisterzo looked momentarily confused. 'I, we don't know.'

Frank approached the younger man. 'I do. Someone scratched her.'

'Mr Cottee, I think we are at the point when Stacy's mother and siblings should come and say goodbye.'

'I'm all she's got.' He looked hard at Bisterzo, desperate to blame the doctor for his daughter's predicament. 'Listen to me, you keep my daughter alive until I tell you not to. Got it?'

'It must be a terrible shock. Take your time. I can bring in colleagues. You don't have to accept my word. I'll leave you in peace.' He walked out of the unit, followed by the nurse.

Frank went back to the bed and picked up Stacy's lifeless hand. 'I'm here sweetheart, Daddy's here. I'll look after you. Now, who clawed your face? Tell me darlin'. I know you can't talk right now 'cause of that thing in your mouth but I promise I'm gonna make 'em suffer. I promise. I love you. I love you.' He could not hold back the tears and Frank felt his whole body overwhelmed with grief as he sank onto the chair. He cried like he'd never cried in his life before. The pain was beyond anything he could have ever imagined. *His princess, his baby girl, his sweet angel.*

A hospital porter pushed Gary in a wheelchair down a corridor and after quite a wait, they entered a lift. The saline drip had been removed but an oxygen bottle rested on his lap and he was grateful for the pure air. Audrey had done her best to smarten him up but he was a far cry from the cocky police patrol officer who had chased after Tina in more ways than one. And now he had to be brave. He had to brace himself. He hoped he had the strength to conceal any shock or emotion when he saw her, but he knew Tina was too smart to be easily taken in.

The porter used his pass to get them through a multitude of locked doors, and with each roll of the chair's wheels, his nervousness increased.

Did Tina still love him?

Even if she did, would she still love him once he'd told her the whole story? He had to tell her, didn't he? Sooner or later she'd find out. Timing was the key; first and foremost they had to get well. Not until they could both stand and breathe could they begin to think about their future.

They entered Intensive Care and Gary steeled himself. He was pushed through the open entrance to her unit and the porter locked the chair's wheels. He looked at Tina, her head and shoulders propped up with a multitude of pillows. An oxygen mask covered her nose and mouth, a drip was in her arm and a bottle was hung on the side of her bed collecting urine. Earlier, Gary had had to use all his persuasive charm to get the registrar doctor to remove his catheter. He lifted the oxygen cylinder. 'I don't need it for a while, thanks.'

The porter turned off the tap and once Gary was standing, placed the bottle on the seat of the wheelchair. Gary took a step towards Tina and her eyes opened. In that brief moment, not even as long as a second, he saw the truth.

# 51

'Mr Cottee.'

Frank turned his head away from his sleeping angel and looked towards the Italian consultant. Standing beside him was a woman wearing a dark blue jerkin top and baggy trousers. Around her neck hung the usual photo ID.

'Mr Cottee,' continued Bisterzo. 'I would like to introduce you to my colleague, Laura Duffy. She's a specialist nurse who helps the unit to support families during particularly difficult times.'

'Are you Irish, Ms Duffy?' Frank got up from the bedside chair.

He saw her smile and was surprised by the small resurgence of his long-dormant lust.

'My husband is, I believe, although I think the bloodline is a little tenuous.'

There was a pause and it annoyed Frank that the Italian doctor felt compelled to fill the void.

'Mr Cottee,' Bisterzo said. 'As I mentioned earlier, we undertook certain brain-stem tests to determine the level of activity.' The doctor took a deep breath. 'Unfortunately, we concluded that all Stacy's brain function is irreversibly lost and that when we remove the ventilator, she will slip away.'

Laura Duffy stepped forward and Frank was able to

get a closer view of her pretty face. He estimated that she was in her late thirties and probably had children. There was a look in her brown eyes that told him she understood what it meant to be a parent of a sick child.

'Frank… may I call you Frank?'

He nodded.

'I would like to discuss with you something that you may find initially disturbing but in time you will derive great pride and comfort from the decision you make today.'

He straightened his back. Frank knew when he was being softened up for a killer punch. 'You want to turn off her life support so someone else can use this room?' He looked down at Stacy. 'No way.'

'That's not what this is about.' She laid her fingertips on his left forearm and he felt a charge. He had to get a grip.

'I have money.' His voice came out surprisingly husky. 'I presume this hospital has a private wing? Move her there and then this room is free for the next mug.'

'Frank, today you and Stacy have the chance, the opportunity to transform the lives of up to eight people.'

'You want a donation?'

'Mr Cottee,' interjected Bisterzo.

Frank turned to the consultant. Why was he still here? Couldn't he see that Frank and Laura were having a moment?

'Mr Cottee.' Bisterzo spoke in a tone of voice that Frank marked down as classic ristorante Italiano. 'I would like to assure you that every decision we have made with regard to Stacy's treatment has been based one hundred per cent on what is best for her. We have done all we can.'

Laura touched his arm again. 'Frank, do you know what Stacy's thoughts were with regard to organ donation?'

Frank stepped away from her. So, that's what the soft sell was all about. 'You want, while her heart is still beating, while warm blood is passing through her veins, to cannibalise her body for spare parts?'

'You and Stacy,' Laura continued in a soothing tone, 'have the chance to help others receive the greatest gift of all – an independent life.'

'Mr Cottee.' Bisterzo interrupted again. 'Stacy has moved on. She cannot suffer anymore. The retrieval procedure is undertaken with total respect and dignity.'

The image of what the doctor had just said hit home and Frank felt his knees going. He reached for the chair, slumped down, and grasped Stacy's hand.

'Frank,' Laura said in her enticing tone. 'Your beautiful daughter will always live in your heart and her heart can live on in the body of another.'

'Get out.'

Laura pulled back. 'Please think about it. There's no rush, but time is short for those who Stacy can help.'

'*Get out!*'

Audrey watched the uniformed police officers leave the ward and hurried to her husband's bedside. 'Everything all right?'

'She was a young woman.' Malcolm spoke sombrely. 'She *is* a young woman. She's on life-support in this hospital. They've gone to examine my car. I told them it's in the pound. When I explained that you'd had to rush one of their own to hospital, I was suddenly their best friend.'

'I'm sorry about the young woman.'

'I am too.' Malcolm squeezed her hand. 'How is Tina?'

'She's still in ICU but well enough to see Gary.'

He took a deep breath and coughed. The sound was horrible and he had to reach for a box of tissues. Once he had recovered, he looked at his wife. 'After two years apart, too much water may have gone under the bridge. Poor choice of metaphor.'

Audrey nodded. 'I hope you're wrong.'

'I hope I am, too. They've both suffered terribly.'

'How are you feeling?'

'I love antibiotics.'

'Don't we all. Have they said when you can come home?'

'I think it's going to be a couple of days. Are you going to be all right?

She forced a smile. 'I'll be fine.'

He paused a few seconds before responding. 'You don't like being on your own, do you?'

'Not anymore. When I first came to Hawksmead, I was happy to be alone in the old school boarding house, living within its Victorian walls. But, when I realised I had fallen in love for the second time, I felt vulnerable, fearful that I could lose someone who is very precious. I get nervous when we're apart.' She gripped his hand tightly. 'You scared me.'

He nodded. 'I think I'm going to quit driving.'

'But it wasn't your fault. I was there. You didn't even hit the other car.'

'It wasn't my fault when I skidded on black ice fifty-four years ago and killed your brother's best friend. I'm old. It's time for me to pass the key on to you.'

She couldn't fight back the tears.

Frank emerged from his daughter's unit and stood to gather his emotions. He saw a medical orderly push a youngish, dishevelled, bearded man in a wheelchair out of another unit and was sure that he recognised him. He stood back and watched the orderly take the man out through the controlled entrance and exit doors.

A loud, demanding beeping sound filled the ICU. A nurse hurried out of the unit the bearded man had just left to join several other medical personnel who rushed into another intensive care unit, one wheeling a trolley with hi-tech electrical equipment which Frank had seen being used in TV dramas but couldn't remember what it was called.

He waited a few moments then checked the patient's name written on the wipe board.

*Christina Burton.*

The scum police officer was visiting his wife! It was only a matter of time before police would come knocking on Frank's door. The pieces that led up to his daughter's race from the boarding school were falling into place. And the scratches on her cheek were typical of a bitch. Now was his chance. His last act to avenge his angel. Without his beautiful Stacy there was no future. The policeman who had deceived him, who had lied through his teeth, who had defiled his beautiful daughter, who had betrayed Frank Cottee's trust, would serve a life sentence.

He entered Christina's unit and stared at the blonde-haired young woman lying with her eyes closed on the raised bed, surrounded by sophisticated equipment, her mouth and nose covered by an oxygen mask. He looked up at the beeping monitor displaying her vital signs.

'Hello.'

Her voice startled him. It was husky but with an endearing silky tone. She had lifted off the oxygen mask and he had a much clearer view of her fine-boned features.

'I was visiting my daughter down the corridor.'

'How is she?'

'Not good.'

'I'm sorry. At least she's in the right place.'

He nodded. 'And how are you?'

'A bit battered. But they tell me I'll live, barring the unforeseen.'

'My daughter has three score lines on her cheek.' He saw a retraction in her eyes and moved closer. 'Gary lied his way into the bosom of my family, he made love to my daughter, promised her marriage, and then betrayed us.' He watched as his words sunk in. The girl held his gaze. She had courage, he'd give her that.

'I was jealous of Stacy,' she admitted. 'Gary told me on a brief visit home that our marriage was over the moment he met her. He may have been working undercover but he was in love with your daughter. Stupidly, I hoped he'd come to his senses, and then waited for him to come back to me, but even after more than two years held as a prisoner, he told me he still loves your daughter and wants a divorce.'

Frank looked intently into the young woman's eyes. 'Why aren't your parents here?'

'They're in heaven. They liked Gary. They trusted him to look after me. They were very disappointed.'

'So you have no one?'

She reached out her hand and touched his fingers. 'In this moment, all I have is you.' He took her hand in his and felt her fine bones. 'Please tell Stacy,' she said, 'that I'm sorry I hurt her.'

He nodded. 'Get well, my dear.' He let go of her

hand and hurried out of the unit. The corridor was empty apart from a young woman sitting at the reception desk. He returned to Stacy's unit and looked at his beautiful girl. He had loved her mother and raged against the cancer that had robbed him and Stacy of so much. He had fought hard to protect his little girl, but angels have wings and she'd wanted to stretch hers.

He walked around her bed and gripped the electrical cable leading to the ventilator in his scarred fist. He pulled down with all his power and there was a blue flash and a surprisingly loud bang. An alarm sounded almost immediately. He switched the power off at the socket and pulled out the plug. There would be no cranking open her chest and plundering her organs.

Within seconds a young doctor and nurse were in the room attending to Stacy. The nurse turned off the alarm. Another arrived pushing the trolley with the electrical equipment.

*Defibrillator.*

That was the word Frank had been seeking.

'Extubate.' Everyone stopped what they were doing and looked at Mr Bisterzo. 'Remove the tube,' he ordered.

Frank watched as the young doctor gently unclipped the mask and pulled the tube out of Stacy's trachea. There was no gagging reflex. The nurse used a tissue to wipe around her mouth.

'Mr Cottee,' Bisterzo continued, 'would like some private time with his daughter.'

Frank watched the medical personnel leave the unit. He looked at Stacy and up at the vital signs monitor. Her heart was still beating. 'I am here, angel. You are about to go on a journey to a beautiful place, far, far away where your mum is waiting for you. And, if you need me, just call. I'll always be close.' He gripped her hand as he fought to hold back his tears. This was a fight he couldn't punch his way out of. He heard another alarm and knew her heart had stopped beating.

Tina held her husband's hand as he sat by her bed wearing a hospital dressing gown and pyjamas. She had been moved out of the Intensive Care Unit and was now in an acute ward. Much nicer. There was more to see. She had hated being alone in the ICU surrounded by all the equipment.

'There's an arrest warrant out for Dermot but he's disappeared.'

'Abel told me he saved my life.'

Gary nodded. 'Yes. But we mustn't forget Hector the dog. Then there's the firefighters. And, of course, Audrey, and the medical staff. All the drugs and specialist equipment. But, yes, Dermot protected you at his own cost. Without him, you wouldn't be here.'

'I hope, one day, I'll be able to thank him.'

'And when that day comes, I'll be waiting with handcuffs.'

'Gary, shall we usher the elephant out of the ward?' She saw him stiffen. 'Did you love her?'

'No.' He shook his head. 'I want to say she seduced me but that would be a lie. I got too close. It was a role. Method acting. I was consumed by lust. Nothing more. I give you my word.'

Tina felt a wave of exhaustion sweep over her and closed her eyes as she pulled her hand away from his. He had slept with Stacy within months of their marriage. Could she forgive him? Could she ever trust him again? Did she want to?

She opened her eyes. He was gone.

When Sam received Audrey's call and she had given him a potted account of what had happened since the funeral, he was stunned and immediately called his husband via WhatsApp.

Luke responded assertively. 'Sam. Get in a taxi and get to the hospital. See your sister. She's your priority.'

'I will but there is one other thing. I don't want to return to New Zealand.'

'What are you saying?'

'I want you to pack up our stuff and come here. I can't deal with my parents' estate from the other side of the world. Once their house is sold, we'll be able to buy our own place.'

'In Hawksmead?'

'Or Undermere. I've been made to feel so welcome. You'll feel it too.'

'What about my job?'

'You'll get a good job here.'

'In London, yes, but Hawksmead? I don't think so.'

'What do you want me to do?'

'I want you to see your sister – then we'll talk.'

# 52

William Longden climbed up into the pulpit of his church. He looked across at the sea of expectant faces and rejoiced in their presence, whether they were here to celebrate or to worship. Everyone was always welcome. He took particular delight in seeing Gary Burton sitting beside William's dear friend, Malcolm; and Tina holding the hand of Malcolm's remarkable wife, Audrey. The reuniting of the estate agent and her policeman had been rejoiced by the whole of Hawksmead. To help their recovery, the young couple were staying in Malcolm and Audrey's spare bedroom where they were receiving the kind of care that only love and good cuisine can provide. However, he was surprised by the urgency of Gary's request, coming so soon after being released from hospital, but he understood the young man's reasoning.

He waited for Eleanor to finish playing *Wind Beneath My Wings* and took a deep breath. 'There's a structure to sermons that most preachers tend to follow.' His voice carried to the back of the pews, without the need of a microphone. 'It's a structure typical of what we often see on TV. It starts with a problem, what writers call the inciting incident. As in drama, the preacher explores various approaches and dead ends until, almost despairing of a solution, we pull out our Ace in the hole, our trump card – *God*.'

He smiled as a few in the congregation tried to control their laughter.

'Detective Constable Gary Burton agreed to work undercover to bring down a ruthless gangland leader. In the line of duty, he was uncovered and held captive for more than two years, and for some of that time up at the old school with migrants who had been trafficked from Vietnam. A brave young man, whose marriage to Tina I officiated, was suffering not much more than a mile or two from here, as the crow flies.

'Was his rescue and the rescue of his wife and others from the subsequent conflagration a miracle? An act of God? Or simply the result of firefighters doing their job? You tell me.' He paused and waited for a response. Of course, all responses were unspoken. He smiled again. 'Today, we are here to celebrate and show our support for a young couple who were torn apart and through Manus Domini Dei, or sheer good fortune, have found each other again.' William stepped down from the pulpit and gestured for Tina and Gary to stand in front of the Lord's table.

Gary stood and offered his hand to Tina. His suit was a size too large and, William thought, was probably one of Malcolm's.

Tina did not take the offered hand. 'What's going on?'

'Please. It'll all become clear.'

She stood and studiously avoided his eyes.

'I want to say something.'

Reluctantly, she looked at him and allowed him to take her hands. He turned his face away to give a little cough. It clearly pained him. 'I, Gary Simon Burton, broke the vow I made to you on our wedding day to forsake all others.' His voice was croaky and he tried to clear his throat before continuing. 'I do not deserve a second chance. But, if you have it in your heart to forgive me, I promise, before God and all these witnesses...' He coughed again. '...I promise to love you, comfort you, cherish you for the rest of our days, in sickness and in health, forsaking *all* others, whatever the circumstances, whatever the temptation, and shall be faithful for as long as we both shall live.'

A strange, shuffling silence almost like a Mexican wave, rippled through the congregation as they all waited for Tina's response.

Silence.

The Reverend spoke quietly to Tina. 'Would you like to say a few words, my dear?'

She took a deep breath and stared at Gary. 'Who else knew you were going to do this?'

'Almost everyone who came to our wedding.'

She pulled her hands free and looked at Audrey.

Gary interjected. 'Both Audrey and Malcolm thought it was too soon, but I made them promise to keep quiet.'

Tina scanned the congregation and saw many puzzled faces she recognised. She sat down beside Audrey and closed her eyes.

Gary coughed. He looked at William and then at the people who almost filled the church. 'Thank you for joining my wife and me, today. Once the service is concluded, you are all invited to the Falcon pub where there is an open bar and food courtesy of our dear friend, Lord Abel Cornfield.' He sat down and hung his head.

William waited patiently for the cacophony of whispering to quieten. Finally, he was able to utter the words, 'Let us pray.'

# 53

The Falcon was heaving. Tina parked the sadness of her parents' passing and her annoyance at Gary's unwelcome surprise and relished the company of so many old friends in their Sunday best; people who had been such a part of her life before she and Gary had left for London. She was particularly pleased to see her brother openly displaying his love for his husband, Luke.

'Sweetie, let me see.'

Tina offered her hands to Magdalena. 'Wow, Mags, you look stunning.'

'And you look beautiful.' She examined Tina's nails. 'Nice job.'

'My mother always said, self-praise is no praise, but you do do very good nails.'

'Darling Tina.' Both women looked at the source of the melodious voice.

'Eleanor!' Tina joyously shouted her name. 'You played the organ so beautifully.' She turned to Magdalena. 'I take it you two know each other?'

Magdalena gave Eleanor a kiss on each cheek and then held her at arms' length. 'You should fire Polish girl who work for you in tea shop,'

'Fire Agnieska?' Eleanor replied. 'Why?'

'She is very rude to Polish customers.'

Eleanor looked puzzled. 'I don't understand.'

Magdalena laughed. 'Of course you don't. She speak in Polish!'

*'Christina!'*

All three women turned as one to Abel whose right elbow was still supported by a sling. There were a few marks from the fire on his handsome face; and his great head of hair looked a little patchy, despite a recent trim.

Tina wrapped her arms around his neck. 'You should have warned me.' She kissed him tenderly on the cheek.

'I sent the three Versace dresses to the cottage as a clue. I thought Gary would crack and tell you.' He looked at what Tina was wearing. 'Gianni would be truly honoured.'

She smiled. 'Thank you.' And she kissed him again.

'Will you think about my offer? With your help a fantastic phoenix can rise out of the ashes.'

'I will. I promise.' Reluctantly, she pulled away from him and saw that Magdalena was now in deep conversation with the owner of the Hawksmead Chronicle, but Eleanor was standing by, looking on. 'Abel, I would like to introduce you to Eleanor Houghton, Hawksmead's finest cakeologist and organist.'

Eleanor laughed. 'Lord Cornfield.'

'Abel, please. You have a theatrical air. Were you ever on the stage?'

'I was,' Eleanor responded, smiling.

Tina chipped in. 'Eleanor has sung in London's West End. She has a beautiful operatic voice.'

'I knew it!' Abel responded. 'I do not have an artistic bone, but I have a great nose for talent.'

Tina gently backed away leaving Abel and Eleanor

immersed in conversation. She really liked Abel. He was incredibly exciting company. No. She felt more than that. A lot more.

'He is very handsome.'

She looked at Audrey. 'But way too honourable.'

Audrey laughed. 'There's a man outside who lives to a very different code of honour. He wondered if he could have a few words.'

The man was wearing a long rain jacket with a hood. Tina wondered who it was.

'Geezus, it's good to see you.' He turned his smiling face to her and she fought an instinct to recoil. 'Not a pretty sight, I grant you.'

She leaned forward and pushed back his hood. His once thick hair was in clumps and tufts with skin that was raw and seeping. His face looked as though he had suffered a severe bout of eczema, with red-raw patches, scabs and weeping wounds.

'It's not a problem. I'm wanted by the British police but with this face I can move around with ease. I'm unrecognisable even to facial recognition cameras. There's a plus to everything.'

'I will never forget what you did for me.'

'Gary will never forget what I did to him. I hope he will forgive me, one day. I hope you will, too.'

She took his hand in hers and held his palm against her cheek. 'Farewell my travelling friend.'

'Till we meet again.'

# 54

## *Hawksmead Chronicle*

### *King Cottee Captured in Rio*

Self-styled King of Essex, Frank Cottee, who disappeared following the death of his daughter and the resurrection of undercover police officer, Gary Burton, has been captured on the phone of a tourist filming his girlfriend sunbathing in Brazil. Sightings of the ruthless gangland mastermind have resulted in many *GotCottee* viral videos. He has been, allegedly, spotted in almost every corner of the world but despite an international arrest warrant, remains at large.

Tina pressed her accelerator and felt Gary stiffen in the seat beside her.

'Relax... my mother was a member of the Institute of Advanced Motorists.'

Gary laughed as the white VW Golf zoomed up the long drive. After so much rain, the early winter's sun was a welcome visitor. Within little more than a minute the tyres scrunched on the gravel as Tina swung around in a circle before bringing the car to a halt as far away from the old school as the apron would allow. She turned off the engine and they both released their belts. Without speaking they climbed out of the car and stared in awe.

The once forbidding edifice was a hollowed shell of blackened bricks and timbers, held up by scaffolding, peppered with large signs warning people to keep away from the dangerous structure.

'How did we get out of there?' Gary murmured.

'Burly firemen,' she replied. 'Do you really think he could still be here?'

'I do. But whether he's alive or not, I don't know. Audrey said he was hurt pretty bad. We should've come sooner.'

'We weren't in the best shape.' She looked away from him and coughed.

'Still,' Gary said. 'He was good at catching rabbits.' He turned to her. 'What about Abel's offer? Are you going to accept? I could help you.' He waited for her response. 'Tina?'

*Roff! Roff!*

'Hector!' he called.

The great dog bounded towards them from the abbey ruins. Gary moved away from the car and knelt down to welcome their saviour. The once ferocious-looking hound was all sharp bones but so happy to see him. 'Hello boy. My heroic friend.'

Tina watched as her husband hugged the dog that had played such a pivotal role in saving their lives.

'I prayed he'd still be alive,' he continued, 'but I didn't really think it possible after all this time. We must take him home and feed him up.' He looked at her. 'Audrey and Malcolm said they were looking forward to the patter of tiny feet.'

'With the best will in the world, I don't think those

paws can be described as tiny.'

Gary continued to hug and kiss the dog as Hector covered his face in sloppy licks. 'Look what I've found.' He twisted the dog's collar and revealed the Patek Philippe watch. 'It's still attached. I don't believe it.' He undid the strap.

'I'll take that, thank you.' Tina approached her husband with hand held out.

'It's still working.'

'It's automatic. Doesn't need a battery.'

He turned the watch over and looked at the back. 'There's an inscription.'

'It's a private message, Gary.'

*'To a most remarkable woman.'* He handed her the watch. 'My thoughts, entirely.'

'Thank you, Hector,' she said, as Gary helped her fix the weathered leather strap to her wrist.

'What about giving Hector a thank you hug?' He turned to the dog and stroked both his ears. 'You would like a hug, wouldn't you boy?'

Tina glanced at the face of her new-found watch. 'Well, I'll be off.'

'You're going?'

'I've seen all I need to see.' She slipped back into the car.

'You're leaving without us?'

'I can't have those big claws on my leather seats.' She started the engine. 'I'll see you at the cottage. There's a shortcut across the moor.' She closed the door and quickly drove off. In her rear-view mirror she saw Gary cuddling the excited dog. As she approached the start of the long drive she swung the steering wheel and accelerated back to the reunited couple.

She pushed open her door and held out her arms.

'Hector!' The dog bounded over to her and tried to cover her face in happy licks.

The chop-chop of a helicopter's rotor blades attracted their attention and the familiar sight of the AgustaWestland AW109 came into view. Hector barked with great enthusiasm as the flying beast circled over the school's burnt-out shell and disappeared from view. The dog gave chase, barking happily. Gary followed. Tina grabbed her handbag and ran in her trainers as fast as her damaged lungs would allow. As she rounded the far end of the school, she saw that the helicopter had landed on the playing fields. Hector was some way off, bouncing around, barking.

The rotor blades were still turning as the front passenger door opened and Abel eased himself out, his arm no longer in a sling. He slid open the rear passenger door and removed what looked to be a cool bag. Hector barked with even greater enthusiasm. Tina watched Abel slip on a blue chef's glove and pull out a large hunk of red meat, which he tossed in Hector's direction.

'I don't believe it,' Gary said, breathlessly, to Tina. 'He's been feeding Hector.' Abel peeled off the blue glove and waved as he came out from under the slowly rotating blades. They hurried over to him.

'Abel!' Tina out-paced Gary and gave him a hug. 'It's so good to see you.' She broke away and looked at him, her heart pounding. 'I've got my watch back!'

He smiled. 'So I see. I tried to get it off Hector's collar, but even though Graham and I regularly flew up here to feed him, he never let me get close.' He looked at the dog enjoying the raw meat. 'I'll take care of him. Keep him fed.'

'He's my dog.' Both Abel and Tina looked at Gary.

'Hector means the world to me,' he continued. 'I hope you understand. When we were both chained to this place, he gave me hope.' They all watched as the scarred hound gulped down a chunk of steak. Gary spoke directly to Abel. 'Will you keep your promise and take Tina to swim with dolphins?'

Abel looked from Gary to Christina and back again. 'Of course. When you are both free to go.'

Gary opened the cool bag and used the blue glove to pick up a hunk of red meat. 'Hector!' The dog came bounding over and gulped it down in one. He turned to Abel. 'Tina is free to go now, if she wants to.'

Abel took a moment before responding. 'What about you?'

'Hector needs me to take care of him.'

Tina stared at Gary. 'What are you saying?'

'Take some time. Have a holiday. Swim with dolphins. You deserve it.'

'We both do.'

Gary approached her, tears rolling down his cheeks. 'Thanks to my actions, you lost more than two years of happiness.' He sniffed hard and wiped his eyes with the heel of his hand. 'I was wrong to think we could simply pick up where we left off.'

She touched his arm. 'I can't go. I have to sort out my parents' house.'

'Sam and Luke can handle that. I'll help.'

She turned to Abel. 'What's the weather like in Florida at this time of year?'

He smiled. 'Pretty good.'

'My passport is in Malcolm's cottage.'

'I'll send a car to pick it up.'

She looked from Abel to Gary and back to Abel. 'I don't have anything with me.'

'I'm quite sure our friend, Audrey, can pack a bag for you.'

She stepped close to Gary. 'I think you and Hector had better move into my parents' house. They have... there is a lovely big garden at the back.'

'I'll talk to Luke,' Gary said. He stared into her eyes and took her hand in his. 'Goodbye... Christina.'

'Goodbye.' She kissed him on the cheek and hugged him for all her worth. 'You will always be in my heart.'

'I never doubted that.'

Tears pouring down her cheeks, she pulled away and walked swiftly to the helicopter.

'The car key?' Gary called.

She stopped and used both her hands to wipe her eyes. 'It's in the ignition. But Hector has to go in the back. And tell him not to dribble on the front passenger seat.'

Gary laughed. 'I'll be sure to tell him that.'

She climbed into the rear of the helicopter. The pilot, wearing headphones, turned and smiled. 'Mrs Burton, it's really good to see you again. Welcome aboard.'

'Thank you, Graham. It's good to see you, too.'

A few moments later, Abel sat in the seat beside her and clicked his seatbelt. 'All good?' he asked, as he handed her a set of headphones.

She nodded. 'All good.' And she put them on.

The rotor blades spun in earnest and a few seconds later they lifted the helicopter off the ground. Tina watched Gary as he walked with Hector around the hollowed shell towards the front of the old school. He looked up as the helicopter circled and then opened the Golf's rear door. Hector leapt in.

She turned to Abel and squeezed his hand. 'This time you came to collect me.'

'I was determined to get your watch back.'

She looked at her Patek Philippe. 'The second hour hand is still set to Rome time.'

'Florida is five hours behind the UK.'

She unclicked her seatbelt and removed her headphones. Abel copied her. They leaned towards each other and their lips were about to meet for the first time when the helicopter jolted. They fell apart, laughing. Both clicked in their seatbelts and put their headphones back on.

'My apologies, Mrs Burton,' the pilot said. 'A small air pocket.'

She held Abel's hand and looked into his eyes. 'I love you.' She mouthed the words so the pilot wouldn't hear; then turned to look out of the window. Through wisps of cloud she could see the quietly flowing River Hawk and its historic humpback bridge.

*If you have a moment, please leave a review.*
*Your help to spread the word is*
*very much appreciated.*

Reviews for Romola Farr's debut novel

BRIDGE TO ETERNITY

5-STARS WOW!
"Never a dull moment with lots of unexpected twists! Read it in one sitting. Could not put it down!!!!! Awaiting her NEXT tale." Reviewed in the United States on April 11, 2020, Amazon.com (Bonus Edition)

"I absolutely loved Bridge to Eternity so much, I read it within a day. I look forward to reading more from Farr as this was such a wonderful debut." Jojo Welsh girl, Amazon.co.uk

"The icy bleakness of the landscape is expertly reflected in the lives of many of the central characters. Deeply buried emotions are intermingled amongst present and past events. It is both atmospheric and unnerving in equal measure as characters struggle with their own personal demons. This is a really intriguing and powerful debut novel." S J Mantle, Amazon.co.uk

"Bridge to Eternity is an outstanding debut novel and a hugely satisfying read." Ali Reynolds, Amazon.com

"...this was so well done that I couldn't stop reading." GranJan, Amazon.com

"A brilliant read ...a real page-turner with finely-drawn characters that the reader cares for." Sue from Wimbledon, Amazon.co.uk

"A gripping novel ...a thrilling read. I read it in two sittings." KJA, Amazon.co.uk

"What separates this book from the others is the subtle yet powerful emotions which trip from the first page through to the last. This novel left its mark on me long after I finished it." Lee-Anne TOP 1000 REVIEWER, Amazon.com.au

5-stars Great read
"I am 65 and could so relate to Audrey's young memories as they are mine as well. I liked the character of these people, kind, strong independent but needing to love and be loved." Amazon Customer

5-stars "Gripping read - this book held my attention all the way through and I have since bought it for some of my friends." Ann Furness, Amazon.co.uk

5-stars A STUNNING DEBUT NOVEL
"... I loved this. It's a mix of history, ghost stories and troubled lives. Most of all it's about following your heart and that sometimes you have to take risks to really enjoy life. This is stunning especially for a debut novel - I look forward to more from Romola, whoever you are!" Misfits farm, Amazon.co.uk

R omola Farr first trod the boards on the West End stage aged sixteen and continued to work for the next eighteen years in theatre, TV and film, and as a photographic model. A trip to Hollywood led to the sale of a film script and a successful change of direction as a screenwriter and playwright.

'Bridge to Eternity' and 'Breaking Through the Shadows' are the first novels in a planned series, set in the fictional town of Hawksmead.

Romola Farr is a nom de plume.

romolafarr@gmail.com
@RomolaFarr
www.wildmoorpress.com

Printed in Great Britain
by Amazon

57388248R00196